Also by J. P. Smith

The Drowning
Airtight
Breathless
The Discovery of Light
The Blue Hour
Body and Soul
The Man from Marseille

if she were dead

a novel

J. P. Smith

Poisoned Pen

PRESS

Published by Poisoned Pen Press, an imprint of Sourcebooks
P.O. Box 4410, Naperville, Illinois 60567-4410
(630) 961-3900
sourcebooks.com

Library of Congress Cataloging-in-Publication Data

Names: Smith, J. P.
Title: If she were dead : a novel / J.P. Smith.
Description: Naperville, Illinois : Sourcebooks Landmark, [2020]
Identifiers: LCCN 2018057489 | (trade pbk. : alk. paper)
Subjects: LCSH: Man-woman relationships--Fiction. | GSAFD: Suspense fiction.
Classification: LCC PS3569.M53744 I3 2020 | DDC 813/.54--
dc23 LC record available at https://lccn.loc.gov/2018057489

Printed and bound in the United States of America.
VP 10 9 8 7 6 5 4 3 2 1

NEFF

Will you be here, too?

PHYLLIS

I guess so. I usually am.

NEFF

Same chair, same perfume, same anklet?

PHYLLIS

I wonder if I know what you mean.

NEFF

I wonder if you wonder.

—Billy Wilder and Raymond Chandler,
Double Indemnity (1944)

Part One

1

CLOSE YOUR EYES.

Now open.

She was in darkness, and now there was a point of light aimed at her right eye.

In the beam she could see the reflection, intricately veined, staring back at her, blinking when she blinked. She looked into it as if it were an uncurtained window in someone's house, an opening onto another's life. It seemed oddly intimate, being able to stare into your own stare, to transfix your own gaze.

Look up, look down. Now to the right, now to the left.

After doing the same with her left eye, he switched off the light. A table of letters was projected on the wall, black characters against a white ground. She recited the first four lines, then the next two, and then at his urging two more, and then after she did likewise with her other eye, he propped a printed card on a rack attached to a mechanism close to her face. He asked if she was able to read the text. She squinted, and he began making adjustments with the lenses until she could read the words with ease. They went from gray to a crisp black, and the sensation was like rising out of water after a long, graceful dive. He switched on the overhead light and made a notation on a sheet of paper.

The doctor explained that it was a matter of age. "It happens to all of us eventually," he said. "You notice it when you have to hold a book far away in order to read it. It usually starts when you turn forty."

"Sometimes I can hardly read the time on my watch."

"One last thing," he said, and he wheeled his chair alongside her, their knees almost touching. He opened a spiral-bound book and held it before her. "Try to make out the figures in the patterns," he said.

"Thirty-six," she said, seeing it clearly amid the psychedelic bubble bath of colors.

"And now?"

"The letter *B*."

"And this one?"

"Fifty-seven." She smiled.

"At least you're not color-blind," he said, handing her a prescription for lenses.

He held the examination-room door open for her, and she stepped out into the sunlight and windows of the optician's area. She had suspected it would come to this: for the past three months she'd noticed how difficult it had become for her to read.

The walls and racks displayed a variety of frames. She knew which ones she'd take, she'd seen them in magazine ads and on other people, she'd even tried them on before her appointment and, standing back a little from the mirror, had admired herself in black frames that contrasted dramatically with her blond hair and blue eyes. She wondered if, simply because she had desired the frames, she had willed herself into farsightedness.

She looked over at the optician assigned to her.

"They're only reading glasses," he said, noting the price tag.

"Still," she said, not quite getting his meaning.

He reached toward her and readjusted them on the bridge of her nose. She looked at herself in the mirror. She knew how much they cost without even looking at the little tag on the stem. She knew it because they had been designed by someone who also lent his name to expensive clothes and shoes, things people wore on cruises or at society weddings. It didn't matter. She rarely spoiled herself; she spent her days working at home in jeans or sweatpants, in sweatshirts or sweaters, and in the summer wore shorts and a T-shirt, or a blouse tied at the waist; times when she was invisible. When she went before the public she dressed more stylishly: at readings or delivering a talk, at a restaurant with a friend, or on the few occasions she'd been asked out by a man and accepted it.

"Look at me," he said, "look at my eyes," and it seemed a little dangerous to her, looking a man directly in the face with absolute forthrightness. It had always been uncomfortable for her since the divorce, as if by showing so much of herself to another she might also display in some obscure manner a diagram of her life, the curve that rose and fell in the elegant shape of deception. The code of her face would reveal it in the way her eyes shifted to the side, or in the set of her mouth, the tilt of her head, the way she moved the hair away from her cheek. She felt his hands brush against her temples as he slid the frames back onto her face; she sensed the faint peppermint whisper of his breath. She looked at the dark brown of his eyes, the way his eyebrows met, the slight rise of his upper lip. She wondered how much scrutiny she could bear before the inevitable flaws became visible.

"They suit you," he said. "A good choice."

They would be ready in a few days.

2

THE INTERVIEW HAD BEEN ARRANGED FOR FOUR, LESS
than an hour away, and the moment she got in the car she
remembered it. She tightened her lips and said *Oh shit* and drove
out of the parking area and onto the highway. She was sorry
she hadn't arranged it for the next morning, or even canceled it
altogether. She tried to recall the voice on the phone, the way the
interviewer asked for directions. She lived in the city, the woman
from the newspaper said. "I'll take the highway up."

Amelie described her home, an old farmhouse set on a rise
off the road, the low stone pillars that stood on either side of the
entrance, a red mailbox that, like her, had seen better days. She
said that her car would be in the driveway, a dark-blue Volvo.
This was the house she and Richard had taken so much trouble
to find, to renovate, to enjoy. She wondered if it needed to be
cleaned, if she should haul out the vacuum and run it over the
wide pine floors, or if she should give a quick dusting to the tables
and lamps, even though the cleaning woman had been there two
days earlier. She knew it didn't matter, that no interviewer had
ever passed judgment on how she lived, the imagined squalor of
her living room.

She turned on the radio and opened the window. A driver in
the next lane turned to look at her. His little mustache rose in

a smile, and she looked at him through dark glasses and eased her foot slightly off the accelerator. She watched as he pulled ahead, his head tilting to catch her image in the narrow slit of his rearview mirror. She turned up the volume on the radio: a woman was singing in German while an oboe twisted its melody into hers. It was obviously something by Bach, from a cantata probably, a piece that her mother would certainly have been able to identify. She tapped her fingers lightly against the steering wheel, for there was something comforting in the rhythm, the mathematical regularity of the pizzicato behind the woman's yearning voice, as though each beat were a step higher on some celestial staircase.

It was three thirty when she arrived home. She opened the refrigerator and put her finger to her lips. She would have to offer the interviewer something, and because it was warm and they could sit out on the deck under the umbrella, she wondered if she should make a pitcher of instant iced tea. She herself would have preferred a dry martini, but that could wait. The last time she had made drinks for an interview, the writer had mentioned in the article her subject's evident lust for alcohol, and both her agent and her publicist had called her, gently suggesting she stick to a more neutral beverage in future.

She walked quickly upstairs and changed into a skirt and blouse. She stood before her mirror and pulled a brush through her hair. She put on a different pair of earrings; she took her sandals from the closet and slipped them on. She went into the bathroom and brushed her teeth and then took some mouthwash directly from the bottle and spit it into the sink.

She smoothed the covers on her bed and banged at her pillow

until it no longer showed the imprint of her head. She wondered if she would have to give the interviewer a tour of the house, or if when she excused herself to use the toilet the journalist would bolt up the stairs and take a look for herself, rifling through her medicine cabinet, discovering her pink vibrator in a drawer by her bed.

On her bedside table were stacked a biography, a novel, and the latest *New Yorker*, sitting next to a lamp and a clock radio. The drawer was slightly open and she nudged it shut. Over the bed was nothing but the shadow of what had once hung there, a framed exhibition poster so beloved by her ex-husband that when he left, she insisted he take it with him. She still hadn't found something to replace it. She wondered if it now hung over his and his wife's bed.

On the dresser stood a framed photograph of her daughter, Nina, taken in September when she'd started college at Wellesley. Her eyes glowed with pride and excitement and terror. Behind her were other students with their families, arms around shoulders, scenes of farewell. Amelie and Richard had together driven Nina there, and she remembered the day as having passed without incident.

Without incident: it was in just those terms that she recalled it, as if she were referring to some zone of mayhem in the Middle East, a place of terror and spiritual malaise, where peace, when it came, shimmered into uneasy stalemate. Afterward, after they'd seen Nina into her room at the college and made small talk with her roommate's parents, after they'd fussed with her and kissed and hugged her, the two of them stopped for lunch at a restaurant in town, instantly ordering drinks, saying nothing of substance for the entire hour, as if, were they to trespass on a subject of depth, small wars or skirmishes might break out.

Since Amelie and Richard had split up she'd added little to the house. It had been difficult enough when her mother had died and Amelie had emptied her Scarsdale home of china and chipped candy dishes and paintings. They still remained in boxes in the cellar, and they would stay there for years, decades, centuries. It didn't matter because she would never unpack them to reconstruct the suburban Westchester house in which she had been raised. Every time she descended to the bowels of her home she would see them jutting out of their chardonnay and merlot boxes, brief reminders of the dead and gone, silent reproaches for her having overlooked them. The pity of it was that none of it represented what her mother had been: once a respected concert pianist, in later years a beloved teacher and lecturer at Juilliard. Nothing that defined her remained: the filing cabinets full of sheet music now long gone; a baby grand Steinway sold a few weeks after her death to a private school in Connecticut.

At rare moments the thought of her mother's death would return to her in unexpected ways. She thought of the half-light of the landing as her mother walked up the stairs, her knuckles white against the dark wood of the banister as she stopped to catch her breath three steps from the top.

Amelie walked into the living room and looked at her watch and then out the window. Now it was ten past four. She hoped it wouldn't last long, not that she minded being interviewed—in fact, she adored publicity. It was like being bathed in the glances of others or caught in the intersection of a thousand conversations. She enjoyed being photographed. She liked the *snick* of the camera, the intrusion of the lens into her wistful smile, her blue eyes. She thought ahead three hours, projecting herself into the future, trying to see herself at that moment, lifting the phone, pressing in the numbers, letting it ring once. Then she would hang up. Then she would wait. Then she would pick up the phone and try the number again. Then he would pick it up. This is how it went.

A routine that had so far lasted two years.

3

AT TWENTY PAST FOUR SHE BEGAN TO CONSIDER
making herself a drink. She thought of her eye examination that
day, how the blurred world had grown crystalline and distinct. It
was like the resolving chord in a piece of music, the great satisfying
clang of clarity and reason that comes at the end of a symphony.

She heard a car coming up the road, she saw it drive past the
pillars, she saw it stop, there was a pause, it backed up, the turn
was made, here she was. Amelie caught her image in a mirror
and touched her hair with her hands, she smoothed her blouse,
she cleared her throat and went to the door. She watched the car
door open, and swinging her long, dark hair as she got out of the
car, the woman sent by the magazine stopped for a moment and
looked at the front of the house.

She was young and slim and rather pretty, with hair extensions
that she probably didn't need. She rolled her eyes. "I'm sorry I'm late."

Amelie saw with dismay that the young woman was carrying
not just a notebook but also a small recorder. The agreement had
been that she would be permitted to have a preliminary look at
the piece before it was published. Now she would have to give it
careful scrutiny. Things could be said and forgotten. Idiocies and
first thoughts could be captured in the machine. Maintaining her
image was vital to her career.

The interviewer stepped in ahead of her. She looked around. "What a nice house," she said. "Is it very old?"

Amelie smiled. "It's only meant to look that way. I think we'll sit outside. If that's all right for you."

"Great."

"It's so nice out. Would you like something cold to drink? Iced tea?" They went into the kitchen and she opened the refrigerator. "I can offer you a glass of wine, if you like."

"That would be great."

She was pleased there would be something stronger to drink. Things would move along smoothly; time would pass quickly: an easy slipstream moment. She pulled the cork from the bottle and poured out two glasses, one slightly fuller than the other.

They sat near each other under the big umbrella. A huge splat of bird shit marred the white enamel table. Often she would print her latest pages and bring them outside to edit, and, pencil in hand, witness the endless defecations of the birds that roosted in the tree above the deck, the insane chatterings and cries of the rabid squirrels that terrorized them and stole their seed from the feeder. "Let me get that cleaned up," she said, going inside for a wet paper towel.

Now they were ready. She sipped her wine. The interviewer said, "The photographer is supposed to get in touch," and Amelie said, "He was here two days ago."

The interviewer seemed confused. "Oh," was all she said.

"He's actually someone from this area."

"I guess so. I didn't make the arrangements."

"He lives in the next town," and instinctively she nodded her head in a westerly direction. The photographer didn't look like a photographer, or rather having imagined a Richard Avedon coming to her house, she found herself greeting what looked more like a stevedore who'd been sitting in a bar for a week in his Black Sabbath T-shirt, his saggy blue jeans, and several days' growth of beard. And yet a moment later she changed her mind. *Charming* wasn't the word at all. Nor *captivating*. *Devastating*: that was more like it. And instead of setting her at ease for what turned out to be two hours of posing and clicking, it left her tongue-tied and wondering, once he'd left, why, while he was there, she hadn't thought of Ben for a single moment.

The interviewer looked at her. "I just finished your new book last night. I thought it was wonderful." She dug about in her shoulder bag and took it out, placing it on the table between them as if to provide some proof of her deed.

"Thank you."

The woman took out a pen. "Would you…?"

"Of course. I'd be happy to."

Amelie opened it to the title page. Beneath it, just above her printed name, she added the long, loping line of her signature, all loops and curves and serifs. The interviewer thanked her and closed the cover. "Amelie Ferrar. Is it your real name?"

"Yes. But it's pronounced with three syllables: Ahm-eh-lee. It was my grandmother's name. She was French, she lived in Paris until just after the war."

The interviewer looked at her.

"The second one," Amelie said. And no, she wanted to add, the lady wasn't a collaborator. Or so the woman had claimed a little too often.

"It's pretty."

"Thank you," she said, though for years she'd hated her name. As a child she would berate her mother for having stuck her with it, for having named her after someone she had seen only in faded photographs taken in the distant monochrome past, a shapeless woman of eighty, her mouth sour and drawn. Now she liked it. She'd grown into it and had in some funny way taught herself how to use it, as though it were a stylish fashion accessory, something feathered, a veil.

She looked up at the new leaves on the trees, gently and imperceptibly uncurling over the long April afternoons beneath the impossible blue depths of the sky. She remembered the soft darkness of the examination room, the elaborate instruments designed to test the surface of her eye, the curve of each orb, the strength of her vision. She remembered the photographer holding his hand in the air over his shoulder, requesting stillness, and then suddenly reaching over and moving a lock of hair from her face. After he had taken what seemed to be hundreds of shots she asked if he'd like something cold to drink.

"I'd love it, but I have another session in an hour."

"Another writer?"

He told her who it was and she winced a little. "Yes, I know him."

"What's he like?"

"You'll find out soon enough, I'm sure," she said, and they both laughed. For a long moment he gazed at her. It was an open, brazen look, the kind she wasn't used to seeing in men, not even in Ben, who, now that she thought about it, was never quite there with her. But the photographer wasn't mentally undressing her; it was more that he was absorbed by her.

The photographer said, "Sorry I was staring. It's your eyes."

"What's wrong with them?"

"Well, that's the thing. Nothing's wrong. They're killer eyes. It's a shade of blue I don't think I've ever seen before. It's probably why the camera fell in love with you."

The words had lingered with her, and returned to the front of her mind as she sat out on the deck with the interviewer, who seemed to be anticipating a response to an unheard question.

Amelie said to the interviewer, "I'm sorry. Could you say that again, please?"

"I was wondering if there's been any film interest in the new book."

"I know that people have been reading it. Producers. Studios. No option has been taken out yet."

"Were you happy with the movie of your last one?"

Amelie smiled a little. "Well," she said, and together they laughed. Yet she'd been pleased it had been made, imperfect as it turned out to be. She'd enjoyed meeting the actors when they shot on location on the Cape, she'd liked the attention she received for the one day she was invited to be there. The actress playing the lead ate lunch with her at one of the folding tables that had been set up for cast and crew. She talked to Amelie about things that appeared in the script—peculiar things, uncomfortable things, naked things, dance things, word things, touch things—and Amelie had to point out that these things were not in the book and in fact had never crossed her mind when writing it. The actress turned to look at the director, who was eating a turkey sandwich and having a difficult conversation with one of the producers. "Scumbag," she said quietly, returning to her lunch and her tête-à-tête with the author.

"It was an interesting experience," Amelie said to the interviewer.

"Would you do it again?"

"Sell film rights to one of my books? I have to make a living, don't I?"

The young woman considered it. She fingered her glass and began to get a clever look on her face. "Even if they screw it up again."

Amelie smiled. "You thought so too?"

"Well, no. Not exactly."

"I certainly did."

"But you'd do it again."

Amelie smiled. "Without a moment's hesitation," she said.

4

AFTER THE INTERVIEW WAS OVER, AMELIE AND THE woman stepped off the deck and walked down into the garden and onto the gentle slope that eventually led to the brook. The interviewer said, "It's nice here. Do you live alone?"

"I'm divorced. My daughter's in her first year at college."

"It's quiet here," the interviewer said.

She'd seriously considered selling the house and moving elsewhere, perhaps to Manhattan or Los Angeles, a place where people ate in interesting restaurants, where people smiled and grew thinner by the day. It seemed ridiculous for her to remain alone in a house large enough for a family of four, and yet she was used to it, she had learned to fill the spaces. She worked in a small room overlooking the garden, she took her meals alone or with invited friends in the dining room, she read and listened to music in the living room. In this house nothing remained of her life with Richard, as if a crime had been committed and all evidence destroyed.

Even her memory had grown cloudy, and sometimes she would try to summon certain recollections of him, to picture him when she'd first known him, when she'd found joy with this man, and although for a fleeting moment she would catch sight of him, or remember some detail, a moment of laughter, an interesting conversation, he would inevitably slip away into another life, another place.

There were a few photographs from their earlier days together, the two of them with longer hair and the worst jeans ever designed, and though she had always meant to throw them away, she had stuffed them in a shoebox with other snapshots on a shelf in the cellar. It was strange how nothing was ever truly final. People might return, change their minds, take back their words. The dead might haunt, cross your path, chill your blood.

They spoke more often than most divorced couples she knew, mostly about Nina, about which of them was visiting her and when it would take place. For most of the summer before she left for college, Nina was fine. She enjoyed the job she'd taken at a local bookstore. And then everything seemed to tumble into disaster.

As August wore on, she grew moody and combative, and then a week before she was due to leave for college she decided she wasn't going to go, that she was taking a year off to travel. By then deposits had been made, loans had been granted, a whole new wardrobe purchased, and she sat and stared at her mother and folded her arms and said nothing. Precisely what Amelie had done before she left for Mount Holyoke all those years ago. Except in her case it was a statement of independence. Amelie had told her mother that she was going to move to New York. What she was going to do there was still up in the air, but that it would involve visits to Studio 54 and maybe sweeping floors at CBGB, a comment that compelled her mother to take up drinking straight gin after three years of sobriety. In the end, Amelie did go to Mount Holyoke and graduated magna cum laude four years later.

Amelie tried reasoning with her daughter, something her

mother had utterly failed at. "But Wellesley was your first-choice school, remember? And when we toured it you said you loved it," and Nina said, "Yeah, so?"

Amelie called Richard and insisted he come over so they could provide a united front, and he turned out to be as helpless as she was, battered by his daughter's absurd counterarguments. To Amelie's dismay, he tried bribery, pulling twenties and fifties from his pocket and holding them in the air like live bait at a crowded fishing hole, and Nina only said, "I don't want your money. I've decided I'm going to hitchhike to LA, and then maybe one day if I feel like it I'll go to college." In California she was going to be a fashion designer, she said, and when Amelie explained that the competition for that sort of thing was, well, a bit stiff, especially as her daughter's experience with clothes was primarily in buying and returning them, Nina told them she would get a job at a TV show, as a production assistant or something. "Or maybe I'll write a script. Or take up acting." She shrugged a sullen *whatever*. Which looked more like one giant *fuck you*.

"Do you have any idea what it's like, thumbing rides across the country? Do you have any idea what's out there?" She pictured her daughter on a lonely road in the hot Mojave Desert, and saw motorcycles and outlaws descending upon her, and then one day, long after she'd disappeared, they'd find her remains in a gully off Mulholland Drive.

"You'll meet some cool guy in his vintage Mustang, and he'll tell you how beautiful you are and invite you to a party, and you'll go and meet all these other girls like yourself and these cool guys, and before you know it they'll be sending you out to fetch firewood, or taking you down to the Valley to dive for food in dumpsters, and then you'll start sleeping with them, and one day you and your pals will drive to someone's house in Benedict Canyon and butcher them in cold blood. And when they hunt you down and arrest you..." Exhausted, she let her words drift into silence. It was a story she'd heard before, and it didn't seem worth the recounting.

"You have a really twisted mind, Mom, you know that?"

She knew it all too well. Sometimes Amelie wished she'd been born without an imagination; she found that it only led to grief and nightmare, as though by simply dreaming up things she allowed them a kind of life apart from her, like some monster in a film, growling and roaming the countryside, throwing innocent children to drown in the lily pond.

Usually it just led to just another book, although when people misbehaved in hers they didn't cut people's throats or shoot them in the back of the head. They said hurtful things, and sometimes walked out of their lives; yet behind the gentle sarcasm of the dia-logue and the apparently innocent actions—phone calls, afternoon visits, meals with friends—seemed to lurk something much darker, touching upon the baser human feelings of betrayal, revenge, the bleak mindful joy of people destroying one another: things that never usually made their way to the forefront of her mind.

She always felt that was why her readers remained faithful to her. Somehow she knew just what they were thinking and plot-ting, sensing what kept them awake at night. It was why she'd built such a wide readership, mostly of other women. *We read, we speculate, we live vicariously outside the confines of our own existence. And then life, in all its dull passing of time, always seems to get in the way. Until someone makes the next move.*

She sat beside Nina and looked her in the eye. "I understand how you're feeling. Believe it or not, I was a lot like you."

"You wanted to murder people?"

She couldn't tell whether Nina was serious or simply treating her mother like the idiot she appeared to be. In fact, Amelie had been nothing like Nina. Never beset with the usual adolescent complaints—weight gain, excessive acne—she became the object of admiration and then lust of the boys in her school, leading to outright resentment from the other girls. Presumed to be a slut, she was instead bookish and solitary, happy to sit with an apple and a novel in a corner while her mother practiced Bach preludes on the piano downstairs.

"Because I'm *nothing* like you," Nina went on, and Amelie waited as the words hung in the air.

"And I'm glad you're not," Amelie said. "You're your own person. Just like I did, you'll make your own mistakes, you'll earn your own rewards, and I can't stop you from doing any of that."

"So I can go to LA?"

"Yes. But I just want you to be safe when you do this, not find yourself lost in some, I don't know, some roadside saloon surrounded by a bunch of tattooed bikers with beers in their fists. This is your life and I need to respect your choices. Just watch out for the guys with no teeth."

Nina laughed, and Amelie was surprised to find her daughter hugging her. And without another word, the matter was settled. A few days before they were due at Wellesley, Nina asked if they could leave earlier on the first day so she could tour the town one more time before classes began. "And I need a new pair of jeans."

Amelie gleefully shared the news with Richard over the phone, and he wondered aloud how she did it without waving cold, hard cash in front of their daughter.

"She came to the decision on her own," Amelie said. "Isn't that the way it's supposed to be?" She wondered if that's how he'd won the heart of his new wife, by offering monetary bribes to make up for all his many shortcomings.

When her new book appeared in the shops only a week before her interview on the deck, Richard had taken the time to congratulate her and say he was anxious to read it. "Your jacket photo's different," he said, and she explained that her publisher thought it was time to update the portrait. This time the photographer, who actually did remind her of Avedon, had been careful to retouch it in subtle ways: the lines around her eyes, the ones that had begun to show about her mouth. Like a copy editor of human physiognomy, he granted her the veneer of eternal perfection.

"You look good," Richard said. Did she detect the slightest nuance of desire in his voice, did some hazy vision of her from years earlier suddenly rise up in his memory like a mist?

"How's Sharon?" she said.

"She's fine."

There was a pause.

"Actually," he said, "she's expecting," and at first Amelie didn't quite grasp what he was saying. Did he mean something was supposed to arrive in the mail, or delivered by the UPS man, shoes or a skirt or something for the kitchen?

"Oh" was all she could say when it dawned on her.

"It's due in September."

"Congratulations." She couldn't imagine her ex-husband suddenly thrust all these many years later back into the role of father to a newborn infant, unable to picture him, in the grip of middle age, rising in the small hours to change a diaper or prepare a feeding. She thought of Nina: pink and soft, as though instead of lying in the murky waters of her womb she had been bathing in milk for nine months. Simply holding her little girl had made her feel whole and decent and clean, and watching her grow with all the usual issues had only made her love Nina all the more.

It was as if, with the birth of her daughter, her life had been redeemed in a way that her writing had failed to do. There were no words to spill, no paragraphs to indent, no chapters to plot. There was simply Nina and Amelie, and for a time it was all that she needed. And then, as Nina grew, Amelie saw with a kind of melancholic satisfaction that she'd given birth not to a perfect creature but to someone very like herself, a person who stumbled into error, who rose to the occasion when called upon, who at times worried over her life a little too much. She hoped Nina wouldn't become a writer, spending her life hiding behind fictions, composing sentences to be worn like a mask. At readings, people had no idea what Amelie was really like, how utterly messy her life had become, and the thought of it brought her a degree of joy. Because it was the mess that she loved: the risks, the secrets, the utter deceit of the thing. It was like living on the lip of a cliff, like surfing in a hurricane sea.

"I'm glad for you," she said to her ex. "And Sharon."

"Thanks. We're…" And he left the sentence unfinished.

Amelie said, "I'm thinking of driving down to see Nina next weekend." The idea had just come to her.

"Really."

"Yes."

"Well."

"I'll send her your love."

"I was thinking of calling her myself," he said.

"Then I won't bother," she said.

5

IT WAS STRANGE HOW DISTURBED SHE WAS WHEN SHE called the second time that evening and Ben hadn't answered, as though the rules of their universe had somehow been broken. Although it wasn't the first time it had happened, it didn't often occur. She pictured his wife at that precise moment: getting ready for bed, undressing in the bedroom, unbuttoning her blouse, making small talk while he slipped off his shoes, looked at his watch, conveniently forgot Amelie Ferrar. His wife, Janet, remained an enigma to her, like a suspect in a mystery story. Yet they had one thing in common: each, in her own way, was the Other Woman.

Now it was time for another drink. She got up and threw some ice cubes into her glass and poured vodka onto them. The blue of the day had given up to darkness, the air filling with sounds she had known for most of her life, yet which remained unidentifiable in origin: the strange minimalism of peepers, the odd chipping of some insect. The natural world played little role in her books: when people touched the bark of a tree it remained unnamed; when a bird sang prettily in the early morning it was just another winged creature. Once she had spent two months traveling in England, where she'd made an effort to learn the names of things, the blooms and grasses of Kew Gardens, the great antique trees that lay toppled in the ancient West Country woods, the wildflowers that twisted their insidious way into the hedgerows of Dorset and Devon. They had names like wolfsbane and woundwort, bird's-foot trefoil, petty whin, and Carthusian pink, and it was just like her to forget the plants but remember the words.

She put her hand on the phone and considered trying again. How many times could she do it before his wife would grow suspicious? Technology had overtaken the lover's ruse: buttons could be pushed, numbers identified, calls blindly returned.

She slid open the door and stepped from the kitchen onto the deck. It was too early in the season for mosquitoes, though moths had begun to appear with their pale nocturnal bodies, their powdery wings. She put her hands on the wooden rail and looked out into the darkness of her garden, and beyond it the brook, the fields, and farther on the woods and the sky, eventually the sea. She sometimes wished there'd be something to look at, something to see into, other lives, just as when she was young she would watch the wordless little dramas unfold through the windows of other houses on her street: marital spats marked by the baring of teeth and the shedding of tears; scenes of amorous abandon, the pressed faces, clasping arms, the curve of a woman's back, the gestures and poses of people losing their balance at the edge of a cliff. The world of adults, as she thought then, and how dead right she'd been.

She turned her head slightly, her eyes went out of focus, now she could hear it, now it was closing in. The car came to a stop, a door opened. Now everything was better.

6

SHE WOKE EARLY, HAD FRUIT AND COFFEE, AND walked for half an hour at the edge of the road, stepping onto the grass whenever a car or truck passed. The morning air was cold and the breeze bit into the skin of her face, and yet the sun was warm and she could feel herself breaking into a sweat. Although most of her friends belonged to a local fitness center with its treadmills and weights and spinning classes, she preferred a quiet, solitary amble, a time when she could gather her thoughts, prepare for the day's work.

Idling and kicking next to their backpacks, children waited in front of their driveways for school buses. An appliance-repair van drove slowly by, and the driver caught her eye, turning his head to look at her as he passed. A month earlier a car had pulled up alongside her, and the driver, a heavyset man in dark glasses, asked if she needed a lift. She said, "No thanks," and then he said, "Hop in."

"I'm taking a walk," she said, as if it weren't obvious.

"I'd like you to get in."

"No."

She remembered the sudden pain in her stomach, the loss of breath, the immediate realization that things were moving into another dimension, a fun-house room of distorting mirrors and uncertain footing. She thought of Nina before she left for college, considering a three-thousand-mile hitchhiking trip into the unknown, and here was her mother, fifteen minutes from her house with a creepy man in a rusty car.

"I want you to see something interesting," he said, reaching to open the passenger door.

But by then she had glanced at his license plate and begun to back away, knowing he would have to reverse or turn around, and she started to run. But he didn't reverse or turn around; he drove on at speed. She had left her phone at home, and reminded herself never to do that again.

When she got back she called Ben at his office. "There was this man," she began, and then she lost control, she was in tears, and her stomach continued to churn.

"But nothing happened," he said after she told him about it.

"Nothing had to happen. I was frightened anyway."

"Come on."

"You don't understand."

"But—"

"Go to hell," she said, hanging up.

By the time she called the police she had forgotten even a single digit or letter of the man's plate number. She described the car, she described the man, and the officer asked how tall he was.

"He never stood up."

"Can you estimate it at least? I need to put something down."

"I told you, he was sitting in his car."

"Six feet?"

"I don't know."

"Five nine?"

"He was in his car."

"He never touched you?"

"He was going to rape me."

The officer cleared his throat. "You said he asked if you wanted a lift."

"He was a complete stranger to me."

"Maybe he was trying to be friendly," the cop said. "A lift is not sexual assault."

"He insisted on my getting in. Do you call that being friendly?"

"Maybe it's a matter of interpretation, Ms. Ferrar."

"He said he wanted to show me something interesting. Do you think he was going to whip out a Blue Period Picasso?"

"What he said doesn't in itself indicate anything of a criminal nature."

"So you're not going to look for him, is that what you're saying?"

"I just need to know how tall he is," he said, and she clicked off and called Ben's office again.

"My secretary is wondering who keeps phoning me, I can see her face through the glass."

"I don't give a damn, Ben. I just need a little sympathy," she said.

"Now?"

"Forget it," and she hung up again.

For a few weeks she kept off the roads in her area, walking instead in a state park twenty minutes away. Now she was back to her routine and she felt safer and more secure, only because time had softened the fear.

When she returned from her walk the morning after the interview she saw a message had been left for her on her cell. She brightened when she saw who it was, and then his voice came on. *Janet just left to take Andrew to school, so I'm going to the office. Last night was amazing. I'm sorry you were upset that I didn't call you first, but I just wanted to surprise you. So. But. It was really nice being able to get out. Um. To see you.*

She smiled to herself, not because of the call or the sound of his voice or his choice of words or the little hesitancies she had always found charming, but because she remembered how it had felt twelve hours earlier, how even though it was just a quick one it pleased her more than he could imagine. She took off her sneakers and socks and yoga pants and sweatshirt and T-shirt and underwear and stepped into the shower. She lifted her face to the water and shut her eyes as it streamed into her hair and ran down her body. She began working the shampoo into her hair. She lathered up the soap and, with a mitt, rubbed it on her skin. She shaved her legs and rinsed off and then she was done.

The drive to the bookstore would take nearly an hour. Though her reading was scheduled for seven thirty, she left a few hours early. She would pick up her glasses and then continue on to the city. She would have a light supper at a nearby restaurant and then meet with the people at the store at seven. She sat in traffic on the highway and listened to NPR and watched the haze of the afternoon thicken over the unspectacular skyline. Things came to mind: the possibility of taking up smoking again, a habit she had ended because a few years before the divorce Richard had stopped and she felt it would be unfair to light up in the house. She wondered if she'd visit Nina on Saturday or Sunday, and on the little pad she kept in the car wrote *Call Nina*, and added an exclamation point. Perhaps she'd bring her something, food or something to wear, just as she used to at camp. Or she would take Nina shopping and then out to lunch, and would this entail inviting her roommate as well? She remembered the young woman's parents, the brass-buttoned blue blazer the father wore, his tasseled loafers and his striped necktie. While other parents tramped casually about the campus in jeans and sweaters, the roommate's mother for some reason wore a yachting outfit, white slacks and a little jacket with piping, and Amelie wondered if there was also a cap involved, something naval she'd left in the car or on her boat or at the marina. The woman had asked Amelie what sort of books she wrote.

"I write about… Well, they're kind of hard to describe. They're about people like you and me," and she waved her hand in the air to indicate every other well-off adult wandering the campus. "I'm mainly interested in how our inner lives are so different from how we act in life. The contrast. I mean, we're all so preoccupied with how people look, how they dress, if they're famous or not, but it's what's inside that interests me. What they're hiding."

It seemed amazing to her how such a literate person could sound so inarticulate. She wondered why people were so interested in what writers thought, or even in describing what they wrote, while in fact authors' lives were usually rounds of self-destructive behavior alternating with baroque fantasies about themselves and others; it was what they put on the page that mattered most. That was the face they wanted others to see, not the thing that startled them every morning in the blaze and glare of the unforgiving bathroom mirror.

The woman sniffed and said she only read cozy mysteries.

Amelie remembered that Nina was not overly fond of her roommate, and that was just as well, for she was a large girl with an unmistakably hungry look in her eye, and lunch might have become something more than a salad or a sandwich; it might have turned into an expensive, three-course feast. No: she would take Nina on her own, they would shop, they would eat, they would walk and talk, and Richard could go to hell if he couldn't find the time to leave his new wife even for two hours.

The woman on the car radio asked her to call in and pledge fifty dollars, in return for which she'd receive a coffee mug with a picture of some other announcer on it. If you pledged seventy-five dollars you received a voucher for dinner at some exotic bistro, and if you pledged five hundred dollars you got to eat with the man whose picture was on the mug. Next week Amelie was due to tape an interview for broadcast on this very station, and stations like it all across the country would be syndicating it. The whole thing would take less than half an hour, to be edited down to something like eight minutes.

She liked to be interviewed, she liked to be photographed, she liked to be talked about. It went along with the job, and yet there were areas in her life that could not suffer the light of day, places of whisper and code that, if discovered, would cause misery and grief to others. She thought of Ben's two children and his wife. How long would it go on, this subterfuge? Twice she'd seriously asked him to leave his family and live with her, and twice he said *Not now, it's not the right time*, and she asked when the right time would be, and all he could do was shrug and say that he didn't know.

She was off the highway now, moving from stop sign to red light, pulling off the road and parking in the little strip mall. The man working at the optician's recognized her from a few days before. He said her glasses were just about ready, that he was giving them one last cleaning, and he held them up to the light and examined the lenses. He stepped around the counter and asked Amelie to sit, and then he slid them over her ears and let them rest on the bridge of her nose. Amelie glanced at herself in the mirror. Now that they had been mounted with glass they seemed less becoming. The man asked her how they felt, and Amelie said they were a little tight over her ears. He took them off and made an adjustment. This went on for ten minutes, off and on, off and on, and then they were done. She was handed a laminated card with printing on it. She looked through the lenses and read the lines to herself, *You can change your life simply by changing the color of your eyes. Ask your optometrist about*, and she looked up and smiled. "That's so much better." It was like magic.

The man took some cases out of a drawer. Amelie chose a soft blue one, and he slid the glasses inside it.

"If there's any problem just bring them in," he said.

In the car she took the glasses out of the case and slipped them on. She looked at her watch and the numbers were distinct and black, and then she took the glasses off and the numbers sizzled into a smoky blur. She looked at herself in the mirror attached to her visor, settling the glasses on her face, moving her head this way and that. She wondered how they would look when her hair was loose instead of being pulled back and clipped, and she reached behind and released her hair and then everything fell into place, glasses, hair, face, and attitude.

She drove away and pulled back onto the highway. She wondered if she would have to wear the glasses for her reading. Still a novelty, they would make her feel uncomfortable, stared at, awkward. She wouldn't wear them, then. She would manage without them, she would stand at the lectern and read the first twenty pages of the book and then answer questions from the audience. She wondered if anyone would actually show up. She remembered when she'd first started doing these events years ago, how sometimes a few people would come and introduce themselves, only to reveal they had never heard of her but they wished her the best of luck anyway, leaving with someone else's latest book in their mitts.

Once, after her last novel had broken onto the bestseller lists, Ben had come to a reading at a bookshop two towns away from hers. It had been scheduled for a Sunday afternoon, and something like forty people were there to hear her, the majority of them elderly women who sat with their arms crossed, their mouths firmly shut, their eyes flashing as she read her tale of suburban lust. She remembered looking up and seeing Ben and his wife, Janet, arriving and sitting on folding chairs in the first row. Janet smiled at her. Ben looked away. She had seen Janet before, because their daughter had been in the same class as Nina, and at school functions they would occasionally politely greet each other.

Amelie stood at a lectern in the back room of the bookshop and for the first time was able to look all she wished at her lover's wife. It was odd. It was odd not so much because she was in the same room as this woman, but because it suddenly dawned on her that she and Janet looked so much alike. Janet was blond, Janet was slim; blue-eyed Janet was sitting next to Ben in her jeans and turtleneck. Amelie took her eyes off Janet and stared briefly and coldly at Ben, and then later when he called her, the first thing she said was, "Whose idea was that?"

"What do you mean?"

"You know what I'm talking about. How could you do such a thing?"

"You mean Janet."

"That's right."

"She'd read your last book. She'd taken it out of the library and wanted to hear you read. What was I supposed to do, refuse to let her go?"

Now her anger shifted its focus. "She didn't even buy it?" she said.

"Oh, come on."

"Okay," she said. "Forget it."

Now when she thought about it she even laughed a little, because time had passed and they were still together, Amelie and Ben. And Janet.

One of them would have to go.

7

WHEN AMELIE ARRIVED IN WELLESLEY ON SATURDAY morning, Nina was waiting for her at the gate. It was astonishing how much her daughter had changed since starting college. Amelie couldn't quite say how, but little things—the way Nina stood, the way she smiled, how the elements in her face had shifted—were subtly coming together to define what was now a woman. She smiled and gave a little girlish wave when she saw the car, and Amelie was pleased that a trace of childhood still remained. She slid down the window. "I'm not late, am I?"

Nina shook her head. Now she was not smiling.

"What's wrong?"

"Nothing." She got in beside her mother. Her eyes were red, and she looked wan and unwell.

Amelie put her hand on Nina's. "What's wrong, baby?"

Nina smiled a little. "Nothing."

"What would you like to do?"

"Nothing."

"Do you want to shop, do you need anything?"

"No. Nothing."

"Do you want to eat?"

Nina shook her head.

"Are you in trouble?"

"No."

"You're not—"

"*No*," and she shook her head with exasperation.

"Let's get out of here," Amelie said, and she followed the narrow road out through another gate. Other students, books in hand, walked toward the library. A few others jogged or rode bicycles. One or two saw Nina and waved at her. Nina seemed beyond tired and looked more like Richard than ever before. "Have you heard from your dad?"

"He called last night but I wasn't in."

Amelie looked at her.

"I called him back this morning," Nina said, pushing some hair back behind her ear. "He said he'd called to say you were coming."

"But you already knew that."

"That's what I told him."

"Did he really think I wouldn't let you know in advance?"

"I don't know," said Nina.

"I mean, really. *Jesus*," Amelie said, and she felt like tearing the steering wheel off its column.

"Slow down," Nina said.

"Let's get some lunch." Amelie pulled the car into a space. On the bumper on the car ahead of hers a sticker read *Mean People Suck*. She turned off the ignition and looked at her daughter. "What's going on with you?"

"It's nothing."

"It's not nothing, it's something. Is it school?"

Nina shook her head.

"Do you want to tell me?"

"It's nothing," Nina said, and she opened the door and got out.

They had to wait ten minutes for a table. Nina stood with her mother and shyly waved at a man with a trim gray beard and a wife as they were just about to leave. He smiled and waved back and left the restaurant. Amelie and Nina were seated at his table. It was covered with bread crumbs and pools of salad dressing. "My English professor is a slob," Nina said.

"Aren't you feeling well?"

"I'm all right."

"You're not all right."

"I'm just…" Nina said, letting it go.

"I did a reading in town on Thursday."

Amelie remained shaken by what had happened afterward, an event she was still in the process of evaluating. She lived in a world of order and compartment: here she was a writer, here a mother, here a lover. Rarely did any of these intersect. Until now. And it remained troubling to her, like the onset of headache, an incipient pain just behind the eye that has yet to blossom into something disabling.

The waitress came over and wiped the table clean. They ordered their drinks and meals.

"You've been working hard, haven't you," Amelie said.

Nina had always been a reliably good student, not in the way that some were, not because the correct answer or brilliant interpretation was there for the taking, on the edge of her mind, but because she worked through things slowly and meticulously.

"I've been really busy," Nina said. She seemed to hide behind her hair. Amelie reached over and pushed it aside and Nina nudged her away.

"How's your roommate?"

"I don't know. She's not here anymore."

"She's gone?"

Nina shrugged. "She left last week."

"You're kidding."

"She called her father, and he just picked her up and took her away."

"You mean she's not going to finish her year?"

"I guess not."

"Was she sick?"

"Probably," and she tapped her head with her finger.

The waitress brought them each iced tea. Amelie removed the straw and drank from the glass. Nina sipped a little. She said, "How did the reading go? I really should have taken the train in and seen you."

"I would have liked that. You never used to like to go to my readings."

"But I should have gone."

In which case what had transpired afterward might never have occurred.

"What did you do on Thursday?"

The waitress brought their salads. She stood by the table looking at them. Amelie looked up at her.

"Can I get you anything else?" the waitress said, and Amelie said, "No thank you, nothing," and the waitress left them alone.

"There's this guy," Nina said.

Amelie said nothing.

"He's this guy I started seeing."

Amelie waited.

"I'm not seeing him anymore," she said.

8

BEN NEVER TALKED ABOUT HIS WIFE. HE NEVER MEN-tioned what she had been doing lately or what she wore, what she read, the music she listened to, where she wished to travel. Sometimes, in the early days of their affair, Amelie in her inno-cence wondered how Janet must have endured being so ignored by her husband, why she hadn't grown instantly suspicious of him, only to realize that Ben was living two distinct lives, that when he was with his wife he was her husband, and when with Amelie her lover. Whom did he love more? Did he love each woman in different ways? Once Amelie sat up in bed and asked Ben what it was like making love to Janet. She demanded all the details, everything they did, what she said, how she touched him, how long it took.

He said, "Come on, Amelie," and she said, "Just tell me."

"Will it turn you on?" he said.

"Maybe."

"Is that why you're asking?"

"I'm just curious. And I like hearing things put into words. Do you think your wife is pretty?"

"Yes."

She was tempted to ask if he thought her more beautiful than she was.

He said, "It's a lot quicker with her."

"Because of the kids?"

"Because of us," he said. "Because of Janet and me."

He talked around his wife as if with his words he were forming the shape of her, the heft of her, the depth and the scent of her, and sometimes it seemed to Amelie as if her lover's wife were in the room with them, silently watching as they pressed lips and touched each other's skin. Would it have been better if he'd been more forthright about the matter, had he treated Janet as simply another part of his life, and that between both women was a thick and impenetrable wall, leaden and windowless?

She knew that he avoided the subject because it would offend her, because she would have been reminded that it was Janet who lived with this man and not Amelie. It was Janet who had him to herself at night before sleep, and in the morning as they roused in the cool hour of dawn.

Once, early in their affair, Amelie and Ben had made love and then fallen asleep in her bedroom in her house in the heat of the summer afternoon: a brief, delicate sleep on top of the sheets, her leg draped over his, his arm beneath her head. The sun streamed through the window, throwing bars of light on their bodies, and a breeze passed through the room, gently agitating the tiny blond hairs on her arms. It had been so hot that a tiny pool of sweat remained in the cup of her navel. He laughed gently to himself and this roused her. "What?" she said, laughing a little in her own way.

"Nothing."

"No, tell me," and she reached down and touched him in a playful way.

"No."

"Please."

"No."

She poked him in the side of his ribs and he jumped. "Come on, Janey," he said.

She looked at him. "Who the hell is Janey?"

He said nothing.

"Who's Janey?" she said, tightening her hand around his arm.

"It's what I call Janet. What I used to call her."

"You forgot my name?"

"Where are you going?"

He watched as she walked away from the bed, her bare back, her legs, her shoulders.

"Damn it, are you angry?"

"Don't be ridiculous," she said lightly, and slammed the bathroom door so hard that it splintered the jamb.

9

"HIS NAME IS PETER," NINA SAID, AND THEN PICKED at her salad. She said nothing about how long they had been seeing each other, how serious she had been, what they had talked about, what she was going to do. Amelie watched her as she ate, looking at the top of her head, and their eyes only met once, when Nina said, "Guess who called me?"

Amelie looked at her.

"Rachel. You know. Her dad's the architect." She shrugged. "I forget what her mom does. You met them at school, right?"

"Sounds familiar," Amelie said.

Nina said Rachel was going to Smith and had called her for no reason at all, just to say hello, maybe they'd get together one of these days, that sort of thing. They had been at the same private school ever since sixth grade and now they had gone their separate ways. It was how Amelie had met Ben: their daughters provided the excuse for the early course of their affair. Each parent had suddenly developed a passionate interest in school activities, joining the same committees, helping out at the spring workday. It gave them opportunities to be together, to have a public identity that implied hard work and selflessness, and often, when wantonly twisted into the sheets of her bed, they would laugh at this elegant turn of fiction they had created together.

Now, with her daughter at college, there was no excuse for Amelie to be at the school, no reason to be involved, and she often thought of Ben sitting in his car at dismissal time, alone and waiting for his son, Andrew, the lusty eyes of other women turned on him.

"What did she want?" Amelie said, and Nina stared at her because her mother's voice had risen sharply above the din in the restaurant.

"Why? What's wrong?"

"I'm just curious. What's up with Rachel?"

"She likes school." Nina said nothing more.

Amelie called for the bill. There was a line at the front of the restaurant, students and some parents, locals and people who had come to shop for the day, waiting for tables. It was odd that Rachel had called Nina just like that, for no apparent reason, and Amelie began to play with the idea, to dissect it, just as she would a sonnet by Shakespeare in college, seeking out obscure hints, unexpected allusions. She wanted to whip out her phone and speak to Ben, to warn him, to ask him to question Rachel, and yet part of her also knew that it was perfectly innocent, Rachel calling Nina. It was what friends did, after all, they took out their phone and called.

They went out onto the sidewalk. Amelie said, "Did you have enough to eat? Would you like an ice cream?"

"Mm," Nina said, indecisive.

Amelie said, "Is there anything you need?" She gestured toward the window of a clothing shop. "That's a nice shirt."

"It's all right," she said.

"Is there anything you want, then?"

Nina shook her head.

"Is there anything you'd like to do?" She wanted to hear more about what had happened to Nina, she wanted to comfort her in her heartbreak, to hold her in her arms, absorb her tears. They began to walk, saying nothing, looking at window displays, grimacing when a car drove by with its stereo blasting, and then the car moved rapidly into the distance and it was quiet again.

She turned it over: Rachel had called Nina. Now Amelie's mind began to move in another direction, a place of palaces and winged horses, of golden-edged clouds and libation bearers, for the fact that Ben's daughter had called Nina meant that they might rekindle their friendship. It moved in steps: separation, divorce, remarriage. Then the girls would be half sisters. Their friendship would make it happen. And she smiled to herself, for it was a ridiculous thing to be thinking about, and suddenly Nina said, "I'm still hungry."

Amelie had been surprised to see her daughter had finished her salad. With her head bowed, fork moving from bowl to mouth, bowl to mouth, she had said little. Amelie noticed her hair had probably not been washed for two or three days.

"You're really still hungry?" Amelie said. Had a man broken off a relationship with her, she would have lost her appetite immediately, not just for food and drink but for all the pleasures of her life—writing, books, friends, travel, music, sleep, long baths, nice clothes, and, of course, sex.

"Actually, I'd really like an ice cream," Nina said.

"All right."

They walked to a shop around the corner. Nina ordered some absurdly named frenzy of ice cream and fragmented cookies served in a huge cup. Amelie had nothing. At her age her figure could go at any time, and why, she thought, hasten the inevitable process now.

They walked until they reached the park across from the town library. They sat and watched the geese as a woman and her child tossed pellets of bread at the creatures. They took the bread greedily, the fowl. They snapped their beaks and stretched their necks and screamed for more and ran about shitting eagerly and without discrimination, as if their digestive system were a simple tube running from mouth to tail.

"I haven't read your new book yet," Nina said.

"There's plenty of time. You have your studies."

"But I want to read it."

"I know you do, baby. Look, I'm sorry about what happened. About this boy and you. Did he hurt you in any way?"

Nina looked at her.

"I meant did he hurt you physically. You know."

Nina shook her head.

"He didn't try to do something you didn't want him to do," Amelie said, more statement than question, and again Nina shook her head.

"Do you want to tell me about this Peter?" Amelie asked, realizing at once that it was a mistake to inquire, that if Nina wanted to say anything she would do it when she was ready.

At first Nina said nothing. Then she said, "I feel really bad about it."

Amelie put her arm around her. "I know you must. It hurts, doesn't it."

"It's not that, it's—"

Amelie looked at her.

"I just feel really bad for him."

Amelie said, "Why?"

"I mean it just wasn't going to work out. I mean he's a nice guy and he's smart and all, but I just didn't think it was going to work out."

"You mean *you* broke up with *him*?"

Nina looked at her as though her mother were incredibly stupid. "What did you think happened?" she said.

10

TWO EVENINGS EARLIER, THE ROOM HAD BEEN FILLED to capacity for Amelie's reading. The person in charge of these events at the store told her that people had called in advance to reserve places and also to make sure there were books available. "And the reviews have been very nice," he said.

The early reviews had been better than very nice; they had been exceptionally positive. She was already at number eight on the *Times* bestseller list, and she had sold foreign rights to nine countries. A week earlier one of the Boston papers had run an article on her along with a photograph, and it was this piece that had brought in the large audience.

She and the events coordinator sat in a little alcove an hour before her scheduled time. "We've ordered two hundred copies, and of course after you're done, people will want to buy books and have you sign them." He smiled and nodded to a desk that had been set up for her. On it were stacks of books, a carafe of water, a glass, and a pen, though she always brought her own Montblanc. A few shoppers moved quietly from table to table, one or two of them looking her way as she tried out the lectern, adjusted the height of the microphone. He said, "Is there anything else you'll need?"

A large vodka might do the trick, but she only said, "I don't think so."

He looked at his watch. "There's still some time. There's a café upstairs if you'd like some coffee, or..." and she said she really needed to get a proper meal. He suggested a restaurant a few doors away. She was sorry she'd forgotten to bring something to read. She went down to look at the new releases and bought a paperback of a novel she'd been interested in.

When she entered the restaurant the people who were sitting at the bar, mostly men in suits, turned and looked at her. Most seemed young enough to be her sons. A man with silver hair sipped bourbon and brazenly smiled at her. Had she not had Ben in her life, would she have been promiscuous, would she have spent her days and night at bars like this one, and would she have become addicted to dating apps, haunted the nightclubs, stood on street corners, grown desperate in her solitude, died at the hands of Mr. Goodbar? But for Ben. He would always be there for her. Late, as always, but there, and she smiled at the thought of him. And smiled, too, as she thought of the bourbon sipper looking her way.

Which meant what, that a part of her was still outside the bond of Amelie-and-Ben, that she was, one, always keeping an eye out just in case, or, two, that she needed to be flattered, to know that men other than Ben appreciated her? It wasn't as if she needed the occasional dose of self-esteem. She was content with her looks, and more than happy with the work she produced, and maybe it was just that tiny bit of risk she missed. Risk other than, of course, having an affair with a married man. But risk had always been an underlying subject for her: her characters often took risks, and yet the consequences were moral ones, a sustained fracture in a family unit, an emotional breakdown that left permanent scars. Or it resulted in a prolonged regret, the idea that the character could have done something differently. They were risks that most people of her generation understood, and she knew this was what drew her readers to come back for more with each title released. These were the familiar valleys to their shared suburban life.

She just sometimes wished she could create a protagonist who could break the curtain of civility as she had never been able to do in life. Having an affair was a consensual joy; murder was its frontier.

A woman greeted her. "Table for one?"

Soon, eventually, sometime in the future, she would no longer be one. She looked forward to when she would be able to carry on with certain parts of her life in public, to be able to sit across from Ben in a restaurant such as this, to have a drink with him and eat dinner and maybe even spend the evening at the theater or a movie. Like a normal couple, in fact.

The waitress said, "Can I get you something to drink?"

Amelie slipped on her new glasses and looked at her watch. She would like a drink, only one, for to have more would be to court danger at her reading. There would be slurred words and uncontrollable giggling and she imagined she might even doze off in the middle of a paragraph. Of course she could play it safe and order a glass of wine. "And the ladies' room…?"

The waitress indicated a stairway leading downstairs. She walked to the end of the narrow hallway, past the two doors with their stick-figure gender labels, and speed-dialed his cell number on her iPhone. She knew he would be working late, as he always did on Thursdays, her mind traveling the length of the circuit, moving up the coast and then a few miles inland, and then he answered and he sounded tired, and she said only, "It's me."

"I know."

"I'm in the city. I haven't done the reading yet. I'm having dinner. Any chance you could drive down and spend time with me afterward?" and she could hear it in her own voice, the bend of desire for the impossible to happen.

The man with the silver hair stepped out of the men's room and, looking directly at her, smoothed his hair back over his scalp. Passing very close and leaving his scent on her, he ascended the stairs.

"I'd really like to see you," he said. "But I can't."

"I know. I just thought I'd try." She laughed a little. "Can you come over to the house later? I'll be home by ten or ten thirty at the latest."

"I don't think so."

"Why not?"

"I don't think I can get out."

"That's never really been a problem before."

"I just don't think I can do it. I'm exhausted, I've been working all day."

"I'm tired too."

"You know I'm working against a deadline."

"But I'd get out for you."

"Look, Amelie."

"I'd get out for you. I'd get in my car without a second thought."

"Look."

She held the phone away from her ear and stared at it as if

she had suddenly forgotten what it was. Then she clicked off, with a violent downward motion, as though plunging a dagger into his chest.

Her pinot noir was waiting for her. She took a long drink and, when the waitress returned, ordered another glass and some sort of pasta dish, simply pointing to the name on the menu. She looked at the book she had bought. Now everything about it repelled her—the ugly cover, the photo of the author on the back, the simpering smile on the woman's face, the idiotic way she held her hand by her face, almost certainly hiding the wattles of late middle age. Amelie didn't want to read, she didn't want to try out her new glasses, she didn't want to eat or smile and meet her readers, she didn't want to sign her name or answer questions, she wanted to drive home and find Ben and shake him so hard he would suddenly come to his senses and reduce his world to Amelie Ferrar.

She got up and went downstairs and called his number again. "Yes," he said, and it sounded like the hissing of a snake.

"I'm sorry. I just wanted to apologize."

She could hear him sigh, a great, huge dramatic sound.

"I know it's frustrating," he said.

"It's been two years, Ben. Haven't we got this down to a science yet? Wait—are you alone? I thought I heard a door shut."

"It's…nothing. Look, I know it's been tough on you."

"I'm home tomorrow," she said. "I'm visiting Nina on Saturday, and I'll be home that evening and all night and all day on Sunday. On Monday I'm driving back down here to record an interview on a radio station. It's a network thing for NPR, *All Things* whatever. Just so you know. Maybe you can get out for a little while and drop by? I'd love to see you."

He said nothing.

"Ben?"

After a moment he said, "Yes. I'm here." The flinty tone of his voice, his whole delivery, made him sound like someone else, a stranger who might otherwise have tried to assault her. She wondered if he was even at his office; with a cell phone he could be at the local Hooters or lost in the woods or sitting across from his wife.

She looked at her watch. "I've got to go. I've got to eat. I've got to give this reading," and she ended the call and walked back to her table. Her food was no longer hot. Warm, but not hot, and she ate it without a break, one forkful after another, chew and swallow, chew and swallow, and she finished her second glass of wine and ordered an espresso. She sipped it slowly, so slowly that when she reached the muddy dregs at the bottom of the tiny cup they were cold. She felt more herself by then, calmer. She knew that she had made an idiot of herself over the phone, badgering her lover with pointless demands, she knew he knew she loved him, she wanted him, and she would make it up to him.

She handed her credit card to the waitress and looked at her watch. Now she could face her audience, read her twenty pages, answer their questions. She would sign their books and accept their compliments and nod her head when they told her what her books meant to them, how they had been moved to tears or laughter, or that they had spoken up in book groups on her behalf. A few mistakes had been made: the pasta would stick in her throat and affect her voice; an extra glass of wine might have been one too many. Still. Still.

When she opened the door to the restaurant and turned to go

back to the bookstore, the last rays of sun were shining directly on her. For a moment she lifted her face and smiled as she absorbed the heat and the light. Now she could feel summer in the air. Soon it would be full upon her. She would swim; she would go on long walks, and she and Ben would find places where they could be together in the tall grass of August. It would be like starting all over again, just as it was on that hot September day they had first exchanged glances.

They met at the end of summer.

It was how her reading began.

11

AFTER SHE WAS INTRODUCED THERE WAS SOME gentle applause. She looked at the faces. Most were smiling; most were women; all must have seen her photos on book jackets or in newspapers or magazines, and now they were seeing her in the flesh. Until then she had only been the author of a number of volumes, novels that had distracted or amused them or, as she'd learned from readers who had talked to her, had served as a reflection of their own lives. Now they could see her as a person with a voice and a body, they could take in her blue eyes, her blond hair, they could see for themselves the woman loved by the architect.

As she did at all of her readings, she began quietly, with her eyes on her audience, as though she was simply telling them a story off the top of her head, something you might make up for a child at bedtime. She knew when to pause and when to lift her voice, and there were times when she would fix her attention on first one person in the audience, then another, as if speaking to each individually.

"*It was long past the time when the lilacs bloomed and the primroses grew vivid in the midday sun. Spring had come and gone, and peace had fallen upon her like a morning mist. She found the time to be alone, to be calm, to be what she'd always wanted to be...*"

Twenty-two minutes later she was done, nodding and smiling

to acknowledge the applause. The man from the store stood and called for questions from the audience. *Where do you get your ideas? Do you write every day, do you have certain hours set aside? Is Nicole Kidman really as pretty in person?* She answered the questions, as always, as though it were the first time she had ever heard them, with freshness and vitality and humor.

Now it was time to sit at the table and sign books, and she realized that she'd already grown dependent on her glasses. She thought of the two phone conversations she had had with Ben from the restaurant and regretted having spoken to him so abruptly. Perhaps he really couldn't get out tonight, maybe Andrew was sick, and yet if that were the case, why couldn't Janet look after the boy, why couldn't he just make the excuse that he'd left something at the office he needed to look at immediately...? He had done it before, he had told his wife he just needed to pick something up, and at high speed made his way to Amelie's house, to make quick half-dressed love to her on the dining room table, and he was back in his car ten minutes later. So why couldn't he do it now? The thought of it darkened her mind, weakened her smile, prodded at her attention. She'd pushed him, she'd urged and nagged, she'd left the conversation unresolved, and now he resented her.

The line for signed copies was dwindling, and at this stage it had become a mechanical exercise. Smile and sign, smile and sign, a few words here and there.

Without looking up, she said to the woman who had handed her a book, "I'm sorry, what was the name again?"

"Janet," she said.

12

IT TOOK HER A MOMENT TO PROCESS THE VARIOUS implications presented to her.

"Janet. Yes. Of course," and almost getting to her feet, Amelie instead smiled a little and took off her glasses, hoping the moment might lose its focus. "How nice to see you." The usual formulaic words, spoken under extreme duress.

"I had a dinner meeting not far from here and was walking by just now to my car and saw you were giving a reading. Since our daughters are friends, I thought, why not, I'll stop in, say hello, buy your latest novel. I really loved your last one," she added. "I'm sorry I missed your reading tonight, though."

The woman seemed sincere and open about it, and Amelie was too flustered to say anything more. She signed the book with *Warmest regards* and, still suspecting the worst was yet to come, handed it back.

"I wonder," Janet said. "Would you like to get a drink with me, or coffee?"

Without thinking, Amelie agreed that a drink would be nice, just to turn the event into a long and utterly unmemorable blur. As they walked Janet spoke a little about her work as CEO of a medical software company, a fact that Amelie had already learned from Ben. She knew that Janet had made a name for herself as someone who ran an ethical and socially conscious company in a crowded, competitive field full of grifters in lab coats.

They ended up in the same restaurant Amelie had eaten in a few hours earlier, and were seated at a table in the bar section. Janet ordered a cabernet and Amelie settled for her usual vodka martini.

"So," Janet said. "All this time and so much in common and I've never had the opportunity to chat with you."

Amelie smiled uncomfortably and tried to guess where this was going. She wondered if before the evening was over, she might be thrown from a moving car or strangled with Janet's expensive Hermès scarf, the victim of a properly vengeful wife. Until now she had thought Janet was totally ignorant of what her husband was doing; now she wasn't so sure. *So much in common…* The phrase seemed a little loaded to her. What did they have in common apart from daughters who went to school together…? Oh, right.

Now that Janet was barely a foot away from her, Amelie had a long, not-altogether objective look at her. *My rival*, as she thought of her. *The other woman.*

His *wife*.

Janet was pretty in an anodyne way, the kind of pretty you saw in magazine profiles of people like her, heads of corporations, movers and shakers, senators and congresswomen: impeccably dressed, a model of confidence and serenity, utterly unreadable. People for whom the dark side was locked inside a vault within a fortress.

Over the course of their affair Amelie had always wondered what Ben saw in Janet, and now it was evident: she was an independent woman of poise and intelligence, leaving Amelie feeling diminished, like a knockoff thirty-dollar Prada bag at a street vendor's stall. From a distance Amelie seemed the genuine article, but next to her lover's wife you could see the shoddy construction, all the little faults in the details that would eventually lead to its structural collapse and eventual demise in a distant landfill.

"You've met Ben, haven't you?" Janet asked.

Here it comes, Amelie thought. "Once or twice."

"I thought you knew each other better," and there was the briefest of pauses. And the merest of smiles. "You know, from school. Our kids."

"We've met. Chatted a little. The girls, like you said. You know." Funny how a person who made her living from using words in a way that drew plaudits from reviewers and readers alike could be reduced to sounding like a mindless teenager.

"How's Nina?"

"Really good, thanks. Wellesley was a good choice for her."

"Same with Rachel with Smith. It took her a few months and an additional fifteen pounds before she settled down," and both of them laughed.

That had never been Amelie's problem. When she went off to college, she'd subsisted on cigarettes and black coffee, and while her roommate quickly outgrew all the new clothes she'd brought, Amelie had lost ten pounds in the first month.

The waitress brought a little bowl of nuts to the table. Amelie watched as Janet took exactly one cashew and introduced it to her lips. Her husband, on the other hand, was a voracious eater. He ate the same way he made love, as though the food on his plate, like Amelie on the bed, was going to be snatched away from him at any moment.

"Where did you go to college, Janet?"

"Stanford."

Amelie said she'd gone to Mount Holyoke, and Janet laughed. "I applied there and was rejected. Same with Smith and Bryn Mawr and Harvard. I was fortunate that Stanford wait-listed me." She shrugged. "Guess I just got lucky in the end," and they both laughed.

Summa fucking cum laude, Amelie guessed, while she was *only* magna and was now being paid a pittance compared to Janet. Maybe that's why Ben was sticking around with her. Like Amelie, he was paid for his commissions, and as with Amelie, especially in the early years of her career, there must still be periods of drought. But Janet was his insurance policy, and once again the film noir was back in play, Barbara Stanwyck and Fred MacMurray facing each other across the shadows in Phyllis Dietrichson's Beachwood Canyon home. But who exactly was in charge here?

Were it in a movie, the conversation would snake around all the niceties and end up in a barrage of accusations, productions of evidence, photos, and recordings, leading to a bitter divorce, and then, of course, murder, because that's how a noir always ends. In this case it could only lead to her marriage to Ben. So maybe this was all for the best. Two women chatting and getting a little plastered.

"I hear you live alone now," Janet said. "I'm sorry, but—what is his name…? Robert?"

"Richard. We've been divorced for two years now."

"So how has it been for you?"

It was a question no one had ever bothered to ask Amelie, and since she felt she had no need of professional counseling, queries of that order simply never came her way.

"Richard and I get along perfectly well. Pretty well, anyway. Anyway, better than we did in our last years of marriage."

"Isn't it always that way?" Janet said, and again they shared a moment's merry laugh.

Amelie looked at her. Now it was her turn. "I know so little about you, Janet. Is this your first marriage?"

Janet smiled. "First and only. He's the love of my life."

Mine, too, Amelie thought. "Actually, Richard's remarried."

"I didn't know that."

"To a younger woman." A *much* younger woman. "Did you ever meet him?" Amelie asked.

"I think Ben once introduced us at some school thing."

Something her lover had never divulged to her. What else had he kept hidden in the folds and valleys of the mysterious gray blob in his skull?

"And life is okay?" Janet said. "Being alone, I mean?"

Amelie's martini was down to its sad final olive, and she knew better than to order another drink. Driving home would be a carnival of swerves and an eventual hit-and-run, the body of some kid coming home from soccer practice left foaming at the mouth in his knee socks and cleats in the middle of the road. There'd be no witnesses, of course. Except for one, the old woman walking her shih tzu in its tartan jacket. *I seem to remember*, she'd tell the police, *that her license plate began with*—And then they'd come pounding on her door at three in the morning.

Another tricky but interesting plot point to consider.

"Another?" the waiter said, and Amelie paused and looked at Janet, who was just finishing up.

"Why not?" said Ben's wife with a big, expensive bleach-toothed smile, and Amelie cautiously ordered a glass of prosecco. "No—change that. I'll have another martini, please." After all, the highway to hell always led to her door.

"I can't imagine living alone," Janet said when their drinks were delivered. "Ben and I have been together for so long that it's… Well, it becomes something of a habit, doesn't it," and she laughed.

Funny how addicts always ended up bonding over the same drug.

"I understand Ben's an architect," Amelie said, pulling the olive off her little bamboo phallus with her teeth.

"He is," and Janet smiled openly and happily. "He's very successful, too. He has a number of potential projects lined up for this year and next. I guess he's a little like you, though."

Amelie gazed at her. *Yes? And so?* said her expression.

"I mean, you both create things out of thin air. You must have an amazing imagination. Unless, of course, you're writing from life. In which case I have a whole bunch of questions to ask about your novel before this one," and with a smile she tapped her copy of Amelie's book that lay bagless on the table.

This is how a detective questions you. Makes you comfortable, gives you refreshment, Big Macs and Big Gulps before the lamp goes on for the third degree.

Amelie offered a nervous laugh and chewed on a few nuts. "Were you shocked by it?"

"That your main character walked out on her husband after twenty years of marriage? It came as a complete surprise to me, but then the more I thought about it, the more it seemed, well, inevitable, if you know what I mean. You tell us all about her outer life, which seems so perfect, but inside her it's all different."

She thought for a moment. "And then, when you close the book you realize that all along you sensed exactly what her heart and soul were really like."

"It's the logic of chaos," Amelie said. "Inner turmoil has a way of creating its own perverse order. One face for ourselves, another for everyone else. When it works, no one can really read what you're thinking." Now she was letting the alcohol speak for her and, in a way, it was rather fun.

Janet pointed a finger at her. "Exactly. And that's what the book ends up being about, right? How we live in these wonderful little towns and do all the same things, and then we find out how radically different we all are. It kind of subverts the whole suburban novel thing, doesn't it?"

They sat in silence for a few moments while they sipped their drinks. The bar was busy for a weekday night. The people drinking earlier while Amelie was having dinner had been replaced with a younger crowd, seemingly always on the edge of rowdiness as they burst into inappropriately raucous laughter. When she was young, she and her mother would often go into Manhattan for a matinee and dinner, and all the people at the bar seemed so much more worldly and tasteful with their tailored suits and designer skirts, their subdued laughter and their hats and handbags and Dunhill lighters. She'd longed to be one of them, to outgrow her seemingly unending childhood and leave home and smoke and drink highballs and make amusing small talk, and now here she was, having an affair with the husband of the woman across from her, an arrangement very much of that time, in a story that in fiction could only end with angry words and gunshots on a rainy Los Angeles night.

As though she had read Amelie's mind, Janet's mood suddenly darkened. "Things could be better between us, between Ben and me," she abruptly said, watching as Amelie's blue eyes grew larger and, if possible, bluer. "We argue more than we used to," Janet went on, "and sometimes he just seems, I don't know, distant…? Like he's not really there…?" She shook her head, rattling the words around inside it. "Like I'm being locked out of his life. Sometimes I think he even resents me. That I'm, I don't know, the odd one out? You know what I'm saying?"

Three's a crowd, Amelie thought, wondering if, as happened to her, Ben had inadvertently called his wife by a different name, one just as dangerously close to Amelie, such as Amy or Leigh. In which case she had to assume Janet suspected her as being the object of his distraction. Had she allowed herself to be hijacked by this woman?

"But then again," Janet said, "whose marriage is genuinely perfect? Is that even possible? And then we absorb all the guilt for an inattentive husband, as if he'd done nothing wrong. What did we do or say that drove him astray? How could we have made things better? It's always on us, isn't it?"

Amelie said that, yes, she understood exactly what she meant.

"And then," Janet went on, "if we find out that our husband has taken up with someone else, what's our recourse other than divorce?"

Amelie cleared her throat. "Do you think your husband is… deceiving you?"

Janet considered it. "Don't we all end up with that conclusion at some point or another? Even if it's not correct?" She took a few more moments. "I think if I had proof that was the case I'd take things into my own hands."

Amelie nodded a little and said *I see*, which was a bit of an understatement.

Now Janet was on a roll. "I really do pray that Ben and I will actually stay together. For the sake of the children as much as for ourselves. And, of course, one day Andrew will be leaving for a whole new life." She smiled a little, as though in anticipation of his departure. "College. You know."

The packed bags, the overstuffed SUV, the tears, the waves.

"That's a long way off, I imagine," Amelie said.

Janet set down her glass and leaned in, her eyes glistening in the light. "Enough of that. So tell me. Give me a hint as to what you're plotting out now."

13

THIS IS THE GAME OF IF SHE WERE DEAD.

If Janet were dead, Amelie would allow Ben a period of mourning, three or four weeks, five at the most. She would go to the funeral and embrace him like just another mourner before the eyes of friends and relatives. "Amazing Grace" would be sung, tears would flow. She would be dressed in muted gray and sit across the aisle from him, two rows back.

If she were dead.

If she were dead, Rachel would leave Smith for a while, maybe two weeks. She would see a therapist, she would comfort her father, she would get edgy and miss her friends and worry about her work and then saying that she really wanted to stay, *Just say the word, Daddy*, she'd hop on the bus and go back to Northampton and her dorm and her friends and her music and her classes in Western Civ and creative writing.

If she were dead.

If she were dead, her things would have to be sorted out, given away, discarded. There were undoubtedly clothes in her closet, drawers full of pretty little undies and Wonderbras, shelves filled with expensive perfumes and things to keep her looking young. Ben would beg Amelie to do it, and she would do it alone, or at least when he was in another room, she would fill garbage bags with Janet's things and then drop them in a dumpster behind the supermarket, along with the rotting vegetables and week-old chicken parts.

If she were dead.

If she were dead, little Andrew would miss his mother. Every night he would cry, *Mommy, Mommy,* and Ben would not be able to give him succor because he was not Mommy, he was incapable of being Mommy, in fact he was Daddy. But Amelie would help in this matter, she knew just the right words, just what little boys needed. She would hold him in her arms, say *Shh, Shh,* and rock him gently. She might even sing quietly to him. There were songs appropriate to every occasion, and she would find them. She would have them on the tip of her tongue, just as her mother would sing songs of broken hearts and longing from Broadway shows that had opened and closed long before her daughter was born.

If she were dead.

If she were dead, Ben would find himself helpless in the kitchen. Every night would be Tuna Helper or ground chuck with things added to it, macaroni and green peppers, and more and more he would come to rely on frozen dinners, *Here, Andrew, here's your Salisbury steak, eat up, buddy.* Amelie wasn't much of a cook, lately she'd been much better on the phone, poring over a Chinese menu or a leaflet from Cluck Plaza, the chicken palace, even ordering a pizza that would be delivered in under twenty-five minutes by the boy with tattoos of defunct heavy metal groups up and down his arms. But she could handle an omelet, she could broil a steak, she could make twenty different kinds of pasta, in a pinch she could even poach a fish. She would be there to serve them; she would be there to wash the dishes. She would sit with them. She would begin to fit in.

If she were dead.

If she were dead, Ben would have to attend functions by himself. He would sit beside a vacant chair, in time being placed next to someone totally inappropriate, someone who didn't suit him, some elegant divorcée with long fingernails and cheap jewelry or an ecstatic widow who would speak to him of her husband's coronary as he ate whatever sat on a plate before him. He would suddenly be invited to hundreds of parties where his stature as widower would increase his popularity a hundredfold.

If she were dead.

If she were dead, it would take him about three weeks before he began even to consider having sex. Naturally he would be thinking only of her, his late wife, of how beautiful she was, how good she was, how tender, how sweet. He would lie alone in his bed, as he never lay alone now that she was alive, he would lie there and watch the movie that was his marriage play in the screening room of his mind.

If she were dead.

If she were dead, he would have to reexamine his life. No: he would have to *examine* his life. He would have to examine his life because he'd never done it before. He would catch glimpses of himself in the gazes of others and see that he was attractive. He would look at the walls and ceilings of the house he'd designed, at the artistic corners and fantastic details, and know that he was talented. He would consider his age; he would weigh his circumstances. He had a daughter and a son. The girl was pretty; the boy handsome, the very image of his father. He would have to be there for Andrew, for Rachel was at Smith and could very well take care of herself, or be taken care of; such a high tuition must cover such needs. He would have to be there for Andrew's Little League practice, for his lacrosse games, for his piano recitals and school plays.

If she were dead.

If she were dead, they could attend the theater in a city near them. They could buy plane tickets and sit next to each other and see the world through each other's eyes. They could go to concerts, and he could finally see Paul Simon and James Taylor in stadiums the size of Rhode Island. They would go to Springsteen concerts, wildly overpriced events with audiences filled with people half their age zonked out of their minds.

If she were dead.

If she were dead, Amelie could dedicate a book to him. *For Ben with love.* Once she'd thought about simply writing *For B.*, and then realized it would take people she knew not more than two seconds to put letter to name to face to person to truth. *Amelie? Oh yes, she's sleeping with Ben, Janet's husband.* But it wouldn't matter, would it?

Not if she were dead.

If she were dead, Amelie could accept awards and thank her husband, Ben, for his love and patience. Magazine articles would no longer show a woman sitting alone in a room but a woman sitting with her husband in the house he had designed. In fact architectural magazines could show them also. This too had to be taken into consideration.

If she were dead.

If she were dead, Janet would eventually fade into the dusty back room of memory. Andrew would grow up knowing mostly Amelie. Rachel would resent her, it was only natural, but in time she would come to love this woman who had grown to love her. Amelie would take Rachel out shopping, just as she did with Nina. Sometimes she could take them both out together, they could spend the day in the city, they could go to nice stores and have lunch in good restaurants and stop for a quick cappuccino before she drove them back to their respective colleges. Perhaps it would be easier for Nina simply to transfer out of Wellesley and also go to Smith or even Mount Holyoke, where Amelie herself had gone; or, conversely, Rachel could leave Smith and attend Wellesley or Harvard. Amelie would spend time with them both on parents' visiting days, she would be introduced by Rachel as her stepmother, and Rachel would be affectionate with her as they walked through the ochre paradise of autumn.

If she were dead.

If she were dead, she would not be wholly forgotten. Occasionally photographs would surface from the backs of drawers, from shoeboxes that once housed Top-Siders and Nike sneakers, and she wouldn't mind at all if the children looked at them, they needed to remember, it was only right. And naturally it would take Ben a little while before he found his bearings. He would embrace Amelie and for a moment think it was Janet, and he might even call her by the wrong name, but it didn't matter, such things could be forgiven.

If she were dead.

If she were dead, she would be in a box under the surface of the earth. If she were dead, she would be silent. If she were dead, she wouldn't unexpectedly appear at Amelie's readings, sitting in the front row in her jeans and blond hair and nice shoes, or show up to buy a book and ply Amelie with cocktails. If she were dead, they would be able to go to restaurants two blocks away instead of forty miles distant. They could check into hotels not as Mr. and Mrs. White, not as Mr. and Mrs. Ruddigore, not as Mr. and Mrs. Armstrong, like the guy from the moon and his wife. They could simply be themselves.

If only she were dead.

Part Two

14

THE DAY IT BEGAN TWO YEARS EARLIER WOULD always remain in Amelie's memory, as though it were a permanent exhibit in a museum, a gallery in which she could browse at her leisure, letting her eyes roam over the works of art displayed there, each burnished with the pleasure and value and freshness of those collected hours.

Something had happened that morning, and she knew that something would happen, that it was only the start of things, and that from then on her life would no longer be a simple round of routine, of waking and washing, eating and drinking, working and resting. Now it would grow in complexity, it would take on dimension and shade, nuance and hue. It was the life of the spy, where she would have two faces, two vocabularies, two loyalties, two lives.

Certain irrelevant things remained with her from those days. She remembered the TV weatherman drawing his hand dramatically across his brow and speaking of what seemed to be an endless heat wave. She remembered looking out the window into the murky stillness of early evening where nothing stirred and the air bore the faint odor of things that had run their course and begun to decay. She remembered hearing a piece of music that made her lift her eyes from the book she was reading and erase her mind of everything but the voice of the soprano and the accompanying piano, and though the words sung were in incomprehensible Italian, the intent was crystal clear: it spoke of longing and the end of hunger, the light that awaited in the great distance, as though at the heart of love was the desire for oblivion. And every time she heard it, every time she came across it on the radio, she remembered the afternoon she'd realized she was going to fall in love with Ben.

It wasn't the end of summer, not technically. It was the beginning of fall, though it had been as hot as the last days of August. The leaves had started to curl and wither, the green of them having begun the fade into what would become the crisp reds and yellows of autumn. Her kitchen had been invaded by ants, large black creatures, obscenely segmented, moving from poses of watchful stillness to the frenzy of food, their little antennae twitching in anticipation. Moths flattened themselves against her windows, unmoving in their thirst for light, vanishing into the mouths of birds at dawn. Pale spiders found comfort in the highest corners of her rooms, and sometimes she would come upon them hanging from thin strands, swaying in the invisible currents that moved through her house. In the evenings the air grew cooler, the breezes of the day shifting, bearing with them the nocturnal smell of the sea and the fog.

It was the beginning of the school year. She had caught glimpses of Ben before, when Nina and Rachel were younger, at school events, on carpool lines. Only now was she able to read his face, the way his eyes took her in, and she returned his look, she let him know it by the way she raised her lids and pursed her mouth a little. It was a game of mutual regard, as if they were two beasts astir in adjoining cages, turning, watching, narrowing their eyes, waiting. They began exchanging a few words, innocuous things: *Hello, how are you, how are the kids, god it's hot.* They remained the only people left on the morning carpool line, caught in the warm wind of early September and the hollow phrases of small talk. Because it begins not on a certain day in a certain hour at a specific minute. It happens because you suddenly become aware it was there all along, as in a moment of distraction one hears the familiar song of birds beyond the din of city traffic.

There were things she immediately liked about him: his eyes, the curve of his mouth when he smiled. She liked the way he made her laugh. She liked the way he used his hands when he spoke, for they carried with them a gentle elegance she had only ever associated with her mother. She liked the way it felt, this warm sense of intuition, of being sure that, even without knowing anything about him beyond his smile and his hands as they defined figures in the air, he would become a part of her life, woven into her waking hours, there beside her in her dreams. Could she dissect it, piece it apart, as one analyzes a poem? Or was it something that could not be so clearly explained, just as she felt when a scene she was writing crafted its own pace, the words and images clicking off her fingers without a second thought. How she did it, why she did it, was beyond her. It just was. It just had to be.

On the days when she picked up Nina she looked for his car, the red BMW, and when she saw him she would offer a casual wave. Once or twice they passed and stopped, and slid down their windows to exchange brief greetings, always a little awkward, as though they were two children overcome with shyness.

Her writing began to suffer. Sitting down each morning at

her desk she found herself at a loss for words, discovering that characters meandered about a house, touched things, gazed distractedly out of windows. Dialogue became spare, the texture of her prose growing dry and stalky, like a plant starved of nutrients, exposed to the relentless heat of a dry sun. She would sit for five minutes, then stand and find something else to do. She made cups of tea, she tried to read, she lay down with her eyes shut. Sometimes when it became too much for her she got into her car and drove away, making sure she had passed certain places where she knew he went. A few weeks earlier she had run into him at the pharmacy, and although she knew she was being completely absurd, like a character in one of her books, she wanted to touch the things he had touched, to walk the aisles where she had encountered him. The magic of longing, the voodoo of adultery.

She shopped. She went to the mall and bought clothes for herself, and she bought them only in the thought that he might see her in them, that he might think of her dressed in these particular ways. She went to cosmetic counters where garishly painted saleswomen offered her tips and hints, touching her face with Q-tips and complimenting her on her complexion and her wonderful eyes, and then suggesting a little something just there, their fingers gently agitating the rise of her cheekbone.

Did he think of her as she thought of him? She had often written novels in which male characters brooded over the women they loved, or wanted to love, and yet she knew that for her it was all supposition, a leap of the imagination. She wanted to be able to tap into Ben's mind whenever she wished, to explore the images that passed there, the taste of his desire, the music he conjured. She wanted to find herself reflected in his hall of mirrors.

She wanted to spend years with him so that, when the final days came in old age, she would feel she had come to know him completely, as though he were an epic novel that had taken her decades to finish writing.

Reason: it was what she needed, it was different from her work, from the tasks at hand, the flow of a pretty sentence, the bite of dialogue, the bend and span of character she was so good at evoking. She and Ben had connected, that was certain. He never seemed in a rush to leave her, he never said *I'm late, I have to run.* He stayed, he lingered, and as their children sat in classes and learned Spanish or algebra, they stood by their cars in the school driveway, in the dust and heat of September, caught in the corridor between conversation and touch.

This was not love, she told herself. Love required more than just words, it demanded the clutch and breath of another.

But it hadn't begun; not yet. It hadn't begun because nothing had passed between them to make it so, as if love were based on a shared password, a line of code. She wanted to make time move, make it move fast, push the hands of the clock ahead, because she knew that when it happened everything would change, everything in the past would be bathed in a different light, and the time to come would be altered forever.

She realized she had never seen his house, and although Nina and Rachel were in the same class, she had never had the occasion to drive to Rachel's, that in fact the girls had never been close friends, and she looked in the school directory and made sure to remember the number 57, before driving off at speed until she was in his neighborhood, barely twenty minutes from her house.

This was the house of its own architect, unlike any other on the street, sloped and eccentric, with wide windows and skylights and an array of solar panels on the roof. She saw that she would have to return at night, just to see what it looked like inside ablaze with lamps, filled with life, a silhouette of Ben moving darkly, breaking the beams of light.

Time became something palpable, something she wished she could take in her hands as a potter works her clay, softens it, shapes it, watches it slither between her fingers. Then time could be sculpted and toyed with, she could stretch it, make it long, let it thread back into the past. Then things would have been different. The words *childhood sweethearts* came to mind and made her smile: it suggested something that happened far away, in the heartland, or in small towns where houses had front porches and fireflies sparked in the quiet night. In the distance and enchantment of an imagined life she would have known him early, she would have had him first, the seed would have been planted.

She never would have let him go.

15

NOT LONG AFTER THAT SHE DROVE PAST BEN'S HOUSE as he was getting out of his car in the driveway. With a squealing of her brakes she stopped and offered a bright hello. "I didn't know you and Janet lived here," she lied. "It's a wonderful house." She heard herself sounding utterly inane.

He didn't bother approaching the car. He turned slightly, and in that turn indicated that people were inside, people who might misconstrue the meeting, who might spoil it for them in the future. Yet at that stage the future was something that remained only in outline, awaiting further plot development and character study. "How've you been?" he said brightly.

"Good," and she smiled and nodded her head.

Now he stepped into the no-man's-land that divided them. "Nice to see you," he said. He put his laptop bag down and shoved his hands in his pockets and smiled at her, squinting against the sunlight. She didn't know what to say.

"Do you live very far from here?" he asked.

She told him where, and he nodded. She said she was on her way to see a friend. She took off her sunglasses. "Where's Rachel thinking about going to college?"

"She's still not sure. I don't even know why she's agonizing over it. She still has a whole year ahead of her. I mean, we've looked at a few schools, but she's still not into it."

Amelie said, "I know, we're going through the same thing."

"But you only have to go through it once. We still have Andrew," and he laughed.

"Not forever," she said.

"I see you everywhere," he said.

"Well," and she blushed, she had begun to make a nuisance of herself. She felt she was becoming a stalker, the type you read about in the newspaper's police reports and see in courtroom photos once they'd taken a step too far, manacled in prison scrubs and pleading insanity to a homicide charge. "Between school and my work at home there are a million things that keep dragging me away." It was an imbecilic statement that she hoped he hadn't noticed. "The school wants me to become more active now that Nina's a junior. I just don't know if I have the time."

"Now I remember. You're the writer."

She laughed a little. "Only one of many around here."

"I'll have to read your books."

"And you're an architect. I'll have to see your houses."

"We're both in the same business then," he said. "We both make things people can get lost in."

He leaned a little on her car and looked over his shoulder at the front of his house. He turned to her, and his breath was on her cheek. Everything grew quiet, as though a secret was about to be passed. "You know," he began, and she waited.

16

IT WAS CLEAR IN AN INSTANT THAT EVERYTHING THAT had led up to that moment—the looks exchanged, the wisps of small talk—was but small steps leading to an inevitable conclusion. In one of her novels the next chapter would have them thrashing about, making mad love, but it didn't happen that way; anticipation, they both implicitly knew, was half the game.

That day, as he leaned into her car, he suggested that maybe the next morning, after they'd dropped their kids off at school, they could meet for coffee in town. There was a Starbucks, where other school parents sometimes got together to exchange cruel gossip about other parents and rumors about their children's teachers, but he'd suggested a greasy spoon far from the main stretch of retail shops, in a strip mall with an auto parts store and a long-defunct Chinese restaurant. Far from the eyes of others, it was the kind of place, she thought, where the illicit might be given the opportunity to breathe.

The next morning he walked in a minute or two after she did and sat across from her. Before either of them could say anything, the waitress was there, pad in hand. She looked barely old enough to be out of high school, but the ring on her finger spoke of marriage, the hickey on her neck of lust.

"Coffee?" Ben said, and Amelie said that would be great. "Just coffee," he said. He raised an eyebrow. "Unless you're hungry?"

She smiled and shook her head.

When they were alone he leaned in a little. "So."

"Well."

"Funny seeing you here," he said, and at that moment she was already a little in love with him.

"I was about to say the same," she said, and now it was his turn to laugh. "I mean, I see you at school, and our daughters are in the same class, and it's strange, because we've never really connected. Talked. You know."

"You've already made a mess," he said, again laughing, and his eyes dropped to the napkin she'd just nervously shredded, turning it into a debris field on her paper placemat.

"I'll get you another," the waitress said as she delivered their coffees.

"Hot," he said, sipping and setting it back down.

"Yes. It is."

"I mean the coffee."

"Your house is wonderful," she said after a moment.

He wrapped his fingers around the chipped mug. Again he leaned closer.

"Did you design it?"

He nodded.

"It's nice."

"You just said it was wonderful."

She laughed. "It's wonderfully nice."

He sat back and looked at her with what appeared to be admiration. "It's good to see you. Meet you, finally. Like this," he said, and he unclasped his hands and they were near hers on the table. She sipped her coffee, which was already losing its heat to the air-conditioned room.

"So you're a writer," he said, and she nodded and said she'd already told him that when she saw him outside his house the day before. "Right, right," he said.

"Ben." It was the first time she'd said his name out loud. It was like when she came around to naming a character in her books, how it was as if this accretion of sentences and bits of dialogue had suddenly been given the breath of life. Like a plane taking off from a runway, gathering altitude, and the sigh of relief from the passengers as they knew they were on their way.

At the mention of his name he lifted an eyebrow.

"And there's…your wife—"

"Janet, yes—"

"And Rachel and…the boy—"

"The boy would be Andrew," he said, and they both laughed again.

"More coffee?" the waitress said, and she looked at them as though she knew exactly what they were up to. Amelie wondered for a paranoid instant if the young woman also knew who they were, that he was married and she was not, and that sometime soon, that day or the next, they would be naked and sweaty and completely satisfied with life.

"I'm good," Ben said, and she agreed. They were both good.

He looked around. At another table was clustered a group of elderly men who probably met there each morning to discuss their aches and pains and their prostate issues and friends who might have recently died. At the counter was a young guy eating eggs and bacon and reading the screen on his phone. Occasionally the waitress would chat with him and laugh.

"What are we doing?" she asked.

Ben smiled, and his smile made her smile, because it was the smile of someone who had been caught off guard. "You tell me," he said.

"Say my name," she said.

He paused for a moment. "Amelie." He said it correctly.

"You knew."

He nodded. "I looked it up in the directory."

She placed her coffee aside, barely touched, while his mug was nearly empty.

"You know what we're doing," he said quietly, intimately. "We're dancing without being on our feet," and she thought it the loveliest thing any man had ever said to her. Even better than a line in one of her books. And she smiled in gratitude.

An hour later, on the bed she shared with Richard, Ben rolled off of her and, lying beside her, took her in with his smile. She rubbed the back of her fingers along his jaw and felt the stubble that grew there, barely a day's worth.

"Dancing," she said.

17

AT THE SCHOOL'S FOUNDER'S DAY PICNIC SIX WEEKS
after Amelie and Ben started their affair, she and Richard suffered
an hour or two of harmony for the sake of their daughter. Parents,
students, faculty, and trustees assembled on the soccer field while
the woman who had founded the school forty years earlier sat
oblivious in a nursing home in an advanced state of dementia,
convinced it was 1971 and Nixon was president. Her son, the
manager of a local inn, delivered a brief tipsy speech before
climbing into his Range Rover and driving away.

Younger children from the lower school ran after one another
and fell down and cried, while the older ones stood in pairs or
threes, brooding and staring at their peers when they weren't
transfixed by their phones. When Nina walked by she pretended
they weren't there. So oblivious she seemed to her parents' lives that
Amelie never worried her daughter might catch on to what she was
doing with this married architect. Now Nina was in her last year of
high school. In another twelve months she'd be off to college, and
though Amelie knew she'd miss her daughter terribly, the house
would finally be her own. Her house, her time. And Ben.

She moved her eyes slowly across the crowd, rising occasionally on her toes, looking for Ben. Once or twice Richard made
some comment, "Oh look, there's Frank," or "The headmaster

is about to make a speech," and she ignored him completely, as though his words were as commonplace as the setting of the sun or the fall of rain. She smiled and nodded and continued to seek out the face of her lover, the back of his neck, the rise of his hand, features she would have recognized at once in a crowd of a million.

For Amelie, life with Ben was divided into two separate time zones: there was their time working, and their time together, and each seemed to move at a different pace, obeying different temporal laws and requiring coordination, like the intricate workings of a fine Swiss watch. They shared each other's schedules, knew where the other would be, where he or she could be reached. She knew when to call him on his cell at home and when he'd be in the car alone and available to talk, and where they would drive for lunch once a week, thirty-five miles away in a town where they knew they wouldn't be seen. She relied on texts and emails, and once he'd read them he'd wipe them from his phone or laptop, because everything was evidence. Their affair already had something deliciously criminal about it.

In the beginning there was no future: everything happened now. It was for her, it was for him, it was for them. She felt herself moving into moods beyond her control. She burst into laughter at inappropriate moments, in doctors' waiting rooms and on checkout lines at the supermarket, she found herself dancing around her living room to music that for anyone else would be unworthy of movement, the violin concerto by Alban Berg or Verdi's *Requiem*. She began to tune in stations on her car radio that played the music of her adolescence, old songs that, though essentially idiotic, evoked a time when she had been through this before with a succession of boys through high school and college, Paul, Johnny, Greg, Jason, Brian, Dylan, the blur of twenty-five years of dating and loving, abandoning and being dumped.

Even if she had parted from Ben only minutes before, she began to hunger for him, as though love were something you could devour, that you pick up and wrap your lips around, whose rind could be chewed and savored, whose juices could be sucked. He was with her always, as if he had somehow burrowed his way under her skin and was incessantly tickling the ends of her nerves. Everything changed: always hungry, she still lost weight; her periods became irregular, and sometimes she would wake in the night unable to catch her breath. She had to remind herself to grow calm, to shut her eyes and stay quiet.

She sat at her desk. She stared at her computer screen. She picked up the phone and called her agent in New York. "I'm in love," she said, and her agent said, "Is this going to be a problem? Is it getting in the way?"

"Why do you say that?"

"Because otherwise you wouldn't have told me. Look, I have authors who've had heart attacks and gone through divorce and had surgery and sometimes I think even suffered brain death, but the books keep coming, Amelie, we all have to make a living."

"I know. I just wanted to tell you."

"You're an adult, Amelie, you're divorced and you can make your own decisions. You write the books, I negotiate your contracts. Everything else is your business." There was a pause. It began to sink in. "What you're telling me is that you can't write."

She nodded, and he said, "Am I correct?"

"Yes."

"Take a deep breath. Close your eyes. Open them. Start writing."

"Do we have a deadline?"

"By the end of the year, certainly," he said. "I mean, it's been a year since your last book came out. It did well. It did very well, in fact, and people want to see more from you. Just a reminder that you owe your publisher two more titles as per the contract."

Her life filled with distraction. She loaded her washing machine and turned it on without thinking of adding the detergent. She ran out of gas on the highway and sat there laughing because she had just spent two hours with Ben in a motel room equipped with a love tub, cable porn, and a bed that vibrated at the drop of a quarter. Once, walking down the stairs in her own house, Amelie in love missed a step and fell four feet, bruising her thigh.

Even Richard noticed and had commented on it at the Founders' Day picnic. "Is this menopause?" he said, and she stared at him. "I mean, even Nina says that you're not yourself."

"Are you seriously asking me that?"

"She only meant that you weren't very attentive, that's all."

"I'm attentive. And menopause isn't going to come for a long time, Richard. Go ask your concubine about it."

"Don't start," he hissed, smiling at someone who greeted him with a wave.

"I'm glad you didn't bring Sharon," Amelie said. "It was ridiculous of you even to think of it."

"She's very fond of Nina."

"But *I'm* Nina's mother."

"Let's not do this here, okay?"

And she looked at him and realized once again that everything about her former husband was hateful to her—his gold-rimmed glasses, the shape of his ears, the ironic twitch of his mouth. She hated his Dockers and his boat shoes and his flannel shirt and his tweed jacket, and she hated the way his hair lay on his head, she hated the color of his eyes and the hue of his soul, she despised him, period.

He had been sleeping with Sharon for almost a year when he asked Amelie for a divorce. They had been married for almost twenty years, having met at graduate school, in fact in the same class, a Henry James seminar. They had gone to rock concerts and movies together and made friends with graduate assistants on the make. They moved to Vermont to take up teaching positions at the same private school. Now she couldn't bear to look at him. Their marriage came to an end when he had stood in their living room and said to her, "I don't know how it happened, I just don't understand it."

She remembered how the year before, he had stood on the lip of his father's grave, tears dripping from his eyes, and how much she had pitied him, how small and pathetic and childlike he had seemed, and then afterward how he had come home and gotten so drunk he'd begun doing imitations of celebrities, Robert De Niro and Jerry Lewis, before a roomful of other mourners. "You're a ridiculous man," she said to him that night he'd broken the news to her.

"I am truly sorry, Amelie."

"God, you make me sick with your piety."

"But I mean it."

"Just go."

He opened his hands. "It just happened."

"Oh. Like an accident?"

He beamed. "Yes. That's it. That's right."

"You had absolutely no control over yourself."

"Well, that's my whole point, Amelie, it's—"

"When Nina was a baby she had no control over herself. She peed in her diapers, she spat up her food, she drooled on my shoulder. Is this what we're talking about, Richard, did you get a little sloppy?"

"Of course not, I—"

"Nothing just happens," she said.

"This did," and he moved his hands up and down before him as though he were in ten feet of water and suddenly noticed he couldn't swim.

"And what happens to me, Richard? I've lived with you for twenty years, what happens to me?"

"What do you mean? You want money?"

"Jesus. Jesus." She got up and went to the window. She felt like thrusting her hand through it, so dim was this man she had loved for so long. "It's not the money," she said.

"I know I've hurt you," he said, idiotic in his glasses and mustache.

"You're a piece of shit."

He said nothing.

"Why did you tell me, why didn't you just carry on screwing this slut in secret?" And of course the answer was right there, it was more than her body he wanted, more than the pleasure of her arms, the taste of her kisses. He simply no longer wanted to live with Amelie Ferrar. It was this that hurt the most. All of a sudden she was completely without allure for him.

"She's not a slut," he said, and she laughed dramatically and said this woman was indeed a slut. "I know who she is now, I've seen her before at your office. She's that freelance tramp you hired."

"She's a freelance graphic artist, Amelie," he said calmly, as though speaking to a mad person.

For a few minutes he said nothing. She could barely bring herself to look at him. She went into the kitchen and poured herself a large glass of vodka and drank it so fast it burned her throat and then she hurled the glass into the sink where it shattered. "I hate you," she screamed, and the sound of her voice rang in her ears.

"Where is Nina?" he suddenly asked.

"Nina? You mean *my* daughter? My daughter is sleeping over at a friend's house. It's Friday, there's no school tomorrow, my daughter's not here, she has no idea what's taking place at this moment, no idea that her father is walking out on his family for a syphilitic little tramp, no concept that at this moment her family is no more. Why don't you run to your woman, why don't you go and let her have the pleasure of your middle-aged body. One of these days, and this is a guarantee, Richard, one of these days you'll rise from her bed and she'll crack open her big vacant eyes and she'll look at you and say 'Oh my god what have I done, why am I living with this saggy lump of human waste?' and then you'll try to come back and I won't be alone."

"Look," and he lifted his hands a little in the remarkable calmness of his evening, "I don't know if it means anything to you, but she feels as bad about this as I do. She's even read your books, she really likes your work."

Amelie turned and stared at him.

"I just think for the sake of Nina that we should always remain friends," he said. And then he smiled.

18

At the Founder's Day event Amelie heard Richard saying something and she turned and she saw them shaking hands, ex-husband and current lover. She almost said *Oh there you are, darling,* and instead she smiled and continued to look around as if there was nothing unusual in this encounter. "Do you know each other?" Richard said.

"We've met once or twice before, I think," Ben said, not quite looking at her.

"Of course. Here at school," she said. She held out her hand and looked a little away from him. "Amelie Ferrar."

He took it and released it at once. "Right, right, Nina's mother. Good to see you again."

There was nothing untoward or suggestive about the scene. She could be friends with a man without being perceived as going to bed with him on a weekly basis. She was friends with many men—her agent, other parents she'd come to know at Nina's school, husbands of friends. Richard was always friends with women and he never went to bed with them, except he did, and that was with Sharon.

"Is your wife here?" she said to Ben.

"Janet's…" He looked around. "She's somewhere."

Amelie stood back and watched the two men talk. One day

Richard would learn about her and Ben, the moment would come
when she'd tell him she was going to marry the architect, and then
he would put two and two together, he would look back and realize
that this had been going on for some time, that while he thought
she was alone and missing her ex-husband, she was in fact deeply in
love with another man. The irony of it didn't escape her; as a novelist she savored it as much as a connoisseur of wines takes pleasure in
a four-thousand-dollar bottle of Château Petrus Pomerol.

Nina passed by with a friend, again ignoring her mother.
A woman Amelie knew came up to her and it took Amelie a
moment or two before she registered the fact that her friend
Peggy was standing directly before her, ten sentences deep into a
conversation. "So I was hoping you'd be able to be a committee
chair for the auction this year," she was saying. "Or you could
co-chair with Matt Baron's mom on the artistic end of things. I
think you two would be a good team."

Amelie looked at her. "I don't know her."

"I thought you did."

"Maybe I've heard her name before, I don't know."

"I thought I saw her a little while ago," and Peggy looked
around, trying to find her in the crowd, and when she pointed
her out to Amelie, the woman was talking to Janet and both of
them were looking at Ben.

"I'll call you after I've spoken to Janey," Peggy said.

"To be honest," Amelie said, "I don't think I can help out this
year," and what she didn't tell Peggy was that she couldn't find the
time because her hours and minutes were being spent elsewhere,
on other things, on the obligations of fiction and the demands
of love.

Ben suddenly turned from Richard and said to Amelie, "Do you know Andrew?"

"Your son, isn't he?" she said, though she knew very well he was. Yet until then he had only been someone glimpsed from afar, a name mentioned in passing.

When the boy ran up to his father she saw the resemblance at once, and she saw that had she and Ben grown up together this was the person she would have known over the years, a small boy with a big grown-up smile and huge dark eyes. He was not just some kid who only incidentally was the child of this man who meant the world to her, he was something more, a young version of Ben, and the likeness took her breath away. In the distance Janet was coming up to meet them by the food tables. She wore designer jeans and a chambray shirt. Loosely tied around her shoulders was a cotton sweater. This was Amelie's rival. This was the woman who was as woven into the puzzle of deception as she was.

In a way she would have liked to know more about Janet, she would have loved to have the freedom of Ben's house even for just an hour, to go through his wife's drawers, to sift amongst the garments in her closet and the spices in her cabinet, to examine her prescription bottles and sniff her perfumes and glimpse her secrets. She had never been in Ben's house, never seen the pictures on the wall or the furniture he sat on, and yet, as though she were gathering material for a new book, she wanted to start with the most intimate details, to have under her eyes lives that could unravel over the course of a few hundred pages.

She walked over to the food tables and took a plate. Now she was behind him, she could see his back, and she couldn't help smiling because she remembered scrubbing that same back in the shower, she remembered with pleasure pressing up against him in the stream of water and feeling his skin under her soapy fingers, and then inching around to his front and—

"Hi."

She looked at the woman across from her, the one with the overgenerous smile, and had no idea who it was.

"How are you?" she said anyway.

"Not too bad, really. Jeff's gotten into Yale."

"Wonderful news."

The woman's smile dipped. "I think I have you mixed up with someone else. Linda Kinsman?"

"I think I've met her once or twice."

"You look so much alike."

Having now wasted a few lines of pointless dialogue, Amelie took some salad and a roll and a bottle of water from a cooler. She found herself following Ben and then he stopped and she realized he was talking to his wife. "I don't want to stay much longer," he said, and as if she had witnessed a fatal car crash or a hit-and-run, Amelie turned and walked away, dropping her uneaten plate of food in the trash bin.

19

IN THE END, AMELIE DECIDED SHE WOULD NOT TELL Ben about her encounter with Janet after the reading, though she did wonder if his wife had instead told him about it. Wouldn't he be desperate to know exactly what they talked about? And if she in fact had told him, why hadn't he said anything? Who exactly was playing what game here, anyway?

She sat at her desk, fingers on the keys of her laptop, and wrote gibberish, as though she was simply exercising her digits in anticipation of doing some actual work. And, in fact, nothing she wrote had the potential to go anywhere but in the magical discard machine, attainable with a quick tap of the finger.

She stared through her office window, seeing nothing but the same blankness that lived between sentences.

What if she did tell Ben about her meeting with Janet and lied about it, say that Janet confessed to having an affair with— and she came up with a list of names, none of them from the school or from the community, something exotic—Vladimir or Serge or Jean-Pierre or Gunther, the kind of people spies might consort with, meeting them in public parks or in disguise? She could create an entire scenario out of it, describe the look of bliss on Janet's face as she spoke of wild afternoons with Marcello or Zorba, and then what would happen, would he divorce her on the grounds of someone's else fiction? Or would he simply drive home, put his hands around his wife's throat and strangle her in the kitchen, leaving her to writhe and die beside the marinating steak tips?

Murder by proxy, she thought, and tapped the keys, saw the words, and deleted them, at least on screen. As though they might one day be used as evidence against her.

But she liked it. She liked it a lot.

Yet she had come away from her drinks with Janet actually rather liking the woman, understanding what Ben had seen in her in the first place. She was pretty in an Amelie sort of way, and she was also smart, driven, and successful. After two years of being Ben's lover, Amelie realized that hers was a minimalist relationship; she knew very little about him: he was flesh in her arms, warmth on her neck, a mouth engaged with hers. And then he was a cluster of incidental details, he was a red BMW, he was a postmodern house, he was a man with blueprints, with an office in an old Federal mansion. He was six-two, he was fit because he went to the gym three times a week and ran nearly every morning, and had already begun to go a little soft around the middle, something she used to tease him about until, of course, gravity had begun to work its malign magic on her own midsection.

He was raised in Philadelphia, he'd gone to UCLA. He liked Paul Simon and James Taylor and Amy Winehouse, and had more than a passing fondness for Bruce Springsteen, but when he drove he listened to NPR's tasteful delivery of the daily horrors. She knew other things about him, such as that he wore colored underpants, or at least he had several in blue, others in black, and at least two in different shades of gray, charcoal, and what the designer referred to as Twilight Mist. Beyond the shape of his body and the look of it, the taste of his skin, the sound of his voice, there were no other landmarks of which she was aware.

Which now led her to think that perhaps he was withholding facts about himself, in which case what could they be? An arrest record, a grim prognosis, some sort of weird kink he might one day spring on his unsuspecting lover?

It was the beginning of a horror novel, the story of a charming serial killer who also designs buildings, one of these mild-mannered professional men, pillars of their community, who sins lightly with his novelist lover, then at night brings his victims to a storage unit in the hinterlands and slowly tortures them, returning daily to inflict further outrages before burying them like dogs in the smoky wastelands of another state.

It came down to this: she had no idea who Ben really was, and now she placed her hands on the keyboard once again.

She realized she had fallen in love with an idea, not a man, and though a person might die, an idea, like a ghost, could live forever.

Now *that* was something to think about.

20

AMELIE WATCHED FROM HER OFFICE WINDOW AS BEN
pulled up her driveway. She had been on the phone with her
publicist for nearly twenty minutes, and they still hadn't finished
the conversation. She had six more appearances over the next few
months, both in bookstores and festivals from Maine to Northern
California, as well as a remote interview with a man who hosted
a book show on NPR out of Los Angeles.

Her publicist told her that the interviewer considered her
books to be wry commentaries on contemporary life, as opposed
to how some reviewers saw them, as bits of fluff, made to be read
on the beach or over daquiris. Of course they were more than
that. Her novels, ostensibly about people like her, also brought
with them a sense of things impending, future crises and tragedies
that lay just over the edge of the horizon, events the reader was
meant to feel with each turn of the page. What the reviewers most
liked was what she most loved writing: scenes of domesticity that
seemed to veer into something darker, the velvety blue of a world
of transgression, leaving her readers the freedom to imprint their
own secret urgings onto the page.

"Uh-huh," she said into the phone, just as his car pulled into
her driveway. "Uh-huh. Okay. Sure. Great. Great."

The moment she saw Ben she lost all interest in what she was hearing. The day would move from the public to the private, from the polite to the passionate, and she felt the anticipation of it as a pleasurable ache. She stood at the window and tried to read his expression as he got out of the car and looked up to meet her gaze. As always, he let himself in.

When he walked into her office she held up a finger indicating a moment more as she finished her call. She felt his hands on her shoulders, and she touched one of them and let it slither away into her blouse. She felt his breath on her neck, and when he nibbled her flesh a little she laughed and said a cheerful goodbye to her publicist. "You smell nice," he said, and she shut her eyes and felt the stubble on his cheek rub up against her face.

When, later, they were on their way to the restaurant far from the eyes of anyone they might know, she was about to mention how she'd had a drink with Janet after her reading, and immediately changed her mind, as though it were something to be held in reserve, just as a plot point born in an odd moment of distraction would be noted down and inserted in a later chapter for greater effect.

But it was absurd, of course, worrying over her lover's wife. Janet had only stopped by, bought a book, suggested they have a drink together. And yet something about it disturbed Amelie, darkened her mood. Knowledge was being withheld; cues remained hidden; plans were gathering like clouds before a storm.

Ben and Amelie had mastered the science of infidelity in the first two months of their affair. She had a private life, while he had a name and a face, occasionally featured in magazines that no one apart from other architects or the wealthy who savored construction porn ever read, and thus, were people ever to see them together, they had to find a perfect balance by creating an entire set of alibis and excuses, something she had already mastered, having spent all of her professional life making things up.

I'm thinking of having some work done on my house and needed to consult an architect.

Ben's car broke down and I happened to be in the neighborhood and offered him a lift.

We're running the school's big fundraising gala, which is why we're having drinks and lunch together. And afterward a quick roll in the hay.

"Do you know that I love you?" she said to Ben.

He turned to her and smiled. Until then neither had said anything of the sort. They had met and climbed into bed for an hour, and words had never come into it, words were things she wrote in her books. Words built sentences and dialogue and character. They were things you thought about carefully and used with cautious flamboyance. Affairs had nothing to do with words; they had everything to do with filling the eye with things imagined and desired, with the dark secret annex to one's marriage. She felt lost in the notion of this man, as if he were some gelatinous, edible substance, sweet and glutinous, forever stuck to the surface of her skin.

"Do you love me?" she asked as they drove north on this spring morning. And she turned and saw her reflection, *Amelie Amelie*, in the lenses of his Ray-Bans.

"Of course I do," he said.

She looked through the windshield at the sky and the cirrus feathers that began to gather over the coast. "Then say it."

"I do."

"I want to hear the words." But this wasn't how it was meant to be. She wanted spontaneity, she wanted Ben to seize the silence, fill it with expression. In their two years together he had said very little. He had talked about things, of course, mostly about his work, but only rarely did he speak about the two of them, Amelie and Ben.

"I love you," he said, and the words came out utterly flat, as though he were reading a sign, *Five Miles to New Hampshire*, or *Burger King Next Right*.

"Are you in love with me, though? There's a difference."

He looked at her.

"Because I'm in love with you, Ben. It means that I'm committed to you." *I'll never let you go*: that's what she meant. Because if she let him go there would be Janet, and maybe others, and that would be unbearable. Better that he never existed so that no one could ever have him.

Committed to you: it sounded absurd. She who used words so well was ineloquent when it came to love. She laughed a little. "You know what I mean," she said, clutching his hand. "It means that I'm not seeing anyone else. It means that we've been together a long time."

It means that I want to live with you: that was what she wanted to say, what she meant to say; it was what remained unsaid.

"I know," he said, and he sounded as if someone had just informed him he was to be hanged at dawn.

"Do you feel that I'm suffocating you in some way?"

"No," he said, though it sounded like *Yes*.

"Tell me the truth, Ben. Do you feel as if I'm putting too much pressure on you?"

"I like it that we're together like this."

She had heard the words before. She wasn't pressuring him, she wasn't suffocating him, she'd never even brought up the subject of him divorcing Janet and marrying her. And yet the notion was always there, like something in the air, a thin wisp of a fog blurring the brilliant landscape that lay in the distance.

"Do you?" she asked. "Do you really?"

"Yes. I do." And this time he said it seriously, with conviction, and he squeezed her hand. "I need you," he said. "I can't imagine not being with you like this. Of course I love you."

She said nothing. His response begged a number of questions, at least one of them coming immediately to mind: needed her for what? For being always available? Once she had asked him about Janet, how she was in bed, and he'd only said that he didn't want to talk about her, he was with Amelie. The gaps in his statements and the great silences of his life turned to chasms and voids.

She said, "So you don't mind that we can't go out together, have dinner in restaurants in town, be seen? You prefer all this clandestine sneaking around? That's okay for you?"

He moved his hand in the sketch of a gesture, defining impatience.

"I just want to know," she said. "I just want it to be clear for me. I need to hear the words."

"This is how it has to be," he said, and it sounded like a litany of things said too often before. "It's just the way it is. I just want to enjoy today. I want to enjoy what we already have." To her he sounded like an idiot, as though she had asked him to repeat what she had said, word for word, and he was only too willing to do it. "Right now anything else is impossible."

"Do you still love your wife?"

"Come on, Amelie."

"I'm just curious. I know I shouldn't be asking it. I just need to," and she shook her head and said nothing more. She thought of Janet sitting across from her in the restaurant after the reading. She couldn't find a thing to criticize about Ben's wife. She was utterly professional, obviously devoted to her work and her family, confident in herself. In her presence Amelie felt more like a ruffian, a day laborer working in the word trenches, dredging up characters and plots, trying to mend a life always on the verge of falling into sentence fragments and unfinished novels.

I just need to find my bearings, she wanted to say. *I just need to know what direction I'm going in, I just need to look out for myself.* That was it: she needed to take care of herself. But she didn't say it. To speak of herself would in some odd way exclude Ben from the picture.

"It's not so easy separating from someone you've lived with for almost twenty years," he said.

"It wasn't any problem for me," she said at once.

"That's because your husband cheated on you, Amelie, it's completely different."

"So if you found out that she was having an affair, you'd walk away from her?"

He said nothing.

"Well, would you?"

"I don't know," he said. He took a moment. "Maybe." And he shrugged. "I just can't imagine Janet having an affair."

"Why not? She's an attractive woman. She probably can't picture you doing it either." She considered it not in light of her own life but as potential material for a novel. *Click-click* went her imagination: two people so bound up in their egotism that neither can imagine the other would stray. And then…it happens.

"I bet she's at least thought about it," Amelie said. "She's very attractive and successful, and she's done it without anyone's help. If you can't see how alluring all this is, then maybe you've just"— she sought the words on the purse of her lips—"grown tired of her."

And then one day would *he* grow tired of *Amelie*? Or would she be the first to do it?

Click-click. Click-click.

He turned to look at her. "Right now I'm with you. This is our time together. Let's not spoil it."

"And if she suddenly died?"

He turned and stared at her, and she mirrored his look as she turned to him.

"It's just a hypothetical. Let's say she got really sick and died. Or was killed. In a car accident, say."

He threw up his hands. "This is crazy, Amelie."

"Anything can happen. That's life. One minute everything's fine, the next…tragedy strikes."

For a few minutes neither said anything. The road they got onto was lined with strip malls and outlet stores, fireworks dealers and gun shops, and the occasional sex den where cursive neon spoke of CDs and mags and toys and peep shows.

Amelie remembered how when Nina was little she and Richard would drive north with her, they would go to the beach and then find a restaurant and eat lobster rolls in the quaint rusticity of a seafood shack, the tables wooden and pitted and stained, the walls covered with old fishing nets and floats. She remembered Nina in her bathing suit, bending over in her funny, awkward way as she collected shells and stones. She and Richard would hold hands and walk as the tide washed gently over the sand. Gulls stood on one leg and stared out to sea.

Now her baby had left home. In less than four years she would graduate. Richard had Sharon and in September they would have a new family. There was little about him that didn't strike Amelie as absurd or comical, and yet he was living with another woman who loved him, who took him seriously, just as she once had. Had she missed something in him, had she overlooked his true nature, the goodness in this man? Or maybe he just needed to be with anyone but Amelie to turn into the man he'd become. And the thought was not just sobering, but depressing.

She didn't deserve it, this solitude: she had the sense that if she thought long enough about it she would see that Ben was a mistake, that as the days and months and years went by he would still be with Janet and Andrew, and she would be by herself. In ten years she would be fifty. And if she didn't think about it, if she didn't allow herself to see things with such cruel clarity, she would be aware of only the bliss and the sweetness of things, the richness of her work.

Right now anything else is impossible: that's what Ben had said to her. Did *right now* imply that later, sometime after now, it would be possible? How long would *right now* last, how long had it been there, was *right now* an illusion, a syntactical error, something he had pulled from the air? Or did it have its margins, was it like an ocean or a desert, where stranded in the middle you thought of it as the whole world, going on forever in limitless, endless dunes, the monotony of waves, and yet you knew that sooner or later you would arrive at some other place, older, exhausted, hobbled by the struggle. She parted her lips, she was about to speak, she heard the words formulating in her head, she pulled off the road and began her descent, and there, like the scattering of broken glass in the sunlight, was the sea.

21

AN HOUR LATER IT WAS RAINING. THEY HAD SENSED
it coming as they walked along the beach and the clouds had
begun to weave one into the other. On the horizon, fishing boats
were stalked by whirling flocks of seagulls, frenzied and ravenous,
their cries filling the air. There were few other people on the
beach; it reminded her of a shoreline she'd visited in England: a
wasteland of broken shells and shingle, the odd spaniel snouting
about for things, the overdressed old people losing their footing
on the stones and the edges of rock pools. The sea seemed to draw
the solitary and the ancient toward it, as if they were slowly being
returned to some former uncomplicated kind of existence.

Today the air was too briny, the color of the sea ugly. She saw
no magic in the waves, nothing beckoning to her. It was dark and
cold and its depths were filled with horror. Ben had said little as
they walked; Amelie felt a gathering sadness, the sense that the
days were rushing past her without delineation. In the richness of
her hours something was breaking down, growing stale. By the
time they got to the restaurant she could feel the onset of thunder
in her head, the swollen pain of it.

She ordered her usual vodka martini. Ben asked for the craft
beer of the day. They still had nothing to say to each other. She
had introduced death into the conversation, just as she sometimes

did in her books, and the mood had darkened. She wondered if he was considering what she'd said. *If Janet were dead...*

A minute later their drinks arrived. *Cheers. Cheers.* She had to put on her glasses to read the menu, the words *sole* and *haddock* and *lobster* coming into focus. A week ago she hadn't had to use glasses and now she did. She wondered if she'd already grown dependent on them, if this was what aging was all about: you picked up a cane one day just to help you get over a sprained ankle and you relied on it forever, teetering toward the grave. Ben looked at her: "I like them on you." His smile faded a little. "They're nice."

After they ordered he said, "I'll be gone for a little while." He said it as though he had been meaning to say it all along, as though what might have come to the boil had reached a steady simmer and had been that way for hours.

She looked at him. "Business?"

"The school vacation's coming up," he said.

She couldn't at first see the connection.

"We're thinking of going away for two weeks. Janet and Andrew and I. Rachel will be at college."

"You're going away with Janet."

"Shh," he said, for her voice had suddenly grown loud and indignant.

Without thinking, she finished the rest of her martini in one swallow and felt it instantly go to her head. "I'd like another, please," she said, and the waitress rushed over to the bar to place the order. A retired couple ate in silence at a table in the middle of the room, looking at everything but the spouse sitting across from them, and Amelie wished they weren't there, she wanted the room to be empty for fifteen minutes so she could have it out with Ben, air her views on this impending leave-taking, and for a crazy moment she seriously considered walking over and politely asking them to go into the bar or simply stand outside in the rain until she was done. Later would not be good; later would be for other things, not arguments, not the changing of minds, not the sadness of the future. Now the gulls were circling low, as though waiting for things to die, things that could be pulled apart with their beaks, things that could be split and devoured.

"When did you decide this?" she said.

"We haven't had a vacation for a few years, and we just thought it was time."

"Just like that. You just thought it was time."

"Please don't start, Amelie." He looked out the window. In the distance a fishing boat was chugging by, followed by a flock of hungry seagulls.

Amelie continued to stare at him. "You and her."

"And Andrew."

"Was it your idea? Yours alone?"

Now he was looking at something over her shoulder. Had she taken a moment, she would have realized they were becoming like the old people at the other table, people who'd heard each other's stories a thousand times, and Amelie wondered if all this arguing, all this debating, was wearing him down.

"Ah. It was hers, then," she said. "It was Janet's idea." Had Janet learned in some obscure manner of their affair? Was she dragging her husband off to Vacationland just to tighten her grip on him?

"It's what families sometimes do on school vacations. We thought Andrew would enjoy it."

She speared the stray olive in her drink with the little plastic épée. "So I won't see you for two weeks." She looked out the window. She saw nothing, as though what before now had been ocean and flowers and trees had been ravaged by earthquake, reduced to gray rubble.

"Where are you going?"

"We're pretty sure we'll head west."

"West." The notion of tumbleweed rolled across her mind.

"California anyway," he said. "Possibly into Mexico. Baja," he added with a shrug.

"I hope you have a good time," she said, and even though her head was killing her she made quick work of most of her second drink just as the food arrived. She thought of asking for a glass of wine and decided against it.

For a little while they ate in silence.

"Is there a problem, Amelie? I mean—"

"I know exactly what you mean."

"It's just."

"Yes, Ben. I know. It's just that this is something you have to do with the family. I understand. I really do."

"We've done this long enough. You should know how it works by now."

She set down her knife and fork. "*This. This* is what this is? It's just *this*? I thought it was something more than just that," she said, and the retired couple in the middle of the room took in this drunk woman with a glance. "An affair is not just a *this*. You have a *this* with a hooker, Ben, not with your lover of two years," and again Ben said *Shh*.

The image of Ben and Janet on a beach left Amelie in a state of vague disquiet. Waves washed over their legs; he oiled her back, rubbed lotion into her freckled skin; in the water they played, he touched her, she touched him. She saw them leave the beach and return to the room. Andrew would sit in front of the television and watch something with monster trucks in it while his parents went in the bathroom and soothed their overheated skin under the shower. She saw Janet soaping Ben, arousing him, and she knew what this was like because they had often done it themselves.

"Please don't go on, Amelic."

She said nothing. She looked only at the slab of fish that lay on her plate. Slowly she reduced it to a mess of flesh and bones.

22

"THANK YOU," SHE SAID AFTER THEY'D BEEN DRIVING
for fifteen minutes. "Thank you for lunch." She looked out the
window. Lunch was something she had quickly forgotten. What
had she eaten, what had she drunk? They could have served her
a plate full of garbage and leftovers for all she knew, crushed sea-
shells and overcooked barnacles. It had become a mere exercise in
the movement of the jaw, open, chew, swallow, open, chew. And
the martinis had not helped, they seemed to have killed not only
the flavor of her food but also the memory of it.

A billboard showed a merry middle-aged couple on diabetes
medicine playing in the ocean. Another said that Lavalle's Guns
and Ammo was a mile up the road. Only the words they had
exchanged remained vivid.

"It was very nice," she said, though of course it wasn't very
nice, it was very horrible.

He was about to say something, she could sense his lips shap-
ing a sound, but he said nothing.

She said, "I'm sorry about that. I was upset, that's all."

He said nothing.

She said, "I've been booked to do another reading next week."

He said nothing.

"It's outside the city. It's a long drive."

He said nothing. Heavy rain started to pelt the car, and the sky seemed to fall onto the highway in thick dirty sheets. She switched on her wipers, to little avail. He said nothing.

"It wasn't fair of me to do that to you," she said.

He said nothing.

"I was just upset. You understand. This...surprise. You going away..."

He said nothing.

"I love you, Ben. It hurts me to love you so much."

He said nothing.

"I love you to death."

23

IT WAS STILL RAINING WHEN AMELIE PULLED INTO HER driveway. She shut off the engine, and they sat in silence as the windshield was blurred by the flowing water. Ben reached over and slid the keys out of the ignition and then got out of the car and let himself into her house. She imagined him wandering around the rooms in a state of anger so fierce that he was methodically breaking up the accoutrements of her life: her paintings and lamps, her tables and laptop, the books she had published and those she was intending to read. But he had no reason to be angry, he was going off to sunny California with its palm trees and sandy beaches, he would sit by the pool with Janet in her bikini. He had, on the contrary, every reason to rejoice, just as she had every reason to be upset. He was going to take Janet and Andrew to California and Mexico and they would behave like a family and she, who was so much a part of his life, would be left behind. Two weeks.

Two weeks of memory and speculation.

She ran through the rain to the house and took in her mail. There was a water-and-sewer bill; there was a magazine and there were four catalogues; there was junk, the endless junk that spoke of auto detailing, of muffler repairs and tanning salons and photofinishers and new pizza parlors and the latest in Chinese cuisine, the junk that seemed to think you were anticipating it, the junk that slipped from your fingers onto the floor, and she felt the anger rising again within her. Ben would be away from her, he would be gone, she would be here in a world of litter.

And the real fear became articulate in her mind, the fear that when he came back he would sit down with her in her living room and like some disgraced politician tell her that he needed to spend more time with his family, that he could only lead one life and not two. She caught a glimpse of herself in the mirror as she walked out of the room, and it occurred to her that she was no longer the self-assured woman who enchanted her readers, who signed books and gave interviews. Her hair was in disarray, her clothes wet from the rain, her stomach uneasy from the speed at which she had eaten her lunch. Their one day of the week together had been shot to hell.

"Ben," she said in a small voice. "Ben, where are you?" She walked up the stairs. He was lying on her bed completely dressed, staring at the ceiling. She knelt on the floor beside him. She said, "I don't want to make love to you today. I'm not very happy and I don't feel I'd enjoy myself. I don't think I could give you any pleasure. Do you understand?"

He looked at her. Very calmly he said, "Take off your clothes."

"Ben, please listen to me. I'm sorry I acted like that. I just. It's just," and she tried to shake the words out of her. "I just don't think it's right today. I'm sorry."

"We're leaving on Saturday."

She looked at him.

"Janet and Andrew and I are flying out on Saturday. I won't see you again for two weeks. I'm going to miss you. I may be going away with my family but I'm going to be thinking about you all the time. Please let me take something of you with me. Please let's make love."

She looked at him, at his eyes, his serious expression, the way his throat moved when he swallowed. *No*, she thought, *look away, look away now, walk out, find something to do*. She said, "I," and he gently pulled her toward him, as though this were her choice and not his. Kicking off her shoes, she mounted and straddled him. He began to unbutton her blouse. She placed her palms on his chest and looked into his eyes. Her breathing grew heavier, she felt herself swell and open to him. She said, "I can't live without you, Ben."

And he said, "And you can't live with me."

But he didn't say that. She only imagined the line two hours later. One day, when it was too late, she would remember to use it.

24

AMELIE SLEPT.

She wore nothing but a white bathrobe and black panties, the garments having been hastily put on just before Ben left the house in the last hours of the afternoon. The belt of her bathrobe had come undone and the panels of the robe were parted. Beads of sweat formed on her upper lip. Her skin had turned pale in the depths of her sleep. She slept heavily, her breathing deep and regular. In her dream someone said that the worm was without merit. Without waking she rolled onto her back, her legs separating in an easy, lascivious gesture. The rain dwindled to a light mist; the sun emerged briefly and the temperature rose until it touched eighty-three. She made a little noise, *ehmmm*, like the sizzle of gravel, a memory of the pleasure of her afternoon. What had taken place in the restaurant was no longer in the forefront of her recollections. She and Ben never mentioned it again that day.

When he left he took her in his arms and held her, he pressed his lips to her head and then her mouth. He told her he would miss her. He said he would try to call and would definitely text and email. She held onto him a moment more and then released him, as though he were a bird she had rescued, nourished, strengthened, and then set free. One day, she sensed, he would not be there for her. Two years of a passionate affair would turn out to have been nothing but a charade, an amusing little trifle that made him feel worthy of this life he led.

But that wouldn't happen. You don't buy a woman's love by going through the motions and mouthing all the scripted words. No: this investment ran deep. He may have thought he owned her, but, in fact, she owned him. This wasn't just his story. Her story, with all its little subplots and thrills, would one day grow all the richer in the telling.

Her eyelids began to flutter as she reentered the playground of her dreams. While she slept things were happening, worlds were in collision, doors were shutting, people were speaking on telephones, packing their bags. In hospitals all over the land people gave up their last breath and expired. Babies were born, people were plotting, fuses were lit, bodies were lowered into the earth. The air was heavy with moisture, the trees glistened in the light, birds sang. She dreamed she was about to go to bed with someone, and she was gripped by the anticipation of it, for the person had never seen her undressed, had never made love to her. She took off her clothes and showed herself to him and then the dream changed utterly because the person waiting on the bed for her was a little boy holding a gun in his hands, and in her sleep she turned over and now she was at a meeting, perhaps with her agent or editor. Now things were fine. Once again thunder was imminent. The sun began to set. Things grew quiet.

Outside, people drove by, a girl delivered the local newspaper to her door, some man with the hands of a bricklayer inserted a flyer into her mailbox advertising his services as a roofer. Her neighbors returned from work, kissed their spouses and their children. They opened their mail, changed their clothes, checked their email, some took to the roads for a quick jog. Amelie slept. One evening her mother went to sleep and never woke up, and Amelie had been the one to find her in the morning, discolored and swollen and silent.

The phone didn't ring. No one came to the door. Now it was time for a new dream, he was once again beside her, just as in the beginning, he was beside her and touching her, and although her eyes were shut she could hear him breathing, she could sense him watching her as she bit her lip in the throes of her pleasure, for he knew precisely how to please her, like this like this like that, and then Amelie woke and blinked her eyes and gasped a little, for the dream had had nothing to do with Ben. She had forgotten about the boy with the gun. All she could remember was that she had just dreamed of Richard.

25

NOW WITH BEN OFF ON HIS FAMILY VACATION AMELIE couldn't write, she could hardly even read, as though her career solely depended on the presence of this man. It was ridiculous. Before Ben, even after Richard, she'd slowly blazed a path to the bestseller lists. Now, having reviewed through a haze of dissatisfaction the patches and sketches she had worked on for two weeks, she decided to start something else, something fresh, a novel not about people to whom very little remarkable happened, who passed their days having perfectly edited conversations, who sat on school boards and worked as travel agents and chatted with friends and consulted their therapists, and who, in the simmering afternoons of their summer, quietly schemed and slept with each others' spouses, but those who take life-changing risks, who break the fabric of what passes for civilized society.

She was sick of dealing with characters who made sheepish transactions with themselves and their lovers, who trusted and then slipped into mild distrust, whose troubling pasts occasionally rose up out of their distant obscure memories to wreak mild chaos. In short, she had grown sick and not a little tired of herself.

Yet, her agent always told her to color within the lines. Go edgy, just not too much. This is your brand. Your readers see themselves in your characters, it's why they stay loyal. Tease them if you like, take them to the frontiers of your imagination, but if your crayon strays too far beyond the lines, if you start to smudge or smear, you may begin to lose your audience.

And maybe, she thought, *even gain a whole new one.*

She wished, then, that she could write about a murderer, someone bright and charming who wielded a knife and slashed the throats of people who opened their eyes and looked the wrong way. She wished she could write about the darker areas of sex, the things that were done in basement rooms in Nevada and in woodsheds in the hill country of Tennessee. She wished she could write about strippers and prostitutes, soldiers of fortune and psychos. She wished she could write anything but what she had made her reputation writing: something new, something startling, something frightening and transgressive and unexpected. Something that would change her image, that would shake up her world.

She looked at the calendar hanging over her desk. She'd put a red dot on the day Ben flew to LA, and a green one on the day he was due to return. Twelve more days. She knew what she was in for, as though she were a madwoman, some tragic figure in a Greek tragedy, day after day cursed to go through the same motions, trapped by the same circular thoughts, thirsting for relief. Even Saturday, a day when calls were primarily from telemarketers, had been totally squandered. She spoke to three of her friends, all of whom had read her new book and called with the intent of praising it. Adulation grew thin, turned to questions: *Is the guy in the book based on Richard, were you thinking of Susan Gartner when you created Leslie Bennett, is the house in the book supposed to be Linda Kinsman's, why did you call the son Cal, is there any symbolism in it?* And she replied to her friends who long ago had taken English Lit 101 by saying that everyone in the book was a product of her imagination, that she would never dream of acting maliciously toward Richard, that Cal was just Cal and not Caliban or Robert Lowell or anyone else they might be thinking of.

Of course the guy was based on Richard, and it was just like Richard not to have noticed the little mannerisms they shared. And as for Susie Gartner, well, if she wanted to see herself in the shrewish character Leslie Bennett, she could just go ahead and please herself.

Amelie went into the kitchen and made herself a salad. Afterward she would take a little walk and then come home and work until four, pecking out words and hoping for a story to emerge. Then she would make herself a drink and dinner and later snooze in front of a streamed movie until bedtime.

On the radio a writer she vaguely knew and intensely disliked was being interviewed. It was obvious the writer was pretending to be shy and retiring, and yet he was spilling the details of his life like a child toting a brimming bowl of milky cereal across a room. He had told these stories so often that they had grown burnished and mannered over time, to the point where they sounded more like tawdry fiction than the grueling life events he so enjoyed recounting. Now Amelie remembered where she'd met him, at a book festival just north of there. The author had strutted onto the stage in his work boots and jeans, and in a halo of preening self-satisfaction read page after page of the most sexually graphic scene from his new novel, looking up with a wry smile to see if he'd either offended or titillated, not realizing that he'd aroused no one but himself.

As she ate she wondered what might happen were she to let it drop through some obscure channel that she had been having an affair with Ben, not just having an affair, something light and airy and occasional, but something unknown to others that had lasted for over two years, something that involved sweat and spit and sperm, an act of moral sabotage with all its promising overtones. Ben would have to admit to it, he would say it was nothing, it's all over, don't worry, but to her it wasn't all over, it wasn't nothing, it was something very large indeed, something that cast a shadow over Janet and her marriage to this man she thought she knew so well.

Ben and Janet would find themselves a therapist, where they would sit in their separate chairs while the good doctor asked questions, offered suggestions, tried to help them patch this torn quilt that had been their marriage. They would begin to drift apart, each to his or her own hour and corner, following the separate times of their divided lives.

Andrew would become difficult, a brooding child blasting hollow men in the twilight world of his Xbox, or idly lighting matches in his bedroom, one after another, flip onto the floor, flip onto the floor. His appetite would change, he would make himself throw up, he would engage in tantrums, he would tell his parents he hated them. He would retire into the dark world of his young mind, a place of vines and caves and tubes of glue, of dead ends and strange dwarfish obsessions, of endless hours of hard-core porn.

Time would pass. Amelie would visit Ben in the cheap motel where he lived out of his suitcase, where the maid came in promptly at ten to vacuum—*Good morning, sir, Good morning,*

Conchita—and where the management of the place offered free HBO and at least one blue channel, and where if he weren't inclined to drive out to the Dunkin' Donuts up the road he could make instant coffee in the machine on the desk. Lawyers would be retained, and a counselor for Andrew engaged, someone to soothe his pain, to help him come to grips with this thing that had destroyed his home.

Of course, Ben would never identify the Other Woman, leaving Janet to speculate at her leisure as to whom it might be. Every woman in their proximity would be a candidate, and every one of them would be considered her enemy. The Other Woman would be unknown to anyone but Ben, leaving Janet only to refer to this woman as *Her. Why don't you go to Her*, she would shout at her husband whenever he visited. *Why are you here, why don't you go and sleep with Her?* And Andrew would watch television and place his hands over his ears or turn up the volume on his music, and life would become something you lived inside your head to the sound of three amplified chords.

The divorce would be described as acrimonious, though blessedly brief and uncomplicated. The name Amelie Ferrar would be mentioned, and Ben would naturally move in with his lover. Janet would get over it, but not until she'd picked up the phone, waited for Amelie to answer, and then called her *Fucking Bitch Whore* at the top of her lungs. Rachel would barely notice what was happening. Andrew would manage, somehow. There might be a spot of trouble with him down the road, of course, difficulties in school, a little weekend vandalism, the occasional binge with friends, Bud Lights and Marlboros on a Saturday night. But he'd manage. He'd manage because Amelie and Ben needed to be together and Andrew would just have to learn to live with it.

But it wouldn't happen that way. Janet would never know what had happened, who had caused it, who was to blame. Of course Amelie would run into her now and again, at the supermarket or dry cleaner, and she would be just as friendly as she had always been. They might even go out for lunch or a drink now and then, and she could imagine Janet spilling all the details of her divorce. *I think there was someone else, another woman. Sometimes I feel that if I ever found out who it was, I'd kill her for the sake of my children,* and the idea—rapidly jotted down on a shopping-list pad she kept in the kitchen—thrilled Amelie to her core.

Part Three

26

THE MAIN RESTAURANT IN TOWN, THE COACH & Four, situated between the Knit One, Kibitz Too yarn shop, and the Second Life yoga studio, was an easy ten-minute drive from the house. Before Nina was born—and because the only other option, near the railroad tracks, was Zeke's Bar & Grill where, after closing time, the odd drunk could be found sprawled outside it on the sidewalk—she and Richard had sometimes gone there for drinks and dinner, though he always spent his meal hunched in silence, a heart full of grievance toward the overstuffed gentry surrounding them.

During the colder months a fire blazed in the hearth in this 1753 house that had now become the most expensive restaurant in town, and the music on the sound system was always quiet enough to be ignored, especially when the place was busy. She hadn't been there since her divorce, and now, desperate to see other people and hear the easy intercourse of conversation, she decided to go for a drink. She would sit with her cocktail at the bar and eat the tasty little snacks provided, and then go home and see if she could get at least one coherent sentence written.

There were only a few tables occupied at this early hour, and as it was spring the fireplace was barren, the air naturally warm on this balmy evening. She took a seat at the bar and looked over at the others sitting along it, a couple she vaguely recognized from someplace, and a younger man opposite her reading a book while he sipped his beer.

Bing! She checked her phone, a text from Nina, a selfie she'd taken the night before at a concert in Boston. Beside her was a guy her age, presumably Peter. He looked like every other twenty-something these days, with the same haircut, the same Heineken grin. Amelie sent back a smiley with two hearts for its eyes, and heard nothing more.

The bartender delivered her usual martini, and when she looked up, the man with the book was staring at her, his eyes quickly returning to his reading.

Well, she thought, flattered by the momentary attention. She was at least ten years older than the guy, something he surely must have recognized, and yet something about her had caught his attention. For that brief moment she felt closer to twenty-nine. He seemed well groomed and decently put together. Because the restaurant and bar weren't busy, she lifted her chin and said, "Any good?" She immediately regretted it. It sounded like a cheap and easy pickup line, not much cleverer than *Do you come here often?* and now she would add to her reputation that of being a tarnished divorcée on the hunt for young flesh.

"I think so." He lifted up the book to show the cover. It was her latest, and her heart shut down before it began to thump all over again.

"Well. I'm flattered."

"I thought I recognized you," and he checked the photo on the back cover, Amelie in full color, her arm stretched across the back of a sofa. "It's really good so far. I'm enjoying it."

"Thanks. Actually, my readers tend to be women. It's kind of unusual seeing a man reading something of mine. Also kind of gratifying."

"I saw a thing about you in the local paper," he said. "I thought what you had to say was interesting, and I thought I'd check out your latest."

It had been an interview that had taken all of fifteen minutes at the Starbucks in town. The journalist, who clearly hadn't read a word Amelie had ever written, asked her the usual generalized questions, and then said she had to rush off to get her dog from the groomer, still leaving Amelie sounding intelligent and provocative.

She sipped her drink and toyed with the little stick that held her olives. "I hope you enjoy the rest of it."

He smiled. "Now that I've seen you in person I'll always think you're the main character."

Ah yes: dear old Caroline who sins impeccably, while Amelie, conversely, preferred to be immoral as messily as possible. And if her protagonist had been a psychopathic killer? Would he have said the same thing to her?

"I wish," she said, and he returned to his reading, saying nothing more to her.

Once again she was forty, alone, and halfway to the bottom of her first martini of the evening.

27

AFTER DINNER AMELIE DROVE FROM THE RESTAURANT to Ben's house. She felt compelled to see it in its vacancy—an act of magic, a way of reaching him three thousand miles away. Before leaving for California he had set timers to mimic the patterns of this absent family, so that early in the evening, life was intimated downstairs, gradually making its way into the upper reaches of the house, ending with the switching off of bedside lamps in this house that was stripped of life. A porch light was on, around which a lone moth darted and danced in its final hour on earth.

She looked at the front of this house to which she had never been invited, not even for one of Ben and Janet's many social occasions. If she thought about it long enough she would see that she was indeed something on the side, and the side she was on was some distant outpost, a backwater village Ben could visit whenever he was up-country. So she was expected to sit at home and wait.

She sat in her car a full five minutes before the flames began, little licks of light like a brushfire in the middle of nowhere, then growing larger until quickly they engulfed the entire house. The outside walls fell away, revealing its inner life: Ben's and Janet's bedroom, the floor collapsing under the weight of the California king and matching nightstands, the bureau and her dresser, the framed prints and paintings tumbling after; Andrew's room with all its little-guy stuff, a lacrosse stick and helmet, some books, a desk, a bed made for one, a laptop melting in the heat; the dining room, into which the bedroom fell, crushing the table and the chairs around it; and finally Rachel's room, left precisely as she had the day she left for college, becoming a heap of burning garbage.

The house was reduced to ashes and glowing embers and broken glass in a matter of minutes, but only Amelie seemed to notice. There were no sirens, no neighbors standing on their lawns in their nightclothes watching this extraordinary display; just Amelie. And while she took one last look at the house in the night, as the last of the timed lamps was extinguished, signifying sleep, she put the car in gear and headed home, catching a final glimpse of the house in her rearview, still standing, untouched by her imagination.

She pulled into her driveway and realized that she had forgotten to leave a light on for herself. The darkness of her home made her think of a death in the family, a prolonged bereavement. Her mother was long gone; her father had left home for another woman when she was twelve. She'd only seen him once since then, at an airport with his new family, children and grandchildren, when she was flying back to Boston from a book festival in Chicago where he apparently now lived. Her mother had never spoken of him again after he'd left, as though the man had only been someone she'd dreamed up one lonely day and promptly forgotten. Until she was old enough to realize that her mother was impossible for him to live with, and her father insufferably unreliable.

At the airport he'd glanced at her, taken a quick second look, then herded his family to their gate. He'd grown distinguished with age, the dark hair of his earlier days gone gray and perfectly coiffed. Unlike most of the other male travelers in the terminal, who seemed to be still in their pajamas, he was in a suit and tie, exactly as she remembered him when she was a child. She'd always felt it was her fault, his leaving, since her parents' arguments always seemed to be centered on her, *What will she think as she grows up? Do you have any idea what this will do to our daughter? Do you really want her to believe men are just like you, endlessly disloyal, always wandering off?* And her father would say nothing. Spied by his daughter from the top of the stairs he would be seen sitting in his usual living room armchair, his arms folded, a glass brimming with scotch beside him.

For years Amelie felt she could have prevented it, could have been a better daughter, could have prodded her father to pay greater attention to his talented and beautiful wife, and such a thought had lodged in her brain like a bullet, only vanishing when she fell in love with Ben and saw, for a brief crowning moment, that she had passed over to the other side of the equation. The side that also happens to consider itself right and just.

She walked past her father and his family and turned abruptly back. She needed to do this, she needed to speak to him, to show that she at least deserved an apology.

She caught up with him at his gate. He'd settled into a seat, while his wife, who looked remarkably like Amelie's mother, walked off to a ladies' room.

When he looked up from his phone he saw her standing there. He said, "Yes?"

"Daddy."

"I'm sorry?"

"Jack Ferrar?"

"Yes…"

"Don't you know me?"

"No," he said after a moment, looking back down at his phone.

"It's Amelie. Your daughter."

"You must be mistaken," he said.

He gazed at her with his rheumy, boozy eyes, while she waited, a moment longer, before walking away. She hated him. She would hate him forever, the cheating, lying, abandoning son of a bitch. There was nothing more to be shared, not now, not ever.

She stepped into her darkened house and thought that something was wrong, something was out of joint: time or topography. She stood still for a long moment and tried to gather her thoughts.

After turning on the lights downstairs, she took a knife from the kitchen, the expensive one she used to demolish garlic cloves and dismember chicken. She pictured someone sitting on the edge of her bed, waiting for her. She would walk into her bedroom and see the guy from the restaurant with the book, and before she could cry out, he would have her on the floor, his hand over her mouth.

She thought of Ben, who would be back in another week and who, not having heard from her after his return, would let himself in to be greeted by the stink of decaying flesh and to find what remained of her bonded to the wide pine boards of her floor she'd had refinished only a few years before, her desiccated unraveled intestines surrounding her naked body like a nest of snakes. But that wouldn't happen. Her bedroom was empty. Nina's room was empty. There was no killer in the house, no one hiding, waiting. There was no bereavement.

What she had lost was any sense of hope, though she sensed once again it had been there all along: Ben wouldn't be in her life forever. That the end of the affair was contained within its first moments: a big bang that would eventually burn out and leave her world a black cinder. She thought of the young man in the bar reading her book. How many more of these would she encounter before she was too old even to be noticed?

She turned on the bathroom light and saw only a crazy woman staring back at her from the mirror, her hair in disarray. She switched off the light and returned to her bedroom. She put the knife on her nightstand and sat on the bed and felt her body begin to shudder, and then the tears came, copiously down her cheeks, and her nose ran and she began to perspire, and when she was done, when everything had begun to cohere, body and soul and heart, she took her bottle of Advil from the medicine cabinet in the bathroom, gave it a shake, assessed the stash. She would take two, not fifty, not ninety-three; she would swallow two and take off her clothes and get into bed.

Take two, she reminded herself, and she opened the bottle and took five and then went to bed.

28

IT WAS NINA WHO ROUSED HER FROM HER SLEEP, AND
when Amelie woke it was instantly into the throes of panic. She
reached for her phone and dropped it and then picked it up and
even before putting it up by her face said *What?*

"Mom?"

"What's wrong?"

"Nothing. I always call on Sunday morning."

Amelie rubbed the side of her face. "I was asleep."

"No kidding."

"Sorry, baby. Sorry."

"Late night?"

Amelie ignored the question. "School okay?" she said.

"I have so much work."

"But you're able to handle it."

"I'm just studying all the time. Can I come home next
weekend?"

"Of course." With Ben away, anything was possible. No
excuses would have to be made, no one would be put off, no lies
were in the offing. "Do you want me to pick you up?"

"I'll take the bus. Or the train. I'll call when I know which
one I'm taking."

"Everything else all right?"

"I saw Peter once or twice."

"How's it going?"

"I don't know," Nina said, retreating into vagueness. "You know, I heard from Rachel again."

Rachel Rachel Rachel. Oh yes: *that* Rachel. "Really."

"We're going to get together one of these days."

"That's a great idea." Amelie looked at the clock: it was nearly eleven, as late as she used to sleep when she was her daughter's age.

"Mom…?"

"I'm here, I'm all right."

"Her parents are in California."

"Really," she said. It was three hours earlier there; Ben was asleep, his arm around his wife. This is what came so vividly to mind.

"What's going on?"

"What do you mean?"

"Rachel said something about you and her father. Some friend of hers saw you and her dad at a restaurant. About a month ago, I guess."

One of Rachel's friends. Some malevolent private school grad with malice in her heart, probably a budding writer with a head full of wanton speculation.

Amelie didn't know what to say. "Go on," she said, and she knew at once it sounded sinister, it rang with guilt. A month ago: she remembered she and Ben had gone to Boston, visited a museum, and afterward ate in a crowded Newbury Street restaurant. It had been foolish of them, a risky thing to do, and now the word was out. It was ridiculous: forty minutes over shrimp scampi and a glass of wine or two were about to become the outward signs of a torrid affair.

"That's all. She was just curious. I was just curious."

"I don't understand what the problem is. We had lunch, that's all. I'm thinking about having some work done on the house."

"You're joking."

"I thought he might have some ideas about it. I mean, he's an architect, right?" She listened as this nonsense issued from her mouth.

"Because if you're having an affair with him, Rachel will go crazy, she will go absolutely insane. Are you having an affair with him?"

"Don't be ridiculous," Amelie said.

They said goodbye and the call was ended. Amelie went directly into the shower. She shut her eyes and stayed there for ten minutes in the heat and noise and the rush of water. It was as if she were drowning, all the breath taken from her as she went under. *Fuck*, she said aloud. *Oh god, fuck.* And she rested her forehead against the wall of the shower and cried real tears.

29

FINALLY SOMETHING LIFTED FROM HER, LEAVING HER
with a stillness she associated with the last days of her mother;
the quiet memory of a woman climbing the stairs, stopping
to catch her breath and gather her strength for her impending
death. Sometimes she tried to imagine how her mother saw
the world in those last days, how the Persian carpet in the
living room became something rich and allusive, the pictures
on the walls panoramas of a lost paradise. It was the calmness
of appreciation, the quiet intensity of self-control, the sense
of something rounding to an end. It was the serenity that
knew only moments, as if time were made up of a million tiny
bubbles, each of them brilliantly reflective, lighter than air. *If
you stop, you will see*, she used to say to Amelie when she was
a child, and in their walks she would come to a halt and point
out a caterpillar on a leaf, or a hummingbird seeking nectar,
vanishing in a blur of wings.

The routine of Amelie's days became an ordered thing, where
hour succeeded hour not feverishly but quietly, each moment
carrying weight and significance in preparation for the next. The
days stretched out before her without event or interruption. Ben
was in California; Friday was hers alone. And the idea of this
solitude left her with an unexpected feeling of muted joy, as if

she had suddenly cupped her hands around the hours of her life to make them all her own.

She began to rise with the sun. She walked and showered and had a light breakfast, and after checking her emails leafed through the newspaper that arrived daily on her doorstep. Through her glasses she read about what was happening in the world and in the country and in the state. She glanced at the obituaries and read the arts reviews and looked at her horoscope and saw that challenging aspects would compel her to make a life-changing decision. She closed the paper and walked up to her office.

Without realizing it she had worked all morning; her engagement with prose had replaced her obsession with love. For one whole day she'd owned her own life, and the only word that came to her lips was *Finally*.

Each day she sat at her desk and steadily tapped out the words until the passing of time became invisible, until the world had been reduced to the sentences she was composing. She thought of Janet sitting across from her in the restaurant: the beginning of a novel, the mistress meeting the wife, and neither knows what is in the heart of the other. Over a few drinks motives become blurred, intentions grow raw, outcomes blossom, inevitably, into fatal uncertainty.

She typed the sentences, one after another, and even before finishing the third page she knew how it was going to play out. All she needed was the one character who would make it work.

30

THE NEXT MORNING AMELIE WORKED UNTIL NOON
and then rose from her desk and prepared a light lunch. She
answered a few emails, she made some calls. She was going to be
recording an interview the next day for a books program based
in Los Angeles, which entailed her driving to a studio in Boston
while she listened to the questions through headphones. The
illusion would be that she was sitting with the host in his Santa
Monica studio, and that afterward she would step out and take a
walk along the beach. It would be funny if by chance while Ben
sat in traffic on the freeway he switched on the radio only to hear
his lover's voice speaking of her work, or reading aloud from it:
They met at the end of summer...

Perhaps she should say something special in the interview,
something meant for him alone. She tried to think of some word
or phrase that was familiar to them from their times together.
He never called her anything but Amelie, save for that time he
had called her Janey. Or Jane, or whatever it was. And to her he
was Ben or Darling. She had never nicknamed his penis, as she
had Richard's, though she did point out to her ex-husband in the
miserable final days of their marriage that in fact he was not, after
all, a Richard but a dick.

But Ben wouldn't hear it. He would be out on the beach

with Janet, or in Disneyland or at Universal Studios, or driving through the streets on the lookout for wandering movie stars. And she consoled herself with the idea that eventually she would be able to take a vacation with him, that they could go off to someplace wonderful, Capri, perhaps, or Portofino, their names forming deliciously in her mind.

That was it.

She looked up.

Here it was.

She smiled.

She would ask him to divorce Janet. She would ask him to marry her. It would be an ultimatum, the logical outcome of their two-year relationship, something he could not possibly dismiss. Because she had it all before her: the narrative she needed to shape the reality. It was so simple, so perfectly logical. The one undeniable element in the story.

The other man.

31

WHEN AMELIE RETURNED FROM GETTING HER HAIR CUT and colored on Friday, Nina was sitting on the deck with her iPhone. Nina held up a finger and said, "Love ya, too, bye-bye," and ended the call. She stood and hugged and kissed her mother.

"How did you get here? Bus?"

"I got a ride."

"Peter?"

"He doesn't have a car."

"I meant on the phone just now. Was that Peter?"

Nina smiled and nodded.

"I'd like to meet this boy."

"This man."

"This young man," Amelie said.

"A girl in my dorm lives, like, ten minutes from here. That's how I got a ride from school."

"Anyone I know?"

"I only met her last week, and school's almost over, so we talked a little about rooming together next year. Her name's Abbie Kinsman."

"I've met her mother a few times. The daughter went to your school, right?"

"Then left for Andover our junior year. So I only knew her a little."

"Let me look at you. What is that?"

"I got my nose pierced."

Amelie resisted the temptation to touch the tiny jewel that lay nestled in the shallow valley above her daughter's left nostril. "Did it hurt?"

Nina laughed. "You can't imagine."

"You didn't get anything else done, did you?"

"No, Mom."

"Is Peter full of holes?"

"Stop it," she said, though she also laughed.

"Do you want to eat?" Amelie walked inside. On the sofa was Nina's laundry, at least three weeks' worth spilling out of plastic garbage bags.

"Peter has a pierced ear," Nina said.

"Is he a student?"

"He's at Harvard."

Amelie went in the kitchen and opened the refrigerator. "And what is he doing there?"

"He's a student."

"I meant what is he studying?"

"Prelaw."

The phone played a few notes from some pop song, and Nina picked it up and smiled, "Hi. Yeah. No. Yeah. Okay."

Nina wandered off with her phone. Amelie opened a tin of tuna and, dividing it in two, emptied each side onto a bed of lettuce leaves. She made a dressing with balsamic vinegar. She poured herself a glass of white wine. Nina came in and finished her phone call, "Love ya, bye."

"Peter again?"

"Sorry."

"I don't mind you talking to him. Why don't you invite him over for lunch tomorrow?"

"I don't think so."

Amelie looked at her. "So…do you want to talk about it? About him, about your relationship…? I mean, it's not my business, but if you want to sound me out about anything, I'm always here for you, no matter what. You know that, don't you?"

Nina came to her, arms outspread, and hugged her mother, holding her close. "Sometimes I guess I just need to hear that."

"Even though you don't want to talk about it," Amelie said, and they both laughed.

Amelie went back to preparing lunch. After a few moments she said, "Sometimes being a writer… It's not just sitting down and working. Your mind is always on it, it's always distracted, you know? So if sometimes I don't sound interested or engaged, it's not you, okay?"

Nina nodded.

"It was always hard for me, having to balance it off, raising you and getting to work. Sometimes, after you finally could sleep through the night, I'd be exhausted, but I'd drag myself to my desk and work until two or three in the morning."

Nina came up beside her and touched her arm. "I'm sorry, Mom."

"No. Never be sorry. I'm the one who should apologize. But, you know, I'm so glad we had you. My life would be so much poorer without little Nina." She tousled her daughter's hair and they both laughed. Amelie handed her a salad.

Nina was the only real constant in her life, the one undivided loyalty she could depend upon. And she smiled at the thought of it.

Nina found a can of Diet Coke in the fridge and popped it open. They went out to the deck. Amelie told Nina about her latest book, how it was being received, how the interviews were going.

"I've been reading it," said Nina.

Amelie looked at her. "And?"

"I haven't finished it."

"Any thoughts?"

"Not until I've finished it."

"Nothing?"

Nina shook her head.

They ate for a few moments. Nina said, "It's about an affair."

"It's about love."

"It's about a love affair."

Amelie looked at her. "Is that a problem?"

Nina shrugged.

"Is it a moral issue?"

"No, Mom."

"It seems to annoy you."

"No, Mom."

For a few minutes they said nothing. Birds sang in the trees, a squirrel hung upside down on the feeder, struggling to extract sunflower seeds. It swung there every morning, its little limbs wrapped around the cylinder, as if there was no food to be found elsewhere, no buried acorns, no nuts, no garbage to rummage through, no slugs to eviscerate. She clapped her hands, and the squirrel swiveled its merry mocking eye to take her in as it continued to gorge and sway.

"Then what is it?" Amelie said. "What bothers you about my book?"

"It doesn't matter."

"It does matter, it matters a great deal to me. It's my book and you're my daughter and you're both important to me."

"It's…" Nina began and then she shook her head and fell silent. Had Rachel's friend seen more the day she was supposed to have spied them at the restaurant, were things going on under the table that could be construed as elements of foreplay?

"I bet Tolstoy's daughters never took *Anna Karenina* out on him," Amelie said, and Nina got up and went back into the house. She returned with a banana and began peeling it.

"Can we have Indian tonight?" she asked, and Amelie smiled.

"Of course."

"I never get it at school."

"Do you ever go out with your friends?"

"Well, yeah, of course."

"I mean for a meal."

"Sometimes."

"And with Peter?"

"Sometimes."

"Have you spoken to your father?"

Nina nodded. "He's going to have a baby. His wife is, anyway."

"How do you feel about that? You'll have a half sister or half brother." She had to stop herself from saying how much she hated the idea, as if Sharon's pregnancy were the result of some intrigue worked out by Richard and his wife to make Amelie appear barren, alone, unloved.

The landline rang and Nina ran inside to answer it. Amelie finished her wine. Nina came out and handed the cordless to her. "It's Rachel's father," she said, and walked back into the house.

32

"I'M OUTSIDE A RESTAURANT IN MALIBU. I CAN SEE THE OCEAN."

"Why didn't you call my cell?"

"I hit the wrong speed-dial number. Is it a problem?"

She could hear the traffic behind him, a siren, someone's car stereo blasting, *I'm a motherfucker, you're a motherfucker*.

"That was Nina," she told him. "Great timing."

"I thought you'd be alone."

She could see Nina beyond the kitchen, in the living room, her bare feet up on the coffee table. Amelie knew precisely what her daughter was doing; she was working out the higher mathematics of her mother's private life.

"She says Rachel has a friend who saw us in a restaurant," and then Nina slid open the screen door and joined her, taking a chair and leafing through a magazine. "So how have you been?" Amelie said with bright interest. "And Janet? And Andrew?"

"Do you really want to know?"

"That sounds nice," Amelie said flatly, and Nina glanced up at her. She wondered if Nina had been endowed with the power to read her mother's mind or the shift of light in her eyes. Amelie put her feet up on the edge of her chair and then changed her mind, because there was something coquettish in the pose. She sat up and crossed her legs. "And how's the weather been out there?" she said with perky brightness.

"I miss you," Ben said.

"Oh, I agree," she said.

"It's been shitty."

"The weather?"

"That too."

"Is that right?" Amelie said, as if Ben had told her of some extraordinary phenomenon he had witnessed, the splitting of California from the continent, the collapse of the movie industry.

"I'll be back in a week. Exactly one week."

"Yes, I know that." She sounded as if she were talking not to her lover, the man who every Friday brought her to the most exquisite orgasms, but to the repairman at the appliance store in town.

"I want to fuck you," he said, and she felt her breath rush out.

"Good," she said. *The washer will be fixed before tomorrow, good, send me a bill,* that was how she made it sound, and Nina pretended to read *Vanity Fair* while all along she was keeping an eye on her mother.

"I want you so badly," he said.

"Hmm," she said.

"They're in a restaurant. I stepped out to get something from the car. That's why I'm calling you while the valet keeps staring at me. You just have to show your face, and they expect a tip."

"Oh I see."

"I'm not going to be able to talk much longer. I'll tell them I called to check messages at my office."

"Uh-huh," she said. "And Disneyland was fun?"

"Are you really interested?"

"Not at all."

"Is Nina still there with you?"

"Oh yes."

"We're flying up to San Francisco tomorrow. We decided not to go to Mexico."

For some reason that pleased her. "How fascinating," she said. "Talk dirty to me."

She laughed. He always liked how she sometimes spoke to him, how she referred to her own body, how she would talk while they were in bed, how she would tell him what to do, where to put things, how to touch her. "And there's the problem with the windows," she said.

"What?"

"Because if we extend the side too far there'll have to be more windows installed. Isn't that what you suggested?"

He laughed. "I've got to get back to the restaurant. I miss you."

"Well, then that's how it'll have to be done. Let me see what solutions you come up with when you're back in town."

"You're good at this, you know. I want to see you naked," he said. "I want your mouth on me."

"And I could always add some sort of, I don't know, little greenhouse at the end, I suppose. You know, lots of glass and…" She shrugged.

"I'll be back late next Friday night. I'll try to get away for an hour or two on Sunday. If not, I'll take Monday off."

"Excellent," she said.

"We'll just stay there all day. We'll screw our brains out."

"It sounds like a great idea. Some sort of walk-in conservatory might be just the answer."

He said goodbye and hung up. Amelie set the phone on the table and looked out over the garden. She could hardly keep from smiling. She felt aroused by her conversation. It was as if the wall had been breached and whatever was inside was seeping out for all to see. It was like an omen, the phone call. He missed her desperately, and now, perhaps, he'd come to realize that she was the woman he should spend the rest of his life with.

Amelie said, "That was Rachel's father."

"I know that, Mom. Remember I answered the phone?"

"He just wanted to discuss something about the addition I told you about."

"While he was on vacation?"

"I guess he brought his work with him."

Nina turned the page of her magazine and said nothing. "Why are you having an addition put on this house?" she suddenly asked.

"What do you mean?"

"I mean, you live alone here, why do you need an addition?"

"I don't know, I just thought it would be nice."

"But you live *alone*, Mom."

"I'm thinking about moving my office downstairs. I don't like the room I'm in. I don't know, it's too bleak in the winter."

Nina looked at her. "How can a room be bleak?"

"Look, I want something a bit sunnier, that's all." It was astonishing how her affair had put her at the mercy of everyone. She had become wary of Janet, she had to tiptoe around Nina, she had to live in a world of code and signal, of distrust and deceit. Now she would have to deal with Nina. She would have to convince her that nothing was going on, nothing illicit was taking place. She went into the bathroom and slid her jeans and panties down to her ankles and sat on the toilet, and then the phone rang and she shouted, "I'll get it," and only half-buttoned, she ran out to hear her lover's voice again.

She stood at the screen door and listened as Nina said, "I'm fine."

Who is it? Amelie mouthed, and Nina looked at her and said, "It's Daddy."

"Oh," Amelie said, and went back to the bathroom.

33

"ARE YOU WRITING NOW?" THE UNSEEN INTERVIEWER in Santa Monica asked, and Amelie said she was working on a new book. "At least I'm trying."

"Do you find it difficult, especially as your latest book has only just landed?"

Amelie said that it wasn't always easy when you're in the middle of publicizing another book. "Sometimes I get a little lost," she said, and she laughed. "I'm still in the world of the last book."

"Will the next novel be anything like the one that just came out? Your reviews have been uniformly excellent."

"I can promise it'll be completely different."

"Then will the setting be pretty much the same?" He went on to say that over her last three novels she had begun to map out a universe of suburban angst, where below a veneer of respectability and conformity was a universe falling into disarray.

She felt a tickle in her pocket, indicating that a call was coming in over her iPhone. She could do nothing about it. She was being interviewed by a man she had never met who was sitting in Southern California asking her the same questions everyone else asked her, except he sounded a thousand times more intelligent.

"Well, I'm not sure actually. I mean, I think all writers try to create a consistent fictional world. The challenge is in always making it new. Exploring different layers of it." In other words, stepping over the line. She didn't know what else to say. Her phone kept vibrating, and she knew instantly it was Ben, that he had managed to extricate himself from the demands of his family. The vibrations stopped; the call had come to nothing.

"Of course a lot of writers don't like to discuss their work in progress, at least not in any detail."

"I suppose I'm like that, too," Amelie said brightly, addressing her invisible audience: people in cars, people in rest homes, actors in their studio trailers. Eight minutes had passed since the interview had begun. She looked at the digital clock on the studio wall, and her pocket began vibrating again. She wanted to say, *Could you please let me take this call from my lover?* Instead she said, "I still have no idea of even the names of the characters."

"So you've just begun work."

"I started it quite recently."

"And I know a lot of our listeners are interested in a writer's working habits."

That again.

"Could you tell us a little about some of yours?"

She wished she could be outrageous as some writers were. She wished she could say that she smoked a joint, or needed to cut her own flesh before sitting down to her laptop, comments that boosted sales and earned their authors spots on late-night talk shows and photos in the pages of glossy magazines devoted to troubled celebrities.

"I like to take a long walk in the morning," she said. "And then I just write."

"So you clear your head in the fresh air."

She was sorry she had mentioned it. Soon the interviewer would be asking her about her religious duties.

"And afterward? How do you wind down for the day?"

Before I go to yoga, I kill small animals and feed them, properly field-dressed, to my cellar full of kidnapped children. She laughed a little. "A glass of wine, some music, sometimes a movie. Then I always read before bed." Then her dear old friend, Mr. Pink, the magic pleasure machine.

After a few more questions the interviewer thanked her for her time, mentioning the title of the book and its publisher, and said it was undoubtedly available in your local library, which wasn't quite what Amelie wanted him to say. She imagined thousands of people putting their names on a reserve list while hundreds of unsold copies in bookstores were being packed and shipped back to warehouses in New Jersey.

"And from our studios in Santa Monica we want to say thank you to bestselling author Amelie Ferrar." She was about to take off the headphones when the interviewer said, "I think that went very well."

"Thank you." She'd forgotten his name.

"You were very, I don't know, unrevealing? In my experience most writers are exhibitionists."

She laughed a little. She knew lots of those. "I think a bit of mystery never hurts."

"I really like your latest jacket photo," he said.

"Oh, thanks." Where was this going?

"Do you ever get out to the West Coast?"

"I have, in the past." With Richard, then with Richard and Nina, then alone when she was touring her last book but one.

"But not with this book."

"Soon, though." The California leg of her current publicity tour would come in another month.

"Well, if you do, I'd love to meet you in person. Maybe for a—"

Again her phone began vibrating, and she took off the headphones and walked out of the studio, still hearing the small voice within them saying *Hello…? Hello…?*

"Hello?" she said into her phone as she walked through the station lobby and out to Commonwealth Avenue.

"It's Richard. I've been trying to reach you for the last twenty minutes."

"I was being interviewed, Richard. I was on a radio show in LA. I'm trying to sell books so I can make a living." She sounded as though she were addressing a delinquent child.

"Oh, sorry. How's LA?"

"I'm not there."

"Then how—"

She briefly explained how it worked.

"What can I do for you, Richard?"

"I just wanted to know how Nina seemed to you."

"You spoke to her on the phone when she was here the other day."

"I know, but…"

"What's the problem?"

"Why this attitude, Amelie?"

"Because I was in the middle of a long-distance interview."

"I didn't know that."

"Don't call me in the middle of the day. You know I'm working."

"You were answering someone's questions."

"That was work, too."

"I'm sorry, I didn't know you were being interviewed. I haven't seen Nina for a few weeks and was just wondering. I know she'd been having some trouble with a boy."

"He's not a boy, he's a man."

"A man?" Undoubtedly he pictured some gent in his fifties in golfing pants and polo shirt with a Buick, someone named Ned.

"A young man, Richard, a college student, prelaw with a pierced ear. And she's back on with him."

"I'm just concerned for her, that's all."

Amelie said nothing. She knew she should appreciate Richard at least for being a good father to Nina. She said, "How's Sharon?"

"Oh, she's fine. Thanks for asking."

"I bet she's big."

"We're having a little girl."

She could hear the smile in his voice. She remembered when she was pregnant with Nina, how pleased she was with herself, how she liked to look at her swollen body in the mirror.

"A girl," she said. "Nina will be thrilled to death."

"We've talked about it, Nina and I. She's going to be okay."

"And you've been all right?" she asked Richard.

"Not bad, thanks."

"Work okay?"

He told her about the recent successes of his design company, his trips to Hong Kong and London and Geneva. Actually she didn't care about his work; she had in fact always found his work extremely boring. He had always wanted to be a writer, and having written one very long, unpublishable novel had given it up, started his own company and made a medium-size fortune within the first two years. "I'm also involved in a project in Berlin."

"Great," she said. "I'm glad things are going well for you," though of course she was nothing of the sort. Or at least she wished she could have come back with something better—not the success of her career, which was evident to him, but of her private life. She wanted to be able to tell him that she was seeing an architect, smart and attractive, but he would catch it at once, he would remember the man he'd talked to on the playing field of Nina's old school, and Richard would delight in seeing his ex-wife mired in the quicksand of what he would perceive as the kind of sordid suburban scandal she'd made a career of writing about. As though somehow, through the words and sentences she'd written over years, she had created her own tragedy.

He said, "I told you how much I liked your new book."

"Thanks, Richard. I appreciate you saying so."

"It's funny, I've been seeing you everywhere."

She shifted forward in her seat. "What?" Had he been spying on her, following her, had he been making inquiries into her private life?

I see you everywhere: it was what Ben had said to her on one of the first occasions they carried on a conversation. Then, of course, she was flattered; he had seen her because he had noticed her the first time, he had remembered her, and he had seen her subsequently because he had sought her out.

For Richard to say that meant something else was afoot, something sinister. He had Sharon. He would have his new baby. What would he want from Amelie?

"You've been getting a lot of great reviews," he said. "Sharon saw the piece in *Vogue*. Wow, I mean, you look amazing."

"Oh, that. Thanks." He had only seen her, as it were, because of publicity exposure. This time her publisher had pumped serious money into her launch, with full-page advertisements in newspapers and the few remaining book supplements, national radio exposure, some TV, readings in New York, Boston, Chicago, San Francisco, and Monterey, where, she was told, she'd fit right in.

She couldn't feel an ounce of pleasure in her book or the reviews. She needed something more, something that would elevate not just her spirits but the whole tone of her life. Richard was going to be a father; she was going to be middle-aged. And having the *Vogue* people fussing over the cushions on her sofa and the hair on her head and the curtains on the windows didn't make it any better for her. She couldn't bring herself to appreciate Richard. She'd been so desperate to have him out of her life, have him and his woman excised from her existence, out of her sight and her hearing, unsmellable and beyond taste, that now they were divorced she could feel only a lingering guilt about this man who treated her with decency and respect.

"Everything else all right?" he said.

"By the way," she said suddenly. "I'm getting married."

34

IT WAS FUNNY HOW RICHARD HAD REACTED TO HER announcement. Amelie herself didn't know why she'd said it, and yet she knew that turning it into words was a kind of magic, setting free the idea as an entity apart from her, much as when she endowed a character with a name: what had been an aggregation of letters on a page became a person with a past, present, and future, someone against whom other characters could be defined.

The phone rang.

"Hi." She hadn't even glanced at the screen. She listened. The breathing was regular, relaxed. "Yes? Hello?"

"Sorry, I just…" The voice, a woman's, was unfamiliar to her. "Amelie?"

"Yes?"

A pause. Then: "It's Janet. Sorry about that, I thought the boys had gone out but Ben had forgotten his phone… Okay, I can talk now."

Amelie sat back and tried to catch her breath. "Janet. Hi. Didn't I hear you were in California?"

"So you knew."

"Um, Nina said she'd spoken to Rachel. How's the vacation going?"

"It's good. Really nice. My husband and Andrew just left to go to the store, and I thought I'd give you a call, just to see how things are."

Amazing how loaded a perfectly innocent question could be. "Things are...good, actually. Busy. You know. The usual."

"Writing?"

"What else is there?" And she laughed, but only a little.

"I was wondering... We'll be back on Saturday, and...I was hoping that maybe you and I could get together. Maybe for an early dinner one evening next week?"

"Um, sure, Janet, that would be nice."

She had called from three thousand miles away. Three thousand miles and four time zones just to set up a dinner appointment...

"I had such a nice time with you after your reading. I just felt, I don't know, that we could be good friends. I mean, most of the women I know are in the corporate world or they're involved in research and development, and sometimes it's good to have someone to talk to outside that whole crazy universe."

"Yes," Amelie said. "Of course." *The call is perfectly innocent,* she tried to console herself. *Nothing to worry about.*

"Good, then," Janet said. "Well, I'll touch base again when I'm home. There's something I'd like to discuss with you."

The call ended, Amelie went into full panic mode. Her heart was racing, her T-shirt soaked with perspiration. She tried to remember the tone of Janet's voice, and was certain it wasn't positive or gleeful or casual or anything even remotely friendly. It sounded serious, and she felt herself going slightly adrift, as if the earth's polarities had suddenly switched and she had no idea which direction she was now facing.

There's something I'd like to discuss with you.

Eight deadly words: like a surgeon about to break the worst news of all to her.

Part Four

35

Now Ben was back, he was home, it was nine in the morning and he was asleep in his house only a short drive from hers. Without realizing it, without even noticing the natural world around her, Amelie walked three rapid miles that warm morning, and everything smelled not so much ripe as decaying on this day she had been anticipating for a fortnight. Nature became a blur, smears of yellow and green, and the sound of bees and the song of crickets were nothing but the undifferentiated hissing of the wind in her ears.

After her shower, just for a change of scenery she drove into town and ran into her friend Laura, who was about to drive her daughter to her riding lesson. She stood by her Range Rover and greeted Amelie. Laura wore khaki shorts and a T-shirt on which was printed the insignia of her daughter's school, a creature bending its tusks against the pressure of her enhanced breasts.

"Congratulations on the book," Laura said. Everyone was congratulating her and yet only once or twice had anyone in her circle of friends and acquaintances actually come up and said she'd read it. Instead she would see them with other people's novels, and always they would say that they were going to read her new one, they absolutely must read her new one, they would do it as soon as possible, and then she would hear nothing more because in fact they never did read her new one. Was it out of fear that they might see something of themselves in her tidy 70,000-word narratives? Or was it simply because they didn't expect very much from Amelie Ferrar, nothing terribly exciting, just the usual tales of lusty suburbia?

Of course Ben read her books, on his iPad, so that no one would see what might be perceived as evidence, and though he would always say how much he liked them, how wonderful they were, she wanted to hear more, about how successful she had been in drawing this character or that, or how moving the central conflict was. She would look at him and smile, because when he showed her photos of the buildings he had designed, she knew she could never intelligently comment on the things that really mattered to him, the flying buttresses and groins, the sense of spatial integrity, and she, too, would only say, "I like it, it's wonderful."

Laura's daughter joined her mother by the car. Amelie said, "I haven't seen Alyssa for, what, a year now? She's really grown." Impeccable in her jodhpurs and paddock boots, the little equestrian gave Amelie a withering look and said, "I ride a horse named Popeye."

Amelie wondered why anyone would name a horse Popeye. "I bet he can see really well," she said, imagining a visually adept thoroughbred raised on oats and spinach.

"No. He's just very strong," Alyssa said, staring at this woman who seemed so amazingly stupid.

"She came in second in her class at the last Labor Day show," Laura said.

"Great," said Amelie.

"Her jumping has improved, too."

"Wonderful."

"Dressage is just around the corner."

"Fabulous."

Laura and Alyssa got into the car. Laura started the ignition. She said, "You know that architect at the school, don't you? Andrew's father?" She seemed about to add something.

"Andrew's in my class. He's gross and disgusting," the little girl said, making a vomit face.

"Why?" Amelie asked Laura, and then realized it was the wrong response. She should have said yes in her bright manner and left it at that.

"No reason," Laura said, smiling and driving away, leaving Amelie mired in a swamp of speculation.

Instead of pulling up her driveway she drove past her house. She had driven into town to buy a croissant and a coffee, though the minute Laura asked if she knew Ben, all her appetite had fled her. Now that she was in her car she could feel it, the vacancy in her stomach, the unlocatable ache that comes with hunger. But she wouldn't stop, she couldn't stop, and instead she drove on until she reached Ben's street, slowing to a crawl as she passed his house, craning her neck to take in the windows, the driveway, the front door. All the blinds in his house had been pulled down. In the depths of his jet-lagged sleep was Amelie the object of his dreams?

She hadn't at first noticed the car that had drifted into view behind her, following her almost all the way back to her house, until she looked at the rearview and caught sight of it. She couldn't make out who was behind the wheel, but there was something sinister about the whole thing. She eased over to the side, slowing to fifteen miles an hour, which the other car also did. And then she came to a stop. And so did the car.

She put her arm out and waved the driver around her as the flashing blue lights of an unmarked police car snapped on from its grill.

"Shit," she said, putting the car in Park.

The cop wore aviator sunglasses and was hatless. He took his time ambling over to her window. She said, "What's the problem, Officer? Surely I wasn't speeding."

"It's that your driving seemed a little suspicious. Going slowly past houses like that. Like you were checking them out, especially as there've been a few break-ins the area lately. May I see your license and registration, please?"

She took her registration from the glove box and the license with its embarrassing photo, making her look like a woman who had been incarcerated for several years for prostitution and narcotics and only now had seen the light of day, prepared to hit the streets again.

He took them back to his car and did the usual thing, made her sweat it out while he probably listened to Howard Stern on Sirius. After several minutes he took his time getting out of his car and moseying over to her, handing back her documents.

"You live just a few doors down from here."

"Yes, I do, Officer."

She tried to see if his name was on his badge or uniform, because she had a sick feeling that this was not going to end well for her, that he would drag her out of her car, cuff her, and throw her in the back of his vehicle, then take her to the wooded road by the recycling facility and have his way with her. She imagined what he'd say to her when he was finished zipping up. *"You say anything, little lady, and I'll tell that architect of yours everything I know about you."*

Even in these moments before a potential citation, she made a mental note of it as something she might use in her new book.

He said, "May I ask why you were all the way over by Bainbridge Road?"

"I'm allowed to drive where I like, aren't I? Free country and all that?"

He grinned like Rod Steiger in that Sidney Poitier movie about the southern sheriff she'd streamed on Ben's recommendation a few weeks earlier. "Well, you are correct about that. You can go now."

Even his words, as anodyne and boilerplate as they were, seemed to carry something ominous about them. Now she was off-balance; now her day had been further knocked askew. In the confusion that followed her encounter first with Laura and now with the law, she felt nauseated and fatigued. She drove up to her house and let herself in. She only wanted to call Ben, to have him hear her out, absorb her fears, settle her nerves. But, of course, that wasn't possible.

Eventually he would get in touch with her by email or text, and even if Janet was constantly by his side, scrutinizing his every action, her eyes bulging with suspicion, he would somehow allow his lover to know he was back and thinking of her. He was like something divine, capable of distant and subtle communication. The light in the sky would change; thunder would roil the cloudless heavens; the wind would carry the whispery ghost of his voice.

By noon he still hadn't gotten in touch, and when five o'clock rolled around Amelie was suffocating in silence. She sat on her deck sipping vodka and leafing through the latest *New Yorker*. She had written precisely zero words that day. That was not exactly true. She had typed the words `She got into her car to meet the` and then had deleted them, because for a moment she felt she was inside a novel being written by someone else, in a narrative moving in a direction of which she was completely ignorant. Was she the main character, or the antagonist? Or maybe just a subsidiary character, a bit of local color, a woman without much dimension who appears here and there to toss out a little witty dialogue?

Instead of trying to write, she shut her laptop and opened the novel she'd bought on the night of her most recent reading. The one followed by the drink with Janet. *That* night.

Chapter two, page seven:

`When Holly's mother called her the second time, she listened to the spiteful words, then quietly set the phone down, uttering not a word in reply to the woman. Earlier, her therapist had reduced her to tears simply by once again referring to her family history and the event that had so marked her client. "Poor Holly," the woman said to her. "You were only nine years old when it happened. Now you're forty-four, divorced, and the mother of three children. You've lived with this burden for so long that, frankly, I think you can't imagine living without it. Which means I'm not sure I can be of any use to you."`

Amelie tossed it aside. She knew exactly what was going to happen. Through blurred eyes Holly was going to drive home, phone her mother, spit accusations at her, then try to kill herself, only to be found by Whatshername, her oldest daughter who's married to that golf pro. She'd read the damned thing a year earlier as an advance reading copy, sent by the author's editor to pry a blurb out of her. Which, of course, she failed to do.

A neighbor's cat wandered into the yard and stopped to stare at her before squatting to drop its daily business. Into her second drink of the evening, Amelie drifted into a light sleep, and when the phone rang it was dark. She cleared her throat and said *Mother?* Had she become Holly all of a sudden?

"It's me," he said.

She blinked her eyes a few times. In her dream the woman had turned and said to her, *I think I'll lie down for a few minutes*, and it was exactly what her mother had said fifteen minutes before she got into bed to die.

"Good morning," Amelie said, trying to sound alert and cheerful. She couldn't understand why she'd woken up so early, why she was sitting on her deck before sunrise. She felt completely rested, if not a bit stiff from sleeping in a chair.

"It's nine o' clock," he said. "I've been sleeping for most of the day."

"It's night?"

"Are you okay?"

"Darling?"

He laughed.

"I must have dozed off," Amelie said.

"Janet's gone to the supermarket. Andrew's in his room

playing a video game. I've been on the phone for the last fifteen minutes with Rachel."

Rachel: Amelie remembered. "Did she say anything?"

"About what?"

"About us in the restaurant."

"I wouldn't worry about it. Janet doesn't know a thing."

But she hadn't asked that. She was asking about Rachel, not Janet. And now Ben himself had become a question instead of the answer he always had reliably been for her.

She took the phone into the house and sat in the living room. Three hours had disappeared from her life. She wondered how she must have seemed, sitting on her deck with a drink by her side, her head slumped, unconscious. Amelie Ferrar the writer; Amelie Ferrar, profiled in *Vogue* in all her perfectly coiffed blue-eyed prettiness; Amelie Ferrar the old drunk. The taste in her mouth was of a foul stickiness. She felt she knew what it was like being one of the old men who convened outside the local saloon each midday, stinking of piss and Camels, their lives fouled beyond repair. "I missed you," she said. She decided she would say nothing at all about Janet's call to her. That belonged to her world, not theirs.

"I missed you, too."

"Did you think about me?"

There was the briefest of pauses. "Of course," he said. "Have you been working?"

"I did a few more interviews. But writing's been slow. Come over and see me, Ben. Try to get out tonight."

"I'm still kind of beat. I don't think I can."

"Just for five minutes."

"I really can't," he said.

Now a silence lay between them.

"Then when?" she said.

"Monday. Like we planned. I'll drop Andrew off at school and come straight to your place," and he hung up, *click*.

"Goodbye," she said. *Goodbye?*

36

Afterward they rested. Her head lay in the bend of his arm, her left hand played lightly with the hairs on his chest, back and forth, this way and that. For some reason she hadn't pleased him, and she didn't know if she imagined it, but he seemed distant, unfocused, somehow separate from her. The dissonance of their failed lovemaking now filled the air. "Should we try again?"

He shook his head a little. "Not right now. I don't think it's going to happen today. I'm glad it was good for you, though."

"But I wish it had been nice for you, too."

He shrugged. The expression on his face was unreadable.

"Tell me what I can do for you."

"Nothing. I don't think it's going to work."

"Do you feel all right?"

"I feel fine."

She placed her palm flat against his chest. "Something on your mind?"

"Besides work?" He looked at her. He smiled.

"Whatever."

"No. Not really."

"Did something happen on the trip?"

He smiled. "Nothing happened on the trip."

"Is there anything you want to tell me?"

He shook his head. She thought about how it would be living with this man, having to shed a long-established routine marked by solitude and work and the small pleasures she had learned to accept since her divorce in favor of carving out an evening or even a whole day with Ben.

Apart from the sex, how would it be? Apart from the sex, was there really anything else to look forward to? And what was he like outside of bed? Although they had eaten in restaurants and driven in cars together, she had no concept of how things would be on a day-to-day basis. Eating breakfast, having dinner, going to bed together simply to sleep. But she would come to learn his habits just as he would learn hers, and sometimes the little things he did or forgot to do would cause some tension. But at least he would be there, even when he wasn't, because eventually he *would* be there.

And she remembered what Janet had told her that night over drinks: that sometimes it seemed as if he wasn't there. Now Amelie was seeing it for herself. He extricated his arm and sat up on the side of her bed. She saw his back, bowed with exhaustion and failure, and when she reached out to draw her fingers across it, he stood and began to dress.

She said, "We'll try again at the end of the week." Already she had begun making excuses for him, because it was what she always ended up doing.

She saw that his body had begun to lose its firmness, that the gravity of age was drawing him down.

"I won't be here," he said, still not looking at her.

"What?"

"I have to travel. On business. I'm flying out Friday morning and won't be back till Sunday night." He was speaking to the air, to the absolute nothing that lay between him and the wall.

She couldn't believe her ears. "But you just got back from LA."

Now he stood and turned to her. "I have to go to Carbondale. Illinois. I'm being interviewed by some people at the university there for an arts center they're hoping to build. This could be a big deal for the firm."

She sat up on the bed and for some reason pulled the sheet up to cover her nakedness. "No," she said, staring at him.

"It's business, Amelie. I'm obligated to do this. I really want this contract."

"No."

"I need to do this."

"You could have told them to schedule it for a different day of the week."

"It's not a day, it's the weekend to tour the site and take photos. And I can't tell them to change their schedule. I mean, I'm the one who wants the damn job. Look, I wouldn't expect you to cancel if your publisher wanted to see you, or if you had to do a signing or an interview."

"But that wouldn't happen. Publishers deal with authors all the time, they allow us to change our minds."

"Look. Amelie. I can't just tell them to alter their schedule. I'm trying to land an important commission. I wouldn't want you to miss something important in your work just for this."

She stared at him, a flaccid man with his hands in the air. "Just for this. Thanks, Ben." She turned away from him. "Just for this." She shook her head.

"You know I didn't mean it like that."

"But you said it. You said the words. *Just for this*. So this is what it's all about. You've had me for two years, and now you've decided you've had enough. Is that what you're saying?"

He pulled on his trousers and zipped them up. He said, "Look. I'm sorry, I didn't mean it to sound that way. You know how I feel." He stepped over and touched the side of her face with his hand. And then he was gone. Just like the last phone call.

Goodbye?

37

IN WORDS IT WENT LIKE THIS: HE WAS SLIPPING AWAY.
Interpreted visually it was the view of him lifting himself from the
bed, stepping out of her reach. There was something emblematic
in the way he presented his back to her. Once, early on in their
affair, Amelie had dreamed that she had reached out to touch Ben
and her hand went right through him, and when she woke, it was
with a laugh, for the dream was like something out of a textbook,
something to make the Freudians put down their cigars and rub
their hands in glee. Amelie sensed that if things didn't change,
the affair would inevitably move into entropy: they would begin
to sicken of each other, their words turning to ominous silence.
It was a rootless thing, devoid of commitment, forever teetering
on the edge.

And where would that leave her?

On Sunday she had been invited to an early dinner party in
the city, hosted by a couple she had known since Nina was a
baby. She knew there would be a few single men there, successful
men, perhaps attractive and intelligent men, men who featured in
magazine articles about "The Hundred Most Eligible Bachelors
with Ivy League Degrees," and she wondered for the first time
in two years whether what she should be doing was dating. Men
with whom she could enjoy an evening, without sex, with whom

conversation would be stimulation enough. Who knows? She might learn to get a little distance between herself and Ben, and maybe this is what he needed, even what she required.

Because if she looked at him objectively, Ben was rather ordinary in his appearance. He was pleasing, not striking. He was certainly not eligible. And he was intelligent but not particularly droll. Often she would say something to amuse him and he would stare blankly at her. She stopped this line of thinking immediately, for by the end of the hour she would have come to despise the ugly witless gnome that her lover had become in her estimation.

She had only dated three or four times since the divorce, and Ben hadn't protested. She once said to him, "I think I need to do this," and he agreed, unhelpfully saying she had to do whatever she felt comfortable doing. "At least for the sake of appearances. Otherwise…" and she let him figure it out.

"Do you like these men?"

"They're not you."

And he smiled and put his arms around her.

"The difference is that I love you."

"Do you go to bed with them?" he asked.

"No," she said. "I go to bed with you."

There had been Stuart, who took her to a restaurant where the waiters were dressed like football referees and where mounted televisions on every wall broadcast nonstop sporting events, and who, when she tried to talk to him, continued to speak to a point just above her head. Over his sixteen-ounce sirloin he suddenly threw his hands in the air and shouted *Score!*

There was Larry, who took her to a comedy nightclub in the

city, where the star of the show was a loud woman who told jokes about fat men suffering from impotence. Amelie remembered the allegedly funny lady saying "Did you ever have a man fart in bed?" and she turned to Larry and whispered "I can't stand this any longer, I want to go home," and she stared at this man with whom she had spent the evening, for he was in tearful convulsions of hilarity.

Early on there was Eric, who took her to dinner at the most expensive restaurant in the city and afterward to a play starring Frank Langella, and she realized that she rather liked Eric, that although he wasn't stunningly gorgeous, he was intelligent and graced with a sense of humor, as well as breath that reeked of an open sewer.

There was Gerry, who was a friend of Patrick and Susie Gartner, and who was in advertising and drove a red Porsche, and with whom she had civilized and amusing conversation over the phone, but of course he had simply never bothered to pick her up at the agreed time. Neither did he call. Nor apologize. Nor anything.

38

AMELIE WAS AT HER COMPUTER. REMEMBERING SIT-
ting in the optometrist's chair in the darkness, she had begun to
type:

    Tell me something that you can't take back, she
    thought as she tried to read her doctor's expres-
    sion. Tell me something that will change this day,
    the night to come, and all the days thereafter.

And then, as though something about that passage had frightened her, she deleted it, one reluctant letter at a time.

And then restored it.

She seemed to come out of nowhere, this woman on the
verge of tragedy. As though with these words Amelie were clearing a path into unknown territory, and even that small step, a
paragraph begging for context, a character demanding a name,
made her uneasy. This wasn't her usual fare; this was dark, ominous even, and to develop it meant she would break out of her
shell; she would write herself into a whole new life, that of this
unknown character. She just needed to find her way into it. And
then find her way to the ending.

The phone rang just as she shut her laptop. .

"I've got a problem," Ben said. It was the day before he was
due to fly to Illinois.

Amelie felt the blood drain from her face. "What's wrong, what's happened?" Her imagination began to blossom, and all the words of catastrophe—disease, death, deception—started to pass through her mind, because not once had he ever started a conversation with her that way.

"I really hate to bother you like this."

"Just tell me."

"Janet's meeting is running late, and I need someone to pick up Andrew from school and bring him to his piano lesson. I'm at the office going a little nuts preparing for the trip tomorrow."

Oh. That was it, then, fetch the boy at school. She let the silence sink in.

"When are we getting together?" she said with as little enthusiasm as she could manage.

"Next Friday, probably."

Probably: one of the great loaded words of the English vocabulary. *Yes, I'll marry you. Probably. Yes, I'll call you. Probably. Yes, I want to see you again. Probably.*

"You've done it for me before," he said. "Remember how you'd sometimes give Rachel a lift home?"

"But this is Andrew," and she didn't know why she said it, why there was something problematic in taking Ben's son from point A to point B, why he was any different from his sister. Somewhere in the crevices of the equation, in the esoteric angles of its logic, lay some further problem, something unclear that might get in the way, throw off the calculation, skew the result.

She opened her laptop and looked again at what she had written. `Tell me something that will change this day, the night to come, and all the days thereafter.`

"Forget it," he said, not sounding the least bit disappointed. "You're working. I shouldn't have bothered you."

"I just need to get into this book."

"You're right. Let me try someone else."

She thought of Andrew, how he seemed like an early draft of his father, a short story that one day would become a novel. Just giving him a lift would make her part of his life, and of course she really did need to get away from her work for a little while, she needed to get some perspective, she needed to take a ride, she continued to make excuses and talk herself into helping Ben. "Actually, I think I might be able to do it," she said.

"I'll give Lindsey Baron's mother a call. Lindsey's in Andrew's class, and they're both out at the same time."

"But I'd like to do it. I'd be happy to do it for you. I want to do it, Ben."

"But your work."

"I don't want you to call anyone else. I'm glad you thought of me."

"Just drop Andrew off at his piano lesson," and he gave her the address. "I'll call the school and have the message passed on that you'll be picking him up. He'll know to look for your car."

She considered it. She said, "And we're definitely seeing each other next Friday?"

"Absolutely," he said.

"If I don't speak to you before then, have a good flight tomorrow."

On her way to pick up Andrew she listened to a news report on the radio about a plane crash in Ohio. All 172 passengers and crew had died in it. Investigators were picking over the wreckage, looking for the black box, finding body parts. She was sorry she had heard it, she was sorry for the people who died and for those who would be told the news, she was sorry she was in her car and finding her thoughts moving in all the wrong directions. In another day Ben would fly off to Illinois. He would board the plane and smile at the flight attendant, eat snacks and drink beer, and then she saw the engine burst into flames over Columbus and the plane tilt and then Ben would grip the armrests on his seat and people would be praying and screaming for god, and children would be crying *Mommy, Mommy*, and then it would hit and there would be a long moment of high-pitched pain and then Ben would become nothing more than a bloody mass of pulp and shattered bone, and alone in her car she let out a little cry and rubbed her brow with her hand.

Because if his plane crashed there would be no Friday.

39

THROUGH THE WINDING BACK ROADS OF NEW
England, past the low stone walls of centuries-old farms, past the
horses grazing in the luxury of their afternoon: it had been almost
twelve months since she'd taken this drive, and it reminded her
of all the years she had done this twice each day, how Nina had
moved from car seat to back seat to front seat, and now Nina was
capable of driving herself wherever she liked. It meant that Nina
had grown up and Amelie was only growing older.

It had begun with the glasses. Until then she had never really
noticed much change. Certainly her skin had lost some of its
firmness, and her body was no longer the trim, shapely figure
she had lived with for so long, but with her eyes weakening she
sensed that she had moved into some new phase of deteriora-
tion. Now she understood why Richard had married a younger
woman and why he'd wanted another baby. Anything to stave
it off, anything to take the mind off the process. What would
happen next? Would it be menopause, deafness, arthritis,
dementia? And aloud she said, "Enough," and turned up the
radio and hummed along with it a little, *hmm-hm-hm-hmm*.
The moment she turned into the school's driveway, people
began waving at her. Here was where she'd see Ben each morning, here they had talked, they had exchanged looks, they had

smiled and waved to each other. It was like wandering into a gallery in the museum of her life.

A woman whose name completely escaped her called out, "How's Nina doing?"

"She's fine, thanks," said Amelie.

"What brings you back?"

"Just doing someone a favor," she said.

"Dougie's at Dartmouth, you know," and Amelie just smiled, because she didn't know who Dougie was. "And Sarah's at Exeter."

"Wow," said Amelie, more at the amount of tuition the woman must be paying than the quality of institution.

"Gotta go," the woman said.

The news was on and Amelie turned up the radio: the news-reader said that only 171 people were killed in the plane crash, as one lucky person, in fact a woman of ninety-two, had decided at the last minute not to board. *A whole new lease on life*, the old girl said in an interview, and Amelie realized that someone was lurking by her window. It was Laura, whose daughter rode the horse named Popeye.

"I got your book," she said. "I bought it yesterday."

"Thank you," an amazed Amelie said brightly. "I hope you enjoy it."

"Will you inscribe it for me?"

"I'd be happy to, Laura."

"We're thinking about doing it for our reading group."

"That's wonderful," she said.

"Would you be interested in meeting with the group on the evening we discuss it?"

"Where do you do it?"

"Usually at Jane Baron's house."

"I don't think I've actually met her," said Amelie, remembering that a few years earlier she had been asked by her friend Peggy to work with the Baron woman at the auction, and had to beg off as she was touring a book. Beyond Laura's shoulder she saw Andrew in his baseball cap, lugging his backpack and dragging his lacrosse stick across the freshly mown lawn.

Laura turned and extended her arm: "She's just over there. In the silver Mercedes."

All Amelie could make out was a face and blond hair and a pair of sunglasses. The woman waved a little, and Amelie smiled and agitated the air with her fingers. Laura said loudly, "Janey, this is Amelie Ferrar," and Jane Baron said, "Ohh." When Andrew got into the car she said, "Is there a kid in your class named Baron?"

"Yeah. Lindsey Baron. She sucks."

She pulled out of the line and turned onto the road. She said, "I hear you went to California. Did you have a good time?"

"It was okay."

When they got to a red light Amelie turned to look at him. "You look just like your dad," she said.

He twisted his mouth in disgust. "Everybody says that."

She wondered if Janet resented that, if somehow she felt left out of the gene pool because there was nothing of her in Andrew. Perhaps she looked more like Rachel, in which case there was some consolation.

"It's not such a bad thing, is it?"

He shrugged.

"How's your mom?" Amelie said.

"Okay."

"Just okay?"

"She's fine."

"Good."

He said nothing. He didn't even look at her, though she occasionally stole a glance at him. The thought again occurred to her that this is what Ben must have looked like when he was Andrew's age.

"She's at a business meeting," he said.

"Your mom."

"Yeah."

She glanced in the rearview to see the same car that had followed her a few days earlier, the one that had turned out to be an unmarked police cruiser. The driver had on the same aviator sunglasses as before. Clearly, she had become a person of interest to the authorities. She waited for the blue lights to come on, and they'd have to go through it all over again. Except this time she was in a different neighborhood with a child who belonged to someone else; as though it were the beginning of a movie that would not end well for anyone in an abandoned cabin deep in the woods.

"You have to make a right here," Andrew said, pointing at the window.

She clicked on her directional and made an overcautious, utterly lawful turn, and saw the other car drive on, though she detected a slight pause. Had he watched where she was going? Now she felt like a fugitive, clinging to the shadows, shunning the lamplight. She had nothing to feel guilty about, really; shreds of innocence clung to her in all its threadbare misery.

She turned the corner and waited at the light. She thought of offering to buy him an ice cream, and then looking at her watch realized he would be late for his piano lesson. "How's school?" she asked.

"It's okay."

"Lots of friends?"

"Some."

"Piano fun?"

"No."

"Why do you take lessons?"

"My mom wants me to."

Amelie smiled. Already there were signs of rebellion against his mother. He would be glad to see the back of her.

"What would you like to be doing?"

He shrugged again and it gave her a tiny frisson, as though she were catching an echo of her lover in this small boy. "I like video games. I like to play chess."

"Really. You play with your dad?"

"Sometimes." She imagined the two of them rubbing their chins over the little horses and castles and bishops, each plotting out a checkmate. "It's just over here," he said, and he pointed at a white colonial and began to gather his things together. Before he opened the door he looked directly at her and smiled. "Thanks," he said, and she stopped herself before leaning over to kiss him goodbye.

40

THE EMAIL FROM JANET ARRIVED THE NEXT MORNING, the same day Ben was leaving for Illinois, asking if possibly she and Amelie might meet for dinner on Sunday at the Coach & Four at seven. Which gave her an excuse to bow out of the dinner party in Boston. It was just as well, as she was in no mood to make small talk. She remembered what Janet had told Amelie: *There's something I'd like to discuss with you.* And now the disquiet had returned, only doubly so.

Her cell phone chimed, her screen displaying *Private Caller.* "Yes?"

"It's Janet. Just wanted to see if I had the right number."

"Hi, Janet. Actually, you called me once before." And then she remembered: that had been on her landline. Then how did she get Amelie's cell number, something Amelie shared only with Nina, Richard, a few close friends, her agent, her editor, her publicist…? Oh, and Ben.

"I know I just sent you an email, but I thought it would be more personal if I called."

"I'd be happy to have dinner with you, Janet," Amelie said, trying to hide her trepidation.

"By the way," Ben's wife said, her voice brightening, "I saw your latest book at the airport in LA. It's just so funny that I kind of know you, and then I see the book, and I think—you have this whole other life."

You can say that again.

"So, anyway," she said. "I'll see you on Sunday?"

"Absolutely."

"Wonderful. I'll make reservations."

Sunday was completely squandered for her. After a quick perusal of the *New York Times*, and anticipating the unknown for that night, Amelie couldn't write a single sentence. She walked out to the backyard and half-heartedly yanked weeds from the garden, something she had always wanted to do, but she could never muster much enthusiasm for what seemed to her a thankless activity. You pull out a weed and another pops up in the same place. The whole exercise seemed without merit.

After ten minutes of this she changed into her yoga pants and a T-shirt and went for a brisk walk as she listened to music. She thought of Ben flying to Illinois. She thought of Ben flying *out* of Illinois, and then of Ben driving to her house the next Friday, she, by then, having already dined with his wife. The whole idea of it was both delicious to the writer she was and dreadful to her as a person. She needed to find that perfect point of balance between the two of them, and by the time she'd dressed to meet Janet, she felt as if finally she might have achieved it.

She put on a pair of earrings, examined herself in the mirror, found herself wanting in certain undefined ways, then said *Fuck it* before turning off the light.

When she walked into the restaurant she nearly lost whatever composure she'd been able to muster, because sitting alone at the bar was the same guy she'd seen before, reading a book. Again, he held the book up and smiled, because it was still her latest. The bartender glanced up and saw Amelie, and then went to serve a customer. It seemed to her like the prelude to a stalking, and there was nothing she could do about it at this stage. Except, of course, worry that he might find out her address and make himself part of her life.

She said to the young woman at the front of the house, "I believe my friend made a reservation," and she said Janet's name.

The woman checked her book and nodded, and took two faux-leather-bound menus with their predictably gold-embossed coach and four, a little too much tallyho for her tastes, leading Amelie to a table for two with a view of the bar. Amelie checked her watch: ten minutes early. Most of the other tables were occupied, and she recognized a few people there from the community, waving a little when they acknowledged her.

"Can I get you something to drink?"

"I think I'll wait for my friend."

When she looked up, the guy at the bar was pointedly staring at her. She looked away, and when she looked back he was looking at someone just entering, with a very different kind of smile. Which is when her phone vibrated. This time she didn't bother checking the screen.

"Hello?"

"Hi." It was Ben. He sounded rushed, harried, confused.

Into her cupped hand she said, "Where are you?"

"Just landed in Boston. I have to go to the office and finish some paperwork, otherwise I'd… Hang on, I'm getting a call."

She waited. She looked up at the bar and saw Janet, having just stepped in, her phone to her ear, smiling and nodding, possibly at the guy at the bar. Then she turned, looked around, and waved when she spotted Amelie.

Ben suddenly said, "Sorry, that was—" and Amelie clicked off as Janet approached her.

"Good to see you again, Janet," Amelie bubbled, and Janet put her phone in her bag and gave her a quick hug.

"That was Ben calling to say he's still on the ground in Illinois. Seems his flight is delayed two hours."

Amelie wondered if she looked as absolutely blindsided as she felt. He'd landed… He hadn't left yet…? What kind of limbo was this man in right now? And why was she being excluded from it? She wondered for half a moment if the two of them, Ben and Janet, were in on this. As if all along Amelie had been set up for a fall.

"Oh, is your husband traveling?"

"Business, yes. He was in Carbondale. So I don't know when he'll be home, probably one or two in the morning. The lower school's closed tomorrow for faculty workshops, so Andrew's spending tonight at a friend's house." She smiled. "So for a change the evening is all my own."

She took a seat across from Amelie. The guy reading at the bar had vanished. "Ben is hoping to do something with the university there," Janet said. "Did you know that he's an architect?"

"Someone told me that, yes. Must be a very interesting career." Words came out of her like spew instead of the gourmet meals she thought most of her sentences usually resembled.

"He never brings his work home—or only rarely. And then he doesn't say much about it. It's just the way he is," and she shrugged.

The waitress came over and they ordered drinks.

"Would you like to hear the specials for this evening? We have—"

"I think we'll wait," Janet said. "We just want to chat for a little while."

The young woman smiled. "Let me know if you need anything."

And then Janet's smile fell. "I asked to meet you because, well, I'm not sure how to say this, because it's not really the kind of thing I'm comfortable talking about…"

Amelie tried to find a way out of this, and though several different excuses came to mind, none seemed of any use in the moment. The waitress delivered their drinks.

"But you being a writer, I'm thinking that maybe you'd have some, I don't know, insight into this problem?"

"Problem?" Amelie sipped her martini, and the speared olives did a single fouetté around the glass.

"It's Ben. And me. I know from what you said the last time we talked that you'd gone through some…difficult times with your husband. That it ended up in a divorce—which is the absolute last resort for us."

"I see."

"But I think my husband—and this is so hard for me to say…" She looked away and composed herself: "But I think Ben may be having an affair."

Amelie nodded and said nothing.

"He's been so…distant lately. And sometimes I see him standing in our yard or in the driveway on the phone. When he comes in and I ask who it was, he always says it was no one. As if he were talking to dead air. But I know he's talking to someone. It's happened a few times. More than a few, actually."

"That must very hard for you," Amelie said.

"It's like…the world suddenly isn't the one you thought you knew." A bitter, brittle laugh filled Janet's mouth, revealing a harder edge to her that Amelie hadn't seen before. "I know that sounds melodramatic, but it's… I don't know, I'm just so confused."

Amelie sat back and realized that she'd already downed her entire drink. "Have you…said anything to B—your husband?"

"I asked him if everything was all right, and he ended up sounding like Andrew—'Yes, everything's fine'—like I was bothering him." She smiled. "What's that line about the child being the father to the man, something like that?"

"That's more or less it," Amelie said, recalling Wordsworth from her college days.

"I have to admit I also checked the calls on his cell phone when he was in the shower…" She reddened and laughed at what she perceived of as her folly. "I mean, wouldn't you do that if you were in my position?"

Here we go. Amelie imagined Janet would invite her outside to slug it out, two middle-aged women smearing each other's lipstick with their fists.

"And I went through his contact list, and they were all the"— she laughed again as she made air quotes—"'usual suspects.' His work contacts, our friends, you know. Relatives. No one I didn't know." She took a deep breath. "And suddenly, after we got back from California, he just seemed to lose all interest in…being intimate with me. I tried to show how willing I was, you know, but he just says he's tired." She looked at Amelie: "Am I saying too much?"

Seeing tears in her eyes, Amelie reached for her hand. "I'm so sorry, Janet."

"I have to make a confession. Ben's the only man I've ever known. I mean, you know, intimately. I'd dated a few guys in high school and in college, but Ben was it. He was the one. And maybe when that's the case it's all the harder to know you're being betrayed. Do you understand what I'm saying?"

"I think I do. It's just…that I'm really not qualified to offer advice about this kind of thing. I'm a writer. I make things up. I'm not a psychologist or a marriage counselor. And obviously in the role of wife I wasn't all that successful," and they both laughed a little.

Now Amelie felt her eyes beginning to mist up, not for herself, but for the woman sitting across from her. Now her life had grown even more complicated; her sympathies had begun to shift and scatter, and what had been the main story, her affair with Ben, had begun to grow subplots that threatened to take it all down.

"But you write so well about relationships," Janet said. "This subject, especially. And I seem to remember one of your characters—is it Lucy?—was some kind of therapist."

Lucy Hoffert, marriage counselor in her third book, whose lover comes in one day with his unsuspecting wife to seek comfort and advice. A difficult situation resolvable only in the most extreme way possible short of homicide.

When the waitress came to their table, Amelie was already holding up her empty glass. They both ordered a second drink.

"Would you like to hear the specials?"

"Not now," Janet snapped, and the waitress looked as if she'd just taken a bullet to her left shoulder.

Amelie quietly said, "We just want to talk for a bit. We'll let you know when we're ready to order."

When they were alone, Amelie said, "Do you have any suspicion of who it might be?"

Janet said, "What? Who what?"

"The…other person."

Janet closed her eyes for a moment. "I think I do."

Amelie also took a moment. "Really. How did you work this out?"

"I know my husband, I know his tastes, I remember how things were when we first met, what attracted him to me." She shook her head. "Now I think it's happening all over again. And I also suspect it's gone on for a very long time. At least for a year. Maybe even two." She leaned closer and lowered her voice. "You know, you look back and you start to see all the little things you missed. Things that took him out of himself. Sexual things, sometimes affectionate things he never normally did with me. I mean, the strange thing is that his first wife looked so much like me."

His first wife?

"Amelie?"

"Yes?"

"You okay?"

"Sorry, I went blank for a moment," and she laughed it off and sucked up some more martini.

His first wife: something Ben had never once mentioned to her; something she never suspected. Not even a hint had been dropped. What else was he hiding, how many other bodies were buried in the murky woodland dells of his past?

"So your husband was married before," Amelie mused aloud. "How long did that last?"

"Just a few years. They married young, when he was just out of college. She divorced him because, well," and Janet reddened, "he'd begun to see me. I was the other woman, you see." She sat back and smiled in that utterly earned complacent manner Amelie knew well.

"After only a few years of marriage," Amelie mused aloud.

Janet leaned in. "Sometimes I still wonder about that. Especially now that I'm so sure he's doing it all over again. Except we've been together for almost twenty years."

At that moment Amelie felt both sympathetic and embarrassed. She hoped Janet would not go into details, for fear of unleashing evidence of her own secret life and its pleasurable byways with some inappropriate response. And yet she also wanted to hear everything, the whole damned backstory to this man she called her lover. This man she intended to marry.

Because in a novel, blackmail, like murder, is always acceptable.

41

AMELIE REALIZED THAT SHE'D FINISHED HER SECOND drink in record time. She held up the three olives on a spear like a prop in a Shakespearean tragedy featuring cocktails. "So what are you going to do about it?"

"Make sure it doesn't continue happening. I'd sooner die than put my kids through a divorce," she said. "It's why I asked to meet you. To see if you had any, I don't know, ideas on how I could handle this."

"Because I'm a writer, is that what you're saying?"

Janet nodded. "And because you'd been through this yourself. And it's your job, isn't it. To write stories, to invent characters, to see how they grow, how they end…? I mean," and she lowered her voice, "how would you deal with the woman who's out to steal your husband and ruin your family?"

Amelie sat back and wished she were anywhere but there. "Well, to be honest, I don't really think that way, Janet."

"But if it were in a book…?"

This is the Game of—fuck it, she'd already played that one once before.

"Well. I suppose if this were in a book, I might consider… eliminating her in some way." She laughed. "Of course, for me it's a matter of hitting the delete key." A lot less blood that way, to be sure.

"Ah, if only," Janet said, also laughing.

Now the waitress returned to shatter the moment and share the specials.

Janet sat back and, looking into Amelie's eyes, smiled. "I think we're ready," she said.

42

THE MAN SHOWED AMELIE A MODEL IN PINK, AND said it also came in yellow and blue. "The ladies like the pretty ones," he said, but she was looking over his shoulder at the wall display. She pointed to one in black, always her go-to color.

He reached for the wrong one, and she said, "No, the big one next to it."

"This baby? She's a lot more expensive, you know. Packs a kick, too."

"Price isn't a consideration." *Neither is the kick*, she thought.

When she held it straight out she could barely keep her hand steady under the weight of the gun. The man seemed amused. "It's why I recommended one of the colorful ones. That lighter weight makes it easier for a lady like yourself to handle."

"I'm not a lady."

He shrugged. "Okay, whatever."

She set down the SIG Sauer, and he handed her the pink one again. She didn't like pink; in fact she hadn't liked pink since she was eight years old and into horses and Barbies and plastic tiaras.

"I'll take the blue one," she said. A fitting color for the thing's primary function.

"Tiffany blue? It's a good weapon. Glock makes some of the best."

It felt like nothing in her hand. She turned and aimed it at the door just as a fat man with tattoos walked in. He threw his hands up in the air and laughed.

"Hope it's not loaded."

"Wes."

"Hey, Al."

Probably a loyal customer. The guy named Wes checked her out with not even a modicum of discretion, breaking her down into three distinct zones, legs, waist, chest, stopping just short of face, because apart from her mouth there was nothing much there that he could make use of, had he the opportunity to do so. She turned back to Al, who owned the store. Apart from firearms he also sold fireworks, hunting bows, various items of clothing, all in camouflage patterns, and magazines aimed at survivalists and mercenaries.

Wes came up beside her. "You got my stuff, Al?"

"Yeah, I got your stuff." His eyes shifted from Wes to Amelie, then back to Wes.

"Where's it at?"

"Hold your horses, will you? Let me finish up here with this customer, and I'll give you my undivided attention until I close up for lunch hour."

Amelie noticed that one of Wes's many tattoos included one of a naked blond riding a tongue protruding from a wide red mouth. He saw her looking at it. He said, "You like that one, right?"

"Not really, no."

"Gutsy lady," Wes said.

"That's right."

Al said to her, "Have you ever fired off a—?"

"No."

"I recommend you take a couple of lessons. There's a pretty decent firing range less than a mile from here." He looked at Wes. "Bert Henson's place."

"Yeah, I know Bert. Went to grade school with him. Still remember how he got his pinkie blown off." He grinned at Amelie. "Guy loved playing with explosives when he was kid."

Al said, "Can I ask how you intend to use it?"

Without hesitation Amelie said, "Self-defense."

"Well, then, this is definitely the weapon for your needs. Once you've properly learned how to take aim, pull the trigger, and fire, no one will get within ten yards of you, guaranteed, without relinquishing his life."

She wasn't sure if he was making fun of her, but he was happy enough to take her money. "And a box of bullets, please."

He slid a cardboard container of ammunition off the shelf. "I'm running a two-for-one special just for this week."

"Good. I'll take two."

"If price is no consideration, I'd suggest you go for these." He took a cartridge from the box and held it between his fingers for a better view, shiny and brassy and reeking of death. "Always best in a self-defense situation to ensure a clean kill."

"Oh yeah," Wes said. "What's good about these is that it goes in, does the job, goes out, and there's very little that ends up on the walls. Very clean, right Al?"

"That it is, that it is."

"Crime-scene cleanup's a snap."

Amelie handed the man her credit card and her license, so he could run a background check. She wondered if he would find anything that could be held against her, some act apart from adultery that would leave a stain on her life. While she waited she walked around the store. There were a few framed photos of Al squatting over dead wildlife in his hunting gear, their eyes blank, their tongues distended. Suddenly Wes was beside her again.

"You got husband issues?"

"Not anymore," she said.

"So you shot him, too?" And he laughed. She thought it was also quite funny, but kept it to herself. "Well, I can figure out your story. You got yourself a sugar daddy, he's married, got kids, the whole nine yards, and the guy decides to dump you and go back to his fat, old, dependable wife instead of running off with a pretty lady such as yourself."

She stared at him, wondering how he knew so much about her. Had Janet hired a private detective, and was this the world-weary Philip Marlowe she'd ended up with?

"Okay," Al said, returning to the counter. "You're all set. Before I charge your card, I'm wondering if there any other accessories you might need or want. A holster, maybe?" He pointed out a display of bra holsters in various colors and designs. She had no idea how something like that might work. Would it nestle in her cleavage? Would it show through a T-shirt?

"You can try it on here. We don't mind, do we, Al?"

"Let the lady make up her mind. Then I'll do my business with you."

"I think we're done here," she said, and by the time she got home she was in a miasma of self-loathing. Though in her imagination Ben had died a million times over in the past twenty-four hours, ranging anywhere from shooting to strangling to stabbing, to one long fantasy about tying him to a chair and torturing him with a curling iron, she knew that in the end she was utterly incapable of killing the man.

As for Janet, well, that was just another twist in the plot.

43

AMELIE HAD BEEN STANDING AT HER OFFICE WINDOW, waiting for over twenty minutes, when Ben's car pulled up late the next morning. She wondered where Janet thought he was going. She wondered if Janet had followed him. She wondered when Janet was going to come after her.

He let himself in and slipped his key into his pocket. He looked up to find her standing on the stairs, looking down at him, not smiling, saying nothing. Like a character in an old movie with an anklet, scarlet lipstick, and a smart Brooklyn mouth. And her new friend, Blue Death, hiding in her nightstand drawer, right beside her other intimate accessory.

"Hi," he said, looking up and notching his thumbs in his pockets.

"Safe flight?"

He opened his arms and smiled. "I'm here, aren't I?" Three steps below her, he buried his face in the crotch of her jeans. She held her hands in the air, waiting for him to finish. He reminded her of a dog who greets you in a friend's home, never offering a paw or a smile, simply coming in for a long, wet, indiscreet sniff.

"What's wrong?"

"Nothing," she said. "It's good to see you."

"Whoa, wait, something's different here."

She walked past him down the stairs and he followed her into the kitchen. Ever the cowboy, he cocked a leg and leaned back against the counter.

"Do you want to talk about it?"

"About what?" she asked.

"About what's bothering you."

She shook her head and fell into neutral. "No."

"Have you been writing?"

"Actually, yes."

"How's it going?"

"One way or another I think I'm getting to the heart of things."

"So it's a breakthrough."

She said nothing. He took a mug from the cabinet and poured himself some coffee. "Thanks for taking Andrew to piano."

"He's very sweet." She heard her voice, made note of her words, and wondered for a small moment who was actually speaking.

"He said you were nice."

"He hates piano, you know."

"Janet thinks he needs to study some musical instrument. As if he didn't have anything else to keep him busy."

"My mother taught piano."

He looked at her. "I didn't know that."

"I also played. Not as well she did, but I played for many years."

She could read it on his face: she had become a mystery to him, someone with unrevealed secrets and facts, just as he had become for her. At least until Janet spilled the beans.

"But you don't have a piano."

"I also took voice lessons from a teacher in Manhattan. And studied ballet when I was a teenager. Now I write books. It's enough for me."

He sipped his coffee. "What did your father do? Is he still alive?"

"I have no idea if he's alive or dead." She shrugged. "What did he do? He lied his way through my childhood and cheated my mother out of having a decent life." She said nothing more about it. Ben knew nothing about her because he'd never taken the trouble to ask, just as she'd never inquired about his early life, which now, it appeared, involved another wife.

For him she was just a head full of blond hair, a body he desired, a mouth he loved, someone other than his wife; a novelty that would eventually become passé. The rest of her, she now saw, was superfluous to him. Like buying a car for its color and shape, and to hell with the engine.

For a few minutes she lost all interest in making love to this man. The shiny object of desire had begun to lose its luster. While Janet yearned for his touch, Amelie wondered if she were slowly losing her passion for it. And yet, like an addict who'd gone cold turkey for a week, as quickly as it dissipated she could feel it bubbling back up inside her. Just looking at him reminded her of what was to come. She might not be able to please him that day, but she could damn well walk away from it with a couple of well-earned climaxes under her belt.

"I missed you," she said, as though it were nothing more exciting than *It's raining*, or *Don't forget your keys*.

"I missed you, too," he said. His words also sounded a little flat. She'd always felt she had a good sense of dialogue, that she understood how a subtext could be hinted at in a line of speech, something her mother had taught her when they listened to music, to detect how a certain touch of a piano key was different from another. She also had perfect pitch, her mother told her. "It's a gift. One day it may save your life."

The line had always puzzled her. Now, without completely understanding exactly how, she was beginning to think her mother was right.

Matter-of-factly she said, "So how was the trip?"

He shrugged a little. "We're on the short list with one other firm. So we have a decent shot at it."

He toyed with a button on her blouse, and she abruptly turned to get more coffee. She said, "When you called me, you said your flight had landed and that you had to go to the office."

He set down his mug. "Yeah. I had to file the paperwork before Monday morning. Email some additional information to the university. It took longer than I thought."

"But at least you'd landed."

He tilted his head a little. "What are you getting at?"

"Well, when you called Janet around the same time, you'd told her that your flight had been delayed two hours. That you were still on the ground out there."

Now he stared at her, as if at a stranger. "How do you know that?"

She smiled. "Because she told me."

Back home that evening after dinner with Janet, she'd looked it up online. His flight had landed fifteen minutes early. Two or three hours lost to both his nearest and dearest.

He turned away and ducked a little. "Janet told you."

She nodded.

"When was this?"

"Around the same time you spoke to her. We had dinner out. She wanted to discuss something with me."

His laugh was brief and full of breath and amounted to nothing.

Dinner with Janet had been a perfectly nice meal, but it was never about the food or the drink: it was about *them*. Nothing more was said about Janet's suspicions. They talked about their daughters, their upbringing—neutral things, the slick lubricants of social intercourse.

But it was always there, hovering between them, a puff of ectoplasm that would, in time, and with the right medium to give it life at the séance table, resemble a human being.

"So which one of us did you lie to, your wife or your lover? And—bonus question—is there a third party that neither of us knows about?"

He topped up his coffee, took a sip, then spilled it out into the sink. He ignored the question, as she knew he would. "What did she have to say?"

"Actually, Janet and I have seen each other a few times. I did promise I wouldn't say anything about it to you."

"She knows we talk?"

"She may even know more than that, Ben." And she took his hand and led him slowly up the stairs, turning to look down at him when she was three steps from the top.

44

AMELIE SLIPPED BACK INTO HER SHORTS AND BLOUSE and brushed her wet hair while Ben finished up with his shower. She prepared a salad with leftover cold chicken. She brought out a pitcher of iced tea and, because they would be seen by neighbors if they ate on the deck, they sat in the kitchen and let the warm air of the day wash over them.

"I have a fantasy," Amelie said, and Ben smiled. "That one day we'll be able to live together." She waited to hear his reaction.

"Haven't we talked about this before?" he said.

"I know. But things are different now." She now knew he was an old hand at infidelity. He'd dumped his first wife for Janet, and in a flash could do likewise for Amelie. "Don't you think?"

"What do you mean?"

She set down her fork. "What if you knew that Janet was having an affair?"

He laughed once. "That's a joke."

"That's not nice. She's your wife, and she's an attractive, independent, successful woman. Would you let her divorce you? That would be handy for us, wouldn't it?"

She decided not to mention his previous marriage. She would save that for another moment of crisis, another twist in the plot.

He reached for her hand. "Look. First of all, Janet's not going to have an affair, and—"

"Because why? She's married to you? I thought the same thing about Richard. I thought, who would want him? Well, guess what, someone did."

She took a few bites of her salad, tasting nothing. She felt something rising inside her, something that fell midway between simmering anger and savage rage. "I bet she thinks the same about you, that you'd never, ever have an affair, and now here we are, reeking of fuck and eating a nice lunch."

He laughed again, as did she. "No, seriously," she went on. "Isn't it good for you? Because it's been good for me, Ben," she said, and an impaled piece of chicken hovered in the air before her mouth. "I mean, twenty-five minutes ago you seemed to be enjoying yourself."

"Where are you going with this, Amelie?"

"This is just too…temporary for me. You have a family, you have a wife, and I'm the one you see once a week."

"You always said it was good for you. So why change it?" he said.

"It's not changing it. It's making it permanent."

"But that would change it," he said.

"Only that it would make it something normal. Something we could depend on. Something that would always be here for us. Aren't you getting tired of all the sneaking around we do? I mean this is our routine, and it's still exciting for me. Isn't it good for you?"

"Of course it is."

"Then why not make it our own?" she said.

"So you're talking about…" he began and she nodded.

"I would like to be married to you," she said.

It was as if she were trying out a line of dialogue in one of her books, just to see how it landed on the page, how it would skew the narrative, where things might take off from that point. It was the bottom line of their relationship, and it couldn't go any lower.

She saw the expression on his face, one she had seen a hundred times before, a look of consternation and puzzlement, and she could only associate it with a child twisted by perplexity over the instructions for a new toy, and who, out of frustration, destroys the thing. "I know it's not something that can just happen overnight. I know it involves other people," and she reached out and put her hand over his. "I know it's harder for you than for me, I know you'll have to deal with Janet and Andrew and Rachel. But if you want something enough, you go out and do whatever you can to get it. I mean—" And she stopped dead before she could add, *you've done it before, haven't you?*

He took a deep breath. He said nothing, though she knew that behind the silence, behind those eyes and closed lips, there were things she should know, words she should hear. She said, "It would be one thing if we just went to bed every time we got together. But we do more than that. We talk, we eat, we go for drives. We do everything but live together."

"So what are you saying?"

"I'm saying that I sit alone in my house every day and then one day a week and possibly the odd twenty minutes or so on other days I get to see you. It's just not sufficient for me. It's not natural that you're staying married to Janet. It's not fair to her and it's not fair to me and, really, it's not fair to your kids."

"So what're you two now, best buddies all of a sudden?"

Amelie said nothing. She just enjoyed the silence of owning the moment. And perhaps even the hours and days to come.

"It's not easy just ending a marriage, you know," he said.

"It was easy for Richard. He stood in the living room and told me."

"And you told me you wanted to kill him."

"But I got over it. And at least you can start the process, you can begin talking to her, you can both consult lawyers. Because right now you have me. And you have Janet."

He looked at her.

"And, now and then, I only have you," she said.

He continued to stare vacuously at her, as though his mind had shut down. She remembered what Janet said, how sometimes he just didn't seem to be in the same room with her. Because in those moments, his mind was with Amelie. Or so she thought.

"So it's not fair," he said.

"Now you've got it."

"Don't be sarcastic."

She said nothing.

"What are you trying to say to me?" Ben opened his hands, weighed the air.

She composed herself. "Remember when you brought Janet to my reading at the bookshop?"

He looked at her.

"It was the first time I really had a good look at her, since you had the tact to seat her directly in front of me."

"That was—" he began.

"Let me go on, Ben. She's very pretty. In fact she looks a little like me. Like half the women in this town, she's made from the same mold. But of course she's different, she has to be different. So let's see what you have. You have me. And you have Janet. You have it all."

"Look."

"You have both of us. And is it the fact that I write novels that allows me to understand that the contrast between her and me is all part of the sexual charge?"

"I," he said.

"Or maybe I'm wrong. Perhaps there is no sex at home with Janet," something she now well knew was the case. "Ah. Well, then, that's all right, that makes it better. So he comes to me for his weekly dose of relief."

He stared at her. "Look. The fact that I'm married should have nothing to do with any of this. I mean, this is the kind of thing you're always writing about, for Christ's sake. You've covered this in how many of your books?"

"That was then. This is now," she said, being a little too cryptic for him. "Just tell me, Ben. Do you love Janet?"

"In a different way," he said after a pause. "I've known her a long time. And she's Rachel and Andrew's mother."

"So what am I, the architect's whore?"

"I don't have to listen to this."

"I don't have to say it."

"You know exactly what I'm talking about."

"More than you can imagine," she said.

He reached across and tried to take her hand, and she slid it off the table onto her lap.

"Things between us, between Janet and me, are different," he said. "We haven't been as close as we were three or four years ago."

"Maybe then she *is* having an affair."

"That would make things a lot easier."

"And if I told you that she is?"

He actually laughed in her face.

"And if I said that I know it for sure?" she went on in utter seriousness.

He took a moment. "Is it true?"

Now she smiled, just a little. And then said nothing.

"So basically you're giving me an ultimatum. You or Janet."

"You forgot the last possible option: or neither."

He set down his fork. Now it was coming. He put down his knife, he pressed his lips together, *here it comes*, he raised his eyes to her, *it was about to arrive*, he sat back in his chair, *it was here with them in the room*, he opened his mouth, *it was imminent and she waited*, he smiled. He said, "I'm not marrying you. Not ever."

45

ONCE BEN HAD LEFT, WALKING BRISKLY OUT TO HIS
car and driving away without even a wave goodbye, once she'd
gotten over the shock of what had just happened, Amelie was
surprised to feel nothing but a strange form of elation, as though
she had shed an early version of herself and had been given the
chance of a fresh start.

The dishes from lunch were still on the table, the iced tea he
hadn't finished, his half-consumed salad she had worked so dili-
gently to prepare: artifacts of absence. She briskly cleared them
away, hiding them from her sight in the dishwasher.

According to him things weren't over, he wasn't going to marry
her, but it didn't mean that they couldn't keep seeing each other,
and he spoke as though she were meant to be grateful to him
for this, as though she was supposed to give him a coquettish
little smile and nod her head and say, *Okay, Ben, it's fine this way*.
Because, once again, he had it all. He had Janet and he had Amelie.

Twenty minutes earlier, instead of dignifying with a response
what he'd said to her, she had risen from the table and walked
behind him. She felt completely calm because she had learned
something important about her lover.

She imagined the back of his head spraying blood and
brain matter, fragments of memory—Ben as a child on his first

Christmas, Ben at college, Ben at his mother's funeral, Ben when he first met Amelie—all of it spattered on her face and her blouse, a pointillist version of the life of this man and of their time together.

"You are the most selfish man I know, Ben," she said finally, and he didn't bother to turn and look at her. She was tempted to call him Benjamin, to reduce him to something childish and ill-named, his face smeared with chocolate as he toddled about in his soiled play clothes.

"I'm trying to be fair," he said.

"And what does that leave me with? Should I just sit around waiting for you to stop by for your weekly bounce on the Beautyrest?"

"You know I don't feel that way about you."

"But it's the way you're treating me, Ben. It's the way I'm…" And she didn't know what else to say. She felt the weight of something not on her body but in it, something heavy and airless that seemed to destroy everything that was light and crisp and buoyant in her life. It was no longer just about them; it was about her—her heart, her life, her future. Ben was rapidly becoming an unnecessary element in her life. Utterly expendable.

She said, "I'm growing older, Ben, Nina's at college, I'm all alone. You have no idea what that's like, do you, being by yourself?" And she lifted her arms from her body. "I have it all, right? I write, I create characters, I give them life, make them do things, make them say things, sometimes even kill them, but I'm always alone when I do it. I eat alone, I watch movies alone, I go for solitary walks, and when I have an opportunity to chat, it's usually just with myself. Thankfully, Nina's coming home in a few weeks, then I'll at least be with someone I can love without having to negotiate one moment to the next."

"I'm getting older, too," he said.

She continued to address the back of his head. "But you're doing it with Janet and Andrew. At least you have company, Ben. Just like you always have. One at home, one on the side. Like the burger-and-fries special at a restaurant."

She knew he would say nothing. She'd gone too far, though she didn't regret it. It had to come to this, and she looked up at the clock: high noon. She was amazed at her calmness and rationality. She wondered how long it would last before there was broken glass, blood, and tears.

"Maybe you should start seeing other men," he suggested.

"I don't want some stranger, someone else, someone…" and again she ran out of words, because he wasn't understanding at all what she was saying. This wasn't just about gratification, it wasn't about *him*, it was about time, how it was being wasted, how she wasn't getting any younger, how she'd—

Forget it, she thought.

"I'm forty, for god's sake," she said. "Two years kicked to the curb, and you're asking me to start all over again with someone else?"

"Just tell me," he said. "Is Janet really having an affair?"

"Yes, and his name is Brad."

She had no idea where the name came from. Maybe the cover of *Us Weekly* she saw at the supermarket the day before. She'd intended Ben to think she and Janet had become fast friends, but the last person in the world she could trust was his wife. She knew something that Amelie didn't know; or, rather, she knew something that Amelie knew perfectly well. But Amelie didn't know how much the woman knew and what her future intentions might be.

Brad, lover of Janet. She remembered him sitting at the bar, reading her book. A good-looking man with a touch of class. Self-possessed. A man of discernment. And she remembered that smile he gave Janet when she walked into the Coach & Four. A smile of recognition? Perhaps. But a smile that lent itself to interpretation; and right now she rather liked the way she was construing it: it worked neatly into the narrative.

She went upstairs and pulled the duvet off the bed, swinging and twirling it onto the floor like a matador's cape. She peeled off the pillowcases and stripped off the sheets that bore the scent of their bodies and dumped them in the washing machine, adding an overflowing amount of detergent, raising the water temperature to *Hot*. She took fresh sheets from the linen closet and remade the bed, slowly and meticulously, finding some small pleasure in the mechanics of the task. She neatened the corners and smoothed the wrinkles.

She heard nothing from downstairs. She wondered what he was doing. Was he quietly weeping into his hands, was he continuing to stare at his watch, was he thinking she might do something irrational? She glanced over at her nightstand, as if the only response were sitting within it, loaded and humming with anticipation.

The bed was made. The room was hers. The moment was hers. And now the pretty Tiffany blue thing tucked into the back of her waistband under her blouse was all hers.

She descended the stairs. He was standing by the window with his hands in his pockets.

"Go," she said.

"It's still early. I thought we'd…" and she said, "No. No more. Not today. Not ever."

"Look, I'm sorry."

"Okay. Good. You're sorry. Now go home. You made yourself perfectly clear. You're not marrying me. Now go to your wife. Like all the other times before."

He stared at her. "Brad. Is that what you said?"

"Maybe it was Kevin."

"Don't fuck with me, Amelie," and his look was fierce and fiery.

"It's Brad," she said calmly. "She'll deny it, of course, just as you would, should anyone ask you about me. It's been going on for a while, she told me. I don't know, maybe you should just let it play out, Janet and Brad, and see where it all takes you."

"You find this funny, don't you," he said.

"I find it utterly ironic. Now go. Scoot." And she waved her hands in the air, as if he were the pet pooch needing a breath of air and a quick shit in the yard.

He looked at her. "Are you going to be all right?"

"Of course I am."

"Are you sure?"

She smiled too brightly and bared her teeth. "I'm fine."

"Do you want to get together on Friday?"

"No."

"What do you mean?"

"I need to have a better life than this. I'm sick of being the object of all your lies."

"I've never lied to you."

"What do you think an affair with someone other than your spouse is, an open book? It's one lie after another—to your wife, your children, your partner at the firm, even to yourself. I don't

know what you've been thinking, but all along I've passionately
believed that we had a future together."

She knew that there were many lies, that woven into the
world the two of them had together created were numberless lies
knotted into the truths, like tiny invisible flaws in an elaborately
woven Persian rug. Having an affair with a married person was a
work of fiction filled with obscure imagery, powered by a byzan-
tine plot, a kind of novel that other people couldn't read for what
it actually was.

"There's more, Ben. To go on with you would mean I'll lose
a part of myself when it's over, and you'll be fine. Intact. Able
to go back to your wife and kids and give them your undivided
attention. And in the end you'll lose, what, whatever pleasure I've
given you? Is that what I am? A morsel to be forgotten? I've given
you two years of my life. Yes, I know, I did it willingly, and if I
were eighteen or nineteen or even twenty-five, I'd be able to land
on my feet. But things are tough for women my age. For men?
Maybe not so much," and she remembered the silver-haired man
in the restaurant, easily in his mid-fifties, who had eyed her. "And
please, don't tell me to go on some internet dating site. That's not
my style. But also don't try to flatter me. I know exactly who I
am. I know what I want, and I intend to go out and get it."

She could see he didn't know what to do. He took a step forward, and she turned and left the room. She was amazed to hear
him actually leave the house. He hadn't gone to her, touched her
arm, whispered a goodbye, he hadn't even allowed her to catch a
glimpse of him as he departed—the back of his hand, the bow of
his head. He started up the car and drove off. Only then did she
burst into tears.

46

O.

It was the next day and it was over.

O fine. O good.

Fantastic. Fabulous.

Lying in bed, Amelie shrugged and made a face as if she had rejected not something significant in her life but an undercooked piece of fish or a defective item of clothing.

And to top it all she had let him off easy. *I'm fine*, she'd told him, and then he'd left. He'd walked out of her life as though he were checking out of a motel after a long night's sleep, just another room in another town in another state. *Have a nice day, y'hear?*

Why had she gotten herself involved with him in the first place? She made a sputtering sound and shook her head. What the hell was so attractive about him? She lay in her bed and stared at the ceiling as images from the early days came to mind, from the time before they had even spoken to each other, when it was the Age of Glances and Smiles, and she knew what it was that was so attractive, she understood immediately what had brought them together, and yet she couldn't define it, put it into words, find the nugget of drama that would bear elucidation. It was because it was all a trick, because at that early stage you can't see the end, you can't imagine a conclusion, life stretched out before you like a cloudless sky on a summer morning, the endless blue of promised bliss.

The fact that he was married? It never came into it at first, because it never does, as her most recent novel made clear. She could write it but not live it. It was a lesson for her characters, not for the woman sitting at her laptop tapping out the words.

And could it really have been only a physical attraction? Now that she thought about it she saw that intellectually he wasn't one of the great minds of the century. In fact he was rather shallow. He disliked reading books, and when he did read, and she knew he only read her novels because he was obliged to, he read dopey techno-thrillers and courtroom yarns. He disliked intelligent films made by underfinanced directors. On the one occasion he went to the theater he spent a small fortune taking his entire family—Janet, Andrew, and Rachel—to *Cats*.

She shook her head: amazing why she had stayed with him for so long.

And then there was his body. Of course it was eminently clear now that in fact he really wasn't very good-looking. His backside was a little shapeless, pear-like and soft. His chest was too furry. His feet sometimes smelled.

As a lover he was unexceptional. His hands were always cool and moist, and they didn't always feel very good against her skin. He was quick while she preferred the long languor of an afternoon, the gentle curve of foreplay that led to the roar of climax.

God, she thought, *what a fool I was*.

She sat up on the side of the bed and looked at her phone. He had walked out and had not even taken the trouble to call her, to attempt to come to an understanding, even to say that his years with her had been wonderful and that he would never forget her. He had simply left.

Actually it was better this way, not having to wait for Ben, to anticipate Ben, to suffer from Ben withdrawal. Now she was Benless, Janet could keep him, and the feeling stood somewhere between a kind of barren emptiness and the sweet iciness of relief. Fridays could now be Amelie's alone. She could have lunch with a friend or drive into the city; she could shop for clothes or make herself available for more readings and interviews.

She could take three-day weekends and, when she was away, not have to think of him. Maybe she would simply move. She could put the house up for sale and go elsewhere, perhaps to a nice apartment in Manhattan, or even out of the country if she liked. She could live in London and go to the theater whenever she wished, she could go to the Tate Modern and look at the paintings, she could travel to the Continent on the Eurostar on a moment's notice. She could move to Paris and exercise her ability to speak French, just like she'd learned at Mount Holyoke. She could move to Africa, for god's sake, she could move to Siberia or Fiji or a miner's shack in Death Valley, as long as she didn't have to think of him or run into him or catch a glimpse of him. She could even drive for three hours and throw herself off a bridge.

She wondered if he would look for her. He would drive past her house and see the *For Sale* sign and wonder where she was going. He would Google her and find nothing, because she would strip herself of social media. He would search obituary databases and the website that told you where people were buried, and come up short. She would have moved or died; she would have vanished. And then his eyes would turn inward: what had he done to make this happen? Why couldn't he have made it work, for both of them?

In a novel he'd hire a private detective to scour the world and look for her in sweatshops in Singapore and tiki bars in Polynesia; in Russian brothels and Italian convents; in fast-food restaurants in all the fifty states, in her little uniform and cap, *Would you like me to supersize that, sir?*

But that wouldn't happen. He would get on with his life, make eyes at other women, and, because someone would be there to replace Amelie, come home unfaithfully to Janet, who of course was seeing a fiction named Brad. Which meant that Amelie had just granted Janet a kind of subtle superpower.

He thinks she's having an affair, and so he'll do everything he can to keep her. Without his wife having to do a thing to salvage her marriage.

Which led her to one simple conclusion: Janet, as nice as she was, as professional and sincere and intelligent as Amelie now knew her to be—Janet was the problem. Sooner or later Janet would discover exactly who the mysterious woman was in her husband's life.

Or maybe she already knew. And then she would do something about it.

There was only one thing Amelie could do, only one final and decisive way of getting back at him. She wondered how she would do it, what would be the best way, and how they would find her body, and now she would have to sit down and compose an email and put it through a few drafts until it was perfect. Maliciously she thought of cc'ing Janet. And why not Rachel? Even Andrew, while she was at it.

Dear Ben, It has come to this because I

Dear Ben, Now you and everyone else knows how much I loved you and

Dear Ben, To say goodbye would have asked very little of you. So now it's time for me to say it.

She went to her office and picked up the phone and, keying in his office number, told the secretary that she wanted to speak to Ben.

"Who's calling, please?"

She thought for a moment. "Amelie Ferrar."

"One moment, please."

There was a pause. She could feel it happening within her, she could feel the press of desire. "He's not able to come to the phone right now," the woman said, and Amelie could not believe her ears.

"Would you ask him to call me back, please?" She gave the woman her number. She said, "Tell him it's an emergency."

47

STRANGERS ON A TRAIN, THEY MET BY CHANCE. SHE WAS
on her usual commute into the city, and at the stop
after hers he entered the car and took a seat across
from her. He looked out the window as the suburban
world slid by him in a monotonous blur.

Normally, she worked during this time of travel,
tapping out emails on her laptop, or reviewing
financial documents and memos, but today she was
reading a book, one by an author she had come to
know a little. She found it thoughtful and percep-
tive and well written, with imagery that made her
stop and read certain lines over again.

Suddenly he said, "It's good, isn't it."

"Sorry?"

"The book. It's good."

"Oh, it's very good. I've met her," and she turned
the book over to reveal the author's photo, filling
up the back in vibrant color. "She's interesting."

"I've met her, too," and he smiled. He extended
a hand. "Brad."

She took it, held it for a second, then released
it. "Janet."

He went back to scrolling through messages on his phone, as she returned to her reading. Once or twice she glanced up at him, and each time he was looking at her with the same smile as before. As though embarrassed to be caught, he would quickly turn away. At first it disturbed her a little, being looked at in that way; but she was nonetheless flattered. Her husband hadn't been all that attentive lately, and to have a man actually show interest in her, now that she was nearly forty, was both a novelty and extremely pleasing.

She said, "Do you work in Boston?" and he said he did, he was head of a research lab at MIT. She asked which one, and when he told her, she dug out one of her cards and handed it to him.

"I know this company," he said, his eyebrows lifting. "It's a good place. You do your due diligence there."

They discovered they lived one town away from each other. He said, "I'd love to talk to you more at length, but…" His eyes went to her left hand and the ring finger, appropriately encircled in gold, nestled beside a diamond engagement ring.

"Actually, I'm in the process of planning to kill my husband's mistress before she kills me," she said. "Would you like to help?"

48

SHE HAD HEARD FROM MORE THAN ONE SOURCE THAT
when you cut your wrists you should immerse yourself in a tub full
of very hot water. That way you felt no pain, and an hour later, in
the glow of all the candles you'd carefully placed around the room,
it would be over. The heat of the water would make you drowsy,
especially if you'd downed three vodkas and most of a bottle of a
nine-dollar pinot noir. You would drift in and out of unconscious-
ness, floating through layers of dream, and death would come as it
had to the ancients, slowly and voluptuously, as though it were a
long journey into a pleasant land of Lethe and lotus. She stood by
the sink and looked at the razor she used on her legs, at the little
cartridge with its slender edge of death. She dried her hair and went
into her bedroom and dressed in jeans and a Wellesley T-shirt she'd
bought when Nina first started college. Now an hour had passed.

Amelie picked up the phone and tried his office once again.
The woman said, "As I said earlier, he's in a conference."

She hadn't said anything of the sort; a conference had never
reared its ugly lying head.

"I'll try again later," and Amelie quietly replaced the receiver.
She looked at her watch. What was later, what defined that
moment, what was a reasonable amount of time that was required
to pass? Eventually his secretary would come to recognize her

voice; there would be the raised eyebrow, the hooded whispers behind his back, the glances out the window as he drove off to get his perfectly innocent smoked turkey sandwich at the local deli.

She looked at her watch again: now another minute had passed. She imagined how he must have looked when his secretary once again came in to tell him that the madwoman Ferrar had called for a second time. She reached for the phone and suddenly it chimed, *Yes?* she said, a little too loudly.

"I got your message."

It took her a moment to catch her breath. "I think we need to talk."

"What emergency?"

"I thought I might have to go to the hospital."

"And did you?"

"Why don't you ask what happened?"

"Okay. So what happened?"

"I think I'm hemorrhaging."

He said nothing.

"There's blood everywhere."

She detected a sigh.

"Call an ambulance, Amelie."

"It's fine. I'll live."

"I need to go."

"We need to talk."

"I thought we already had talked."

"Look, Ben, couldn't you at least have called me back from a place where your partner isn't listening?"

"I'm calling you from the car."

"Then kindly stop talking to me as if I were a damned roofing contractor. I think I need to have a few points cleared up."

"You kicked me out of your house."

"I asked you to leave, Ben."

"You told me to get out."

"I never used those words."

"And that...thing about you and Janet. I don't know if I can really believe you."

"Like I said, Janet and I have talked and we get along quite well. I've sort of become her confidant."

She heard the silence of a man considering things.

"I think it's important that you understand how I feel," she said. "At least try, Ben, try to see it from my point of view."

"I never once said I'd marry you."

"Jesus."

"Look," and she could hear the anger now, she could sense the edge, "what do you want from me, Amelie, what do you want me to say, what do you want me to do? I'm not going to leave Janet, I'm not going to destroy my family."

She said, "Even if it would make you happy?"

"I'm happy enough as it is," he said.

For a moment she was distracted; idling on the road at the end of her driveway, almost blocking it, was a black Audi.

"What?"

"I said, I'm happy enough, thanks."

"And without me on Fridays?"

"I'll manage."

"You'll manage." She waited. "You'll manage, then, right?" She waited. "Ben? Ben...?"

He had clicked off ten seconds earlier.

49

AMELIE THOUGHT THE DRIVER HAD JUST STOPPED TO check a cell phone or send a text, and waited until the car left before getting into her Volvo and pulling onto the road. She wasn't going anywhere in particular; she just needed to get out of the house, to get away from what was starting to feel like a suffocating hall of memories. The painful ones were hard to bear; the pleasant ones even harder.

She drove past houses without really seeing them, groves of trees and open fields, a firehouse, a day-care center, a church. Familiar landmarks, and no matter where she looked, everything seemed to carry a memory, as though these inanimate objects and structures and geographical features contained something of her, and him, and of them. Two years of her life scattered across a few square miles like jacks thrown by a child.

Reaching the end of the road, she headed into town. Which is when the Audi reappeared, four or five car lengths behind her, intermittently glimpsed in her rearview mirror. She turned right and increased her speed, hoping that cop wasn't anywhere near, the Audi following at a distance. Now it was just the two of them, until Amelie made an abrupt left turn toward the road leading to Nina's old school, and the other car disappeared. It was nothing, she knew. The day had been difficult enough without her turning an innocent traffic situation into the beginning of a horror movie.

She turned on the radio, found a station that wasn't broadcasting the hourly misery, and listened to some music. It wasn't the kind of music she particularly liked, but it was something new and different, and right now new and different was exactly what she needed. A fresh start: *Yes*, she thought, though she knew she sounded like a character from that novel with that annoying Holly in it. *A fresh start*: she was well aware that was all an illusion, the product of wishful thinking, the sad optimistic fictions we all invent to make us feel momentarily better.

And yet, oddly, she did feel better. Somehow more *transparent*, though that wasn't quite the word she wanted, yet even as she drove under the slate-gray sky and listened to the music she sensed everything was about to change. Ben was out of her life, and in a perverse way it seemed to set her free. No more waiting for *his* calls, *his* texts or emails; no more thinking about him. The gaps in her life, small and big, would be filled with other things, new people, fresh experiences.

She pulled into the parking lot of the local overpriced liquor mart, a reasonable place to start her new life, and picked up a giant-size Ketel One vodka and a few bottles of wine, put them in the back and drove home. That would do for now. She would go home and return to the woman in the doctor's office. She would give her a name, a story, an age, all her hopes dashed by a simple declarative sentence uttered by this physician sitting before her.

She crested the little rise as she drove up her driveway. Parked in front of her house was the black Audi. Leaning against it was the driver, her arms folded before her.

50

"JANET," AMELIE SAID, AND SHE WAS SO OUT OF breath, so shocked by this turn of events, that Janet must have felt she was thrilled beyond words to be seeing her.

Amelie waited for the smile, and there it was, the same honest, open smile she remembered from their dinner out.

"Hello, Amelie." Janet was calm and in control, looking like she wasn't about to go anywhere. Amelie's mind went in so many different directions that she sensed she wouldn't be able to find a way out.

"How did you get my address?"

"Remember? Our kids went to the same school?" And she laughed.

Right: the parents' directory book, full of addresses and phone numbers and email addresses, too much information for the information age.

"Is everything okay?" Amelie decided to leave the liquor in the car. Otherwise the grapevine would be working overtime tonight.

"No. Everything is not okay. Hop in. We're going for a drive."

"A drive," Amelie said, as though the notion were wholly unknown to her.

Janet opened the driver's side door. "Come on. Let's take some time to talk."

Amelie buckled her seat belt. Janet drove slowly down the driveway and turned right, driving just under the speed limit. She made a left and within half a mile they were in the country, on the road that led to the town dump, formally known as the James Winslow Memorial Recycling Center, though normally it stank of rotting overpriced vegetable matter and myriad bags of dog shit that had burst open.

Janet began to increase her speed until she was barreling along the road leading to the great open vistas of the treeless subdivisions and culs-de-sac that blandly defined the end of the town. Another mile, and you would end up in a whole other economic zone: old money, venerable names, acre upon acre of land held for three centuries by the same families in their more cash-starved generations.

Until then Janet had said nothing, while Amelie felt herself shift into the same space in her mind when she would begin to get an idea for a novel; a place that, seemingly empty, apparently barren, was instead filled with a million invisible possibilities of what might happen to her before the hour was up.

This is not happening, she tried to tell herself, and yet when she opened her eyes she saw that in fact it was taking place, a sequence unfurling before her eyes, the kind of narrative string that could only lead to something horrific. One sunny autumn morning, long after she'd been declared a missing person, someone would find her remains, hastily buried under bramble and scrub, a scarf tightly knotted around what remained of her throat, her fingernails thick with dirt, her nails chipped, her chest torn open by packs of coyotes, her eyes replaced by bundles of maggots burrowing their way into her brain. Just another episode of *Unsolved Mysteries* brought to its usual grisly conclusion.

Quietly she said, "Where are we going, Janet?"

"The long way around," Janet said, turning to her with a smile. "I just wanted to talk to you, because I consider you a friend now, someone—really the only one—I've confided in about this, and I sense that you could be very helpful to me. Remember," and easing to a stop at a crossroads, she turned to Amelie, "how I told you that Ben was so distant lately? Well, I'm now one hundred percent sure that he's having an affair."

Amelie felt like the tennis player who, expecting a shot to her expert backhand, gets one solidly in the face. "Really. That must be devastating. Was it...something you came across...?"

"Just something I discovered."

"I see," Amelie said.

Janet clicked on her turn signal, *clackclack clackclack*, and made a left turn. Amelie had had never been in this area. In a small uncertain voice she asked again where they were going.

"You'll see."

Only when she reached the end did Amelie recognize it as Ben's street, Bainbridge Road.

"Do you have any idea where you are?" Janet said almost gleefully.

"No," Amelie lied. "Not really."

She turned into a driveway and put the car in Park. "Welcome home, Amelie," and Janet laughed and laughed.

51

"BEN'S NOT HERE, THOUGH I THINK I KNOW WHERE he is. He'll tell me he was at work, but that's always been his excuse. He just needs to run to the office for fifteen minutes— that's another good one. Andrew's at a friend's house. But my son, at least, well I *always* know where he is," and she laughed once again, just as loudly.

It was the closest Amelie had ever been to Ben's house, and her legs began to grow weak. "It's a lovely home," she said once they were inside.

"He designed it, of course. Maybe fifteen years ago, I guess? We bought the land and he hired the best people he could find to fulfill his vision." Janet looked up at the structure. "One day he won't be living here," she said as she unlocked the door.

Once you stepped inside, it was as if you'd walked into the atrium of a museum. The ceiling seemed to go on forever, and the windows were oversize, letting in the late-morning light veiled by a thin gray haze. Seeing it for the first time from within was like something sexual for Amelie. This was the dark unknown, a piece of Ben's life she'd never been privy to, like a palace in the Forbidden City. You could imagine what you wished about it, and know that at least one of your darker thoughts was the truth.

There was no oversized furniture here: simple designs, a sofa, some chairs, a coffee table, the odd occasional table or pedestal. Rugs here and there with modernist designs. A wide gas fireplace was situated on the right wall, above which a mantel held several framed photos of the family. There were a few shots of Ben when he must have been in his twenties: in one of them he was shirtless and in white shorts on a sailboat, his hair thicker and darker, his smile as enigmatic as it had been that first time he leaned over her car and told her just what he wanted to do. That was the man she'd fallen for.

"What do you think?" Janet said.

Amelie took another look around. This was theater of a high order. "I think it's amazing. This house, I mean."

Janet lifted the photo from the mantel. "We'd been married for maybe eight months when this was taken. We were staying on the Cape with some friends. Believe it or not, Ben is quite a skilled sailor."

She set it back in its place. "He's good at many things. Lacking in many others. Anyway, that's when I conceived Rachel, those few days on the Cape. Probably the same night that was taken. I'll show you some more, if you like."

She took a photo album from a shelf and patted the cushion next to hers on the sofa.

The wedding photo: two gorgeous people, Amelie had to admit to herself. Janet was a knockout back then, and Ben was, well, Ben. Just younger. And for a moment she imagined herself in that photo, young and beautiful and married to him.

Janet flipped ahead: a miserable little girl on Santa's lap, all frown and tears and terrified eyes. "Rachel was so scared of him, even though he was promising her presents. Maybe because we told her never to take anything from a stranger. And then she peed her pants and he was one very pissed-off Santa, I can tell you that."

Amelie laughed along with her. Of course she had never obeyed *that* rule, even though her mother was adamant about it, warning of a world full of creeps and con men. Anyone who offered Amelie anything when she was a teenager and, afterward in college—a joint, a pill, a bottle of Heineken, twenty minutes of physical pleasure—became her best friend at least for as long as the buzz lasted.

"Nina didn't fall for it, either," she told Janet. But of course she and Richard were insistent that no matter what Nina's friends or movies or TV shows said, there was no such thing as an overweight, heavily bearded man who flew through the air powered by wingless reindeer, bearing enough presents to deliver to every child on earth. Yet every Christmas morning Nina would wake up to a pile of prettily wrapped gifts brought to her by the only people who knew her tastes and desires, Santa Dad and Magic Mom.

The next shot showed a little boy in shorts and a T-shirt swinging a baseball bat. One of his eyes is almost closed, while the other is focused on the ball that his bat has just engaged.

"That's your son, isn't it?" Amelie asked, and Janet laughed.

"That's Ben when he was, I don't know, nine or ten?"

Amelie studied it for a moment before Janet turned the page to a photo of the family, taken some years earlier, just outside a tent. Ben is in cargo shorts and a U2 T-shirt, squatting over what looks like the beginnings of a campfire, his blue eyes catching the afternoon light.

Amelie had never been camping, and Ben had never suggested that she join him in his tent one future day. Another part of his life that had been denied her.

Janet rose and put the album back on the shelf. "Can I get you some coffee, or tea, or maybe something stronger?" And she laughed again and added, "Though maybe it *is* a little early."

"I'm fine," Amelie said.

"Have a seat."

Here it comes.

Janet joined her on the sofa. "You know, I think at some time or another we all suspect our spouses to be at least considering cheating on us. Maybe it comes when we're feeling less sure of ourselves. I mean, I'll be forty-two in two months, and I'm definitely not the same person I was when Ben and I first met. I may be good at what I do, and successful at it, and hope that possibly my work will help many people in the world. Yet I look at myself and see only failure. My body isn't what it used to be—I mean, whose is at our age?" And she laughed again. "And even though it sounds vain, when you start looking at yourself as somehow… less than what you were—do you understand what I'm saying?— physically, I mean, you feel somehow less inside."

Amelie nodded. It made perfect sense to her.

Janet went on, "Look at you. I would say most women my age—or your age, for that matter—would envy you. You have a beautiful face, great hair, and a figure to, well, die for," and she laughed. "I look at those photos of me from all those years ago, and barely recognize that woman now."

Little did Janet know how much Amelie had to spend to maintain those amazing looks. First thing in the morning she looked like a bag lady who'd spent the night cruising the dock-yards and living out of dumpsters behind the supermarkets.

Yet what Janet was saying was raw and true. She was getting to the heart of things without once flinching. Age. Infidelity. The loneliness of the jilted wife. Amelie just wished this little get-together would be over. And soon.

"And I'm tired," Janet said. "From work, from looking after Andrew, from all the things I do outside of the office."

"Are you still active in the school?" she asked, and Janet laughed.

"They're always roping me in for something, and I'm always happy and willing to do what I can. And I sit on the board of two charities, one regional, the other national. It's exhausting, as I'm sure you know. People heap their expectations on your back, and you feel obligated to carry them to the finish line." She looked away and her smile faded. "I suppose that's half the problem with Ben. He's... Well, he's a guy, he's still vigorous and sexual, but he's under a lot of pressure himself. Work is always an issue for him. Getting commissions, you know. But things have been very different over the past year or two. Like I said, he's just not completely...here. Do you understand what I'm trying to say?"

"I think so," Amelie said. She was beginning to feel genu-inely sorry for Janet. She was a woman insightful enough to understand her position from all angles, while Amelie's focus was always a little too narrow, always in the service of the story, the plot, the climax.

"There's always a short list in the back of our minds, don't you think?" Janet said. "Women he might be involved with. Family friends, parents of our kids' friends, you know, that kind of thing.

And then we find out it's not the person we thought it would be. It's always the dark horse. The one we least expected to betray us." She sat back and looked up at the ceiling. "It takes us a little while until we realize, of course, that it had to be *her*."

She turned abruptly to Amelie. After a moment she said, "How did *you* find out?"

Amelie looked at her.

"I mean that your husband was cheating on you."

"I didn't," Amelie said. "I just assumed everything was fine. Until everything wasn't. I was completely blind to it, I never suspected a thing. One day he told me. Afterward I realized it was there all along."

"Like a plot twist in a book or a movie," Janet said.

Precisely, Amelie thought. She realized that Janet was more or less the ideal reader. Just not so ideal that she'd been blind to Ben's infidelity. Until now.

"And was it who you expected it would be?"

Amelie shook her head. "I'd only seen her once before, at Richard's office. She was young and pretty and utterly forgettable, and she fell in love with my husband, just as he fell in love with her."

"And how did that make you feel?"

"Angry," said Amelie. "At first, anyway. Then resentful. Then hurt, of course. It was really, really painful. Then I was...okay with it." Because by then she'd met Ben. "Since you know who it is, what are you planning to do about it? Divorce?"

"Like I said, that's not happening. But look at me. Do I look like the vengeful type?"

Amelie shook her head.

"And if you were writing this story wouldn't I be the last person anyone would think would take matters into her own hands?"

Amelie nodded her head, though she knew, just as Janet obviously did, that even the meekest-looking person could turn on you in a moment and shred your pretty face until you bled to death. But Janet was different. She had a successful career, a son to raise, all her charity work. Too much was on the line for her to do anything out of the ordinary.

Janet excused herself and went into the kitchen. Amelie could hear her rummaging in a drawer full of weaponry, knives and garlic presses and potato mashers and god knows what else she kept in there. She returned a few minutes later with a funky wedge of cheese on a piece of slate; a curved knife like the Gurkhas used, only smaller; and an array of imported crackers found only in the finest of the town's several extortionate gourmet shops. Eight ninety-nine, Amelie guessed, having eyed them herself a few months earlier. Janet went back into the kitchen and brought out two glasses of chardonnay. With a sly smile, she said, "It's not *that* early, really, now is it?"

They clicked glasses and sipped. Janet sat back on the sofa and smiled. She looked pleased with herself.

"That's nice," Amelie said. "Thanks." She was beginning to find herself liking this woman who was so unlike her.

"And now…?" Janet asked, setting down her glass. "Things are okay with you? There's harmony, I hope?"

"I'm fine. Richard's going to be a father again. And he seems really happy."

"So you talk."

"Now and again, mostly about Nina."

"Once this is over I will never again utter a single word to my husband. Because he won't be here. He'll be with *her*. Just as he expects it to be." She tucked her feet under her. "Unless, of course, it doesn't happen that way."

"So you're going to wait until he leaves you?" The words came out just when she was about to censor herself. "Sorry. I didn't mean to go there. I know this must be very painful for you."

Janet lifted her chin a little. "Oh, I'm not giving him up so easily. If he wants to make amends he will have to earn every moment of it."

"So…you'll forgive him…?"

"We're not there yet, Amelie."

Now she was beginning to think Janet was either as crafty as a character in one of her novels—crafty primarily because Amelie had created her—or that she had lost her mind entirely. And then there was the other option, that Janet had this whole thing planned out and had completely outwritten the author.

"Is she someone I know?" Amelie ventured.

"In this town? Oh, probably."

Amelie felt as though she'd walked into this woman's trap, closed the door behind her, locked it, and tossed the key into a floor drain. While her weapon, impatiently resting in her bag, would remain useless to her.

She said, "How I can help make this better for you?"

A moment too late she realized that it was just short of a confession.

Janet tilted her head questioningly. "What do you mean, Amelie?"

"I just want to…help you. You're going through such…

difficult times, obviously. And…I don't know… I guess I just want you to be happy."

Janet shook her head sadly and slowly. "Sometimes I just wish someone would put me out of my misery."

Yes, I see, Amelie wanted to say. It was uncanny how two people who barely knew one another could follow the same train of thought.

"And…what are you going to do next?" she asked.

Janet suddenly seemed vulnerable, lost, adrift in a story she'd never anticipated. "What? What are you talking about?"

"This woman you suspect your husband is seeing. What are you going to…" And her words drifted into nothing.

Janet looked at her in a way Amelie hadn't seen before. This was the flinty, tough-assed CEO look, the look of someone who would fire you and call security to have you escorted out to the parking lot and then ruin your life forever with malicious gossip that would spread like a disease throughout the industry.

Janet said, "I'm going to deal with it in the only way I know how." She cut herself a thin slice of cheese and chewed slowly until it was down her throat. "And then," she said, "everything will be back to the way it should be."

52

SHE'D BEEN WARNED: THAT WAS THE ONLY WAY
Amelie could interpret it. From now on Janet would be woven
into her life, and if fate would allow her to be with Ben, they
would have to go far away, maybe to Mexico, to the mescal paradise of Cuernavaca in the shadow of the volcano, or to a forgotten
hilltop village in Italy where old women hung their laundry out,
where their husbands played bocce and drank grappa, and late
at night their grandsons fought vendettas in the streets when
they weren't whizzing around in their Vespas, ripping jewelry off
wealthy American tourists.

After an uneventful and largely silent ride, Janet dropped her
off at her house. It was the quiet in the car more than what had
been said at the house that bothered her most. As though Janet
were clearing a space for Amelie.

"I'm glad we had a chance to chat," Janet said finally. "Let's get
together soon again, okay?" And she gave Amelie's hand a squeeze
that lasted a little too long.

Amelie's mouth was too dry to do anything but whisper
Okay. Once inside her house, the silence seemed overwhelming,
a soundlessness heavy with memory and apprehension and loss.
She had spent two years with a man who, in the end, she realized
had never really loved her, never cared for her, would never fight

to keep her, and who probably barely even thought about her, a person who was married to a woman who knew something that would destroy him. And probably Amelie as well. Janet *owned* Ben, now and forever.

Which meant that Janet also owned Amelie.

She went into the bathroom and switched on the lights by the mirror. She splashed some water on her face and patted it dry. There was nothing she could do with this woman staring back at her; no amount of makeup could possibly make things better. Her mother was seventy-three when she died, which gave Amelie another thirty-three years. Would she be as alone as her mother had been for most of her life? And yet her mother had ultimately discovered happiness in her solitary life.

Adele Ferrar adored her students, and would sometimes come home with a smile on her face and stories to tell. Amelie had nothing but the sly imaginings of a novelist, the tiny puppets that walked through her mind and did and said things, until a whole new cast of characters took up residence there. And shutting her computer, she'd return to where she'd been for two years now—alone in the late afternoon, at day's end, as night fell. When sleep would overtake her.

Morning would bring a day full of possibilities and promises, and it would start again, the endless round of her routine.

She turned away from the face in the mirror, switched off the light, changed her clothes, and walked out of the house.

She took her usual route, a road bordering a large horse farm. In a pasture a stallion had mounted a mare, humping and gripping and snorting and neighing. Amelie thought of Ben, and then tried to forget about him because, really, these were just two horses having what one might call a rollicking good time. What *she* used to think of as a rollicking good time.

It *was* over, wasn't it?

Wasn't it?

Or maybe it wasn't... If Janet suspected someone other than Amelie of being the Other Woman, then she still had a chance. She had definitely stopped short of confronting Amelie, though once inside her and Ben's house it would have been the right time for it. Which meant, what, that she was certain it was someone other than Amelie? But that was impossible. There *was* no one else.

She knew now there was no way she could ever see Ben again, not after that conversation with Janet. Were she to continue seeing him, Janet would always be the elusive third person, physically invisible but psychically there, watching, listening, waiting. It would take Amelie a little time to get over the breakup, but of course she had felt it coming for months, she had sensed it in her heart but not inscribed it on her brain. It had been there in his hesitancies and gestures, in his lame explanations and pathetic excuses, the sad charade of a weak man.

Good, she thought. It was over, and to hell with the bastard. Now she and Janet had something in common, the contempt for a despicable man who loved neither of them. She stepped into her house just as her cell chimed and she answered it and said, "*Ben?*"

53

"WHO'S BEN?" NINA SAID.

"I didn't say 'Ben.' I said 'But.'"

"It sounded like Ben."

"I was talking to someone."

"You're not alone?"

Amelie looked around. "Laura is here. My friend Laura. She's asked me to talk to her book group."

"Don't forget to pick me up two weeks from Saturday."

"For what?"

"For the end of school," Nina said. "We have to leave the dorms then."

Amelie had forgotten her daughter was not going to be living at college for the rest of her life. "Have you called your father?"

"He said that maybe you'd come down together."

"I'd rather come alone. How much stuff do you have?"

"Too much for the Volvo."

"Fine. I'll rent a U-Haul."

"You don't need to, Daddy's got his Durango."

She shrugged. "Fine. I'll borrow his Durango, then."

"Why don't I just ask him to get me?"

"Fine," said Amelie.

"Are you all right?"

"Everything's fine."

"You don't sound fine," Nina said.

"I'm just tired."

"I finished your book. It was weird."

"You always say that."

"Especially the sexy bits."

Amelie said, "I'm glad you read it, though."

"I liked it a lot."

"Especially the sexy bits."

"No, Mom. I was embarrassed."

"Don't be. They weren't written to make you uncomfortable." She glanced out the window and saw a red BMW drive slowly by. She couldn't believe what she was seeing. She said, "Can I call you back?" and ran out and looked up and down the road and then went back for her keys.

She drove up to the junction with the main road and looked both ways. She turned right and followed the road into the village until she came to the town where he worked. There was the Federal mansion where he and his partner had their office, she turned the corner and saw that his car wasn't there.

"Well," she said.

She wondered if she should drive to his house, and if his car wasn't at his office and not at home, perhaps she should race back to her house and find it parked in front of her door. He would be inside, his fingers tapping impatiently on his knee as he sat waiting for her. She turned the wheel and merged with light traffic. She smiled and shook her head a little. So they had had an argument. People did it all the time. She and Richard were always arguing, and once he had even threatened divorce over her having forgotten to call the exterminator to deal with the squirrels in the attic, and once she had packed a bag and simply walked out on him. After a few hours had passed she returned and life went on as it had before. Until, of course, Richard stood up and walked out on her for good.

But that was inevitable. Had he not left her, she would certainly have left him. She would have met Ben and they would have begun their affair, and then the day would have come when she would have to confront Richard. He would be stunned, he would cry and drink too much and he would hire a therapist, he would go on Prozac and submit to electroshock, but she would speak of her love, her true love, of how absolutely authentic this love was, how in some cosmic New Age manner she and Ben had been made for each other, and Richard would go and live in a cheap motel up by the Hawg's Breath Saloon out in the boondocks. He would gain weight and grow an unkempt beard and start to neglect his physical hygiene. He would begin to frequent adult movie theaters. He would hang out at tattoo parlors and biker shops, and make friends with guys named Al and Wes. He might join a militia with all the other lonely hearts. He would take to wearing fatigues and combat boots, he would become an aficionado of the backwoods, he would get a crossbow and go out and hunt young animals, and then skin and eat them with his bare hands, and while he waited for the North Koreans to invade New England she would be with Ben: traveling through Italy, or spending a dirty Manhattan weekend at the Pierre, or looking for a vacation home on the Vineyard.

But Richard had married and was about to become a father for the second time. The woman he had married had one thing going for her: she believed in Richard. And Amelie had no one. And

Ben's car wasn't there. She turned the corner and began to drive home, she pressed her foot to the accelerator, she gained speed, she made it in record time, she pulled into her driveway.

There was no Ben; no Janet. Just her. And the person in the mirror everyone knew as the author Amelie Ferrar. Poised. Pretty. Utterly professional.

Part of her knew precisely what would happen. Not the actual events, not the day-to-day progression of her life, but the general sweep of things. Eventually the heat and cry of the moment would pass. As the tide carries debris from a past calamity at sea to some distant shore, something residual might surface, and in the detachment and serenity of the future, a time when other opportunities and other people would have slotted into place, she would examine this remnant—this fragment of pain, this pearl that had formed in her heart, something hard and spherical that would reflect the sky-blue memory of her eyes—and set it aside as nothing more than a curiosity, of no interest to her whatsoever.

She had written about these things before. Her first novel was about the end of an affair and the vicissitudes of memory, and now that she was living it, now that she was inhabiting a plot she'd already imagined, she knew that she would never write about it again. She wasn't even sure she would be able to love again, as though everything in her heart had been spent, leaving nothing within her but this vast, uninhabitable desert where nothing could flourish.

This is what it would be like for her: servant to a dream, plaything of the insubstantial, a chaser of illusions. She took her bag, the gun lying heavily within it, and walked with resignation into her house.

Part Five

54

WHEN AMELIE WOKE ON FRIDAY THE SKY WAS DARK and rain fell from it, rain without end. She rose and showered and had breakfast and sat down to work. With Ben's absence, with her hopes and wishes having withered, she felt as if someone had spilled ink over her imagination: now she could write about the darker impulses in people: the homicidal shift in the most unassuming character; the scheming, leveling place in the heart that might explode at any time.

A woman sits on an examining table at her doctor's office. He listens to her heart and lungs, and the regularity and depth of his breathing indicates he is evaluating things, moving toward a conclusion. She can smell the soap on his body and the shampoo in his hair; she can see the thought behind his eyes.

It was as if she were examining him while he was assessing her state of being. She watched his pupils dilate as his hand nestled into the fold beneath her breast, gently pressing the cold disk of the stethoscope against her skin. With each step, she knew, the news would only get darker.

Tell me something that you can't take back, she thought as she tried to read her doctor's expression. Tell me something that will change this day, the night to come, and all the days thereafter.

And then life, Amelie added, can truly begin.

When noon came she had completed a total of three satisfactory pages in a novel that would, she now knew, be about a woman who has little time to live, but who needs to even up the scores in her life. Coloring outside the lines, as her agent once cautioned her against doing. But the time had come for her to do exactly that.

"Good," she said quietly, as she closed her laptop. *Good*, she thought.

She got into her car and drove into town to buy soup, because right now it was what she needed, some liquid comfort that wasn't called vodka. Three blocks from her house on one of the country roads there were flashing lights ahead, and her wipers doing their intermittent sweep revealed at least three police cruisers, a fire engine, and an ambulance. A cop in the road, the same one who had stopped her when she was driving past Ben's house, put up his hand. She came to a slow halt and slid down the window.

"What's happened?"

He said, "Accident." He tilted his head a little and looked at her. "I know you, don't I?" It felt like a pickup line at a bar.

I see you everywhere, she remembered Richard saying. And Ben. And now a stranger in a uniform.

"I don't think so," Amelie said.

"You look familiar."

"I've been told that before."

"We're trying to reach next of kin to the deceased."

"Deceased."

He leaned back and scratched his head. His radio squawked. He said, "Driver didn't make it." Another cop, farther down, waved her on. "Okay, you can proceed."

She passed slowly by the wreck and a line of traffic flares. A silver Mercedes had veered off the road, apparently at a high rate of speed, because its front end was completely crushed against a large oak tree. Officers were pointing at the skid marks on the road, while others worked on extracting the body as EMTs stood by.

Shaken by what she'd seen, Amelie drove even more cautiously than usual, especially as the rain had grown harder. Her phone chimed. Laura said, "So we thought we'd meet next Thursday at Jane Baron's. That'll give everyone a chance to read the book. Actually, everyone's bought a copy. Books 'N Stuff in town ordered copies for all of us."

"Sorry, I'm just... I just saw a terrible accident. Someone was killed."

"Oh my god—you actually saw it happen?"

"No, just...after. I'm a bit shaken by it. Anyway, go ahead."

"So I'm hoping you'll definitely be able to join us."

"Yes. All right. I'll do it."

"You don't sound enthusiastic, Amelie."

"It's just that I've done this sort of thing before." Still disturbed by the scene she'd witnessed, she tried to put a smile on her words. "I'm not complaining, but you end up trapped in someone's living room having to explain every little detail in your novel."

Is the fact that you named a character Oswald anything to do with the Kennedy assassination, is there any symbolism in the river overflowing its banks, how did you manage to write the sex scene without using the you-know-what word, do you have any inside

*Hollywood gossip, how much does your publisher pay you, is your
agent willing to read a little something I've jotted down?*

"Oh no no," Laura protested. "We don't do that sort of
thing. It's just a discussion group. You know. Book chat and
chardonnay."

Amelie considered it. It would be nice to get out with other
women, it would be nice, now that she thought of it, to get out
with anyone but men, and, more particularly, Ben. If she ever
took the time to think of it, she'd realize that she'd made few
friends since moving there twenty years ago. Her work kept her in
isolation, and the little socializing she did was with other families
from Nina's old school. She didn't have one close friend, no one
to confide in or trust. She'd invested all in Ben. And now she had
nothing. Except for Janet, of course. Her brand-new friend with
a heart as dark as hers had become.

"We usually open a few bottles of wine, and everyone brings a
little something yummy to snack on," Laura went on. "As you're
the guest of honor, you bring nothing but yourself. This time it'll
be something of an event as Janey's husband was offered a position
at Berkeley beginning in September and I guess after that someone
else will have to provide the house." She laughed and Amelie
ignored her; she knew nothing about this Baron woman except
what Andrew had told her, that she had a daughter who sucked.

"Sounds great."

"And you can sign our books for us."

"I'd be happy to."

There was a pause. Laura said, "Everything else okay?"

"Everything's fine," Amelie said, and then ten minutes later,
after she parked in front of the shop where she always bought

soup, she called Laura back. "I was just wondering what time you wanted me next Thursday."

"Sevenish, if that's convenient."

"And one other thing. Why did you ask if everything was okay?"

"What do you mean?"

"Because everything's fine."

"That's what you said."

"I mean, you sounded like you'd heard that something wasn't fine."

"No, no," said Laura, and Amelie very clearly heard the laughter in her voice. Now that it was all over, had Ben gone out and told the world about what had happened, did he describe Amelie as a woman unhinged? Was love really akin to insanity? But he wouldn't do that, just as she would never speak of him. They had been joined in love, they had split in silence, and now he had not a moment in his life to spare for her. She was like a doll that wets or cries "Mama": *the Disposable Amelie.* You can brush her hair, take off her little outfits, twist her limbs this way and that, and then, if you like, you can just toss her away. *Bye-bye, Disposable Amelie.*

Because there's always a bright new toy waiting on the shelf.

She clicked off. The rain had gone from drizzle to downpour. Once inside the place, she ordered her soup and looked at who else was there, the odd familiar face without a name. Everyone looked solemn. She wondered if news had reached them about the accident, the victim someone they knew.

She paid for her lunch and ran back to her car. Now everything in it smelled of wet dog, of wet dead dog, and she switched on the heat and turned on the radio and pulled onto the road.

It was the time of day when everything falls quiet, when people are at work and children at school, when the solitary and homeless huddle for warmth beneath bridges, the time when Amelie felt most redundant. Now she lived like a vagrant, moving from errand to errand to sofa to books to four o'clock and eighty-proof vodka on the rocks. Now the hours lay before her not in terms of seven or eight of them, but the subdivisional hell of minutes and seconds, computable in the millionths, one after another.

Everything fell still; time seemed to come to a halt. Her tires whispered on the wet roadway. She turned the corner, pulled into the gas station, and found herself behind the red BMW. On the rear window was a sticker for Andrew's school and above it one for Rachel's college. Ben waited while the attendant filled his tank. He looked in his rearview, looked away, then looked back.

"Well," she said quietly to herself as their eyes met, and something moved in her chest, something grew hard in her throat, she could feel her heart blasting against her rib cage, and for a moment she feared she might be having a stroke. She watched him get out and walk slowly toward her car. He opened the door and climbed in beside her.

"Hi," he said.

"Hi."

He laughed a little. "You look as wet as I am. How've you been?"

She wondered whether she should tell him that she had been miserable and lonely and suicidal and unhappy and angry, or say that she'd been great, fabulous, happy, and satisfied thanks to a long line of suitors who had been waiting for Ben to get the hell out of her world. She said, "I've been all right." She thought of the gun in her bag. These days it went everywhere with her. The itch of a handy weapon: like the urge to self-gratification, it never failed to creep up on a person at the oddest of times.

The attendant came to the passenger-side window, and Ben handed him his credit card before the guy stuck his nozzle into Amelie's tank.

Now she wanted to watch Ben squirm. "I might as well tell you that Janet is aware of us. Or at least of you. She knows you're having an affair."

He just stared at her. "Are you serious?"

"It's why she wanted to have dinner with me. To see if I might have any ideas on how she could handle this."

He took a deep breath and said, "Did she say she knew who it was?"

"Well, I assume she was talking about me."

He looked around and obviously saw nothing but rain. "But *she's* having an affair, right?"

Brad. Like a character who suddenly makes an entrance in one of her books and grows in importance once he's allotted an identity, throwing the plot in a wholly unexpected direction. But Brad was still just a convenient placeholder in the life of Janet. And the life of Amelie.

And, of course, Ben.

"You haven't asked her yet, have you? I didn't think so. Too afraid to learn the truth that you've been betrayed as much as she has? I don't know who to feel more sorry for, you or Janet, but right now the odds are really slithering away from you."

He took a moment as he stared through the windshield. "Who is this guy?"

"Brad? He's with MIT. Runs one of the big labs there. The kind of man someone like Janet would go for."

He seemed in shock. "How long—"

"Has it been going on? I don't know. But I think it's been a while. He seems like a really decent guy."

"You've *met* him?"

She smiled a little. "Did I say that?"

She was discovering that messing with reality was almost as much fun as writing.

He shook his head. "It won't last."

"Is that a wish or a prophecy?"

"Let her have her little fling. It'll be over soon."

"So tell me honestly," she said. "Have you ever mentioned me to her?"

"No, of course not."

"Not let anything slip out...?"

He shook his head. He turned away and looked back out the window. In the closeness of the car, with the windows tightly shut and covered in a thin film of condensation, she could smell him, he was inches away from her, and she turned so that she wouldn't have to see him, that she wouldn't be tempted to touch him, that only words could be exchanged. She felt herself beginning to tremble, not inwardly, as characters in her books tended to do, but literally, her hands jigging in the air.

"Look," he said. "I'm sorry about what happened. Between us."

She let him go on.

"And about how that all came out."

"What do you mean?"

"About the way we argued like that. You know."

"So now you're sorry," she said. "For what, exactly?"

"I just think it could have been done better."

"You might begin by explaining what you meant at the time."

"About," he said, and she nodded, she looked at the mute face of the radio, she said, "Marriage."

"Just what I said. I can't marry you."

"Listen."

"I just—"

"Let me talk, Ben. We've been together for two years. We've been intimate in ways other people couldn't imagine. We've done everything but take out a license and buy the rings. Do you really think it's fair to Janet for you not to ask for a divorce? Especially now that she knows? I mean, how much longer do you want her to suffer?"

"But it's my family."

"That's just a word."

"And you're a writer. You know how important words are."

She also knew how easily they could be juggled in the air and bandied about and tossed to the wind, where all of their edge would be worn away and mutate into just another overpriced Hallmark card with its artless mush and sad drawings of flowers and cats.

"At least Richard did the honest thing. It was hard on me, but he ended it and stopped the deception, and I'm glad he respected me in that way."

Now his hand was on his knee and she crossed her arms. She would not touch him, she would not look at him, she would be pure voice, words and sentences, questions and answers.

"And I can't understand how you can just end it like that. As if you couldn't even say a proper goodbye. It means that everything we've done has no resonance for you."

"It was hard for me to do that," he said. "It's been hard for me since then. I'm not sleeping, and the other night I drank too much and Janet and I fought about nothing important and—"

"If it was all so hard for you, why didn't you call me, or come over and see me? We're perfectly capable of having a civilized conversation without anything getting in the way."

"It's just—"

She waited.

"It's just that I didn't think I could resist you," and then she felt it, his hand on her thigh, and she fell.

55

SHE LET THE FRONT DOOR SLAM BEHIND HER AND began undoing her jeans as she ran up the stairs ahead of him. This was not going to be the long anticipated screw-of-the-week; this was going to be the quick and soon-to-be-forgotten one, and when they got into bed, they moved with speed, the air filling with growling, hungry noises that came from something deep within them as they wrestled each other into position, and in less than a minute it was over, the best she'd ever had, ever, ever.

And, just as quickly, it began to fade.

They lay sprawled against each other, drifting in and out of sleep. Something within her said that she shouldn't have done it, it was like the Just One More Cigarette of the person determined to quit, and yet she couldn't resist him. And this thing that lay within began to rouse her, and without looking at him, without moving her sweaty body, without reaching down to touch his shoulder or his face or any other part of him, she said, "Why did you do this to me?"

He made an inarticulate sound, and it seemed to her that he was no better than an animal.

"Why did you do it? Why did you get into my car, why did you touch me, how can you do this?" The word *corruption* passed through her mind.

"I couldn't help it," he said.

"Then how can we go on living this way if every time we see each other we can't keep our hands to ourselves?"

"You need to have a life," he said. "You need to be able to live the way you want, not always waiting for me."

"Do you really think I'm always waiting for you, Ben? I was pestering you at your office because I thought I deserved better than I got the other day. Otherwise I have a very full life. I write, I promote my books, I'm a mother, I have a mind, I have my imagination. What makes you think my life is spent in the devoted following of a priapic architect?" she said.

"It's really over, Amelie. I mean, it's been fun and all, I've really enjoyed this, but I have a career to protect. Especially now."

She understood exactly what he was trying to say. No loose ends. She was nothing more than an inconvenient thread dangling from the hem of his professional life.

"And you think, what, that I'm somehow hindering your advancement in the world of architecture?" she said.

"You know what I mean. Stability." And he shrugged.

"So you never saw this as anything but a lighthearted little diversion?"

"You had fun, didn't you? Anyway, it's time both of us moved on."

"Wait a moment—I don't have anything to protect? Are you serious?"

"Come on, Amelie," he said, barely disguising the weariness in his response.

"No. Please explain it, because all these words—these little prefab lines you're coming out with—mean nothing to me. Because I always thought I meant something to you."

"You did. You do. I mean, we can still be friends, right?"

She lay back and shook her head in exasperation. The ambiguous exit and a soft landing in the lush meadows of cheap cliché. As though she were expected to be grateful to him for the sentiment.

She felt completely calm. "Did you also say all this to your first wife when you dumped her?"

He looked stunned, as if someone had hit him hard in the back with one of Al's two-for-one bullet specials. "What do you mean?"

She sat up and held the sheet to her chest. "You got rid of wife number one when you met Janet. But you couldn't leave Janet for me. Am I that second-rate? Or just too damned old and used-up for someone like you?"

He shook his head. "Christ, she really is out of her mind."

"What, you're saying there was no first wife? That she's making this up?"

He took a moment. "What else did she tell you?"

"That's between your wife and me, don't you think?"

He sat up on the side of the bed, his back to her. "All right, look—yes, I was married before I met Janet."

"And you were going to tell me this when—?"

He shrugged. "At the right time, I suppose."

"At the altar?"

Now he turned to look at her. "I'm not marrying you. You know, maybe if you and I had met earlier things might've—"

"But you still fell into bed with me. You knew exactly what you were doing, unless, of course, all these years your little one-eyed friend there has been taking you for a joyride down Happy Street. I always felt you were the perfect man for me. We fit together so well in so many ways, and now I'm seeing that all along I was just...an amusement for you. A trifle. You've been lying to me for two years. Two years when you earned my respect and love, and now this. So let's get right down to it, Ben. Am I no longer good in bed—?"

He said, "Of course not, you're amazing."

"Have I grown ugly?"

He sputtered and shook his head. "Don't be ridiculous. You're beautiful."

"Have you grown bored with me? Obviously not, because here we are. Do you honestly think this is just going to end because you want it to? We're going to keep running into each other. At gas stations and supermarkets, and we'll always end up back here. I know it, and you know it, and as much as I may want to resist it, I can't. And neither can you."

Without a word he got off the bed and went into the bathroom. She heard him pee, and without washing his hands he came back, a naked detumescent man framed in the doorway. Now he was serious, he was dead calm.

"That's never going to happen, Amelie. We're not going to see each other ever again. Because I'm not going to be here much longer."

She sat up and looked at him. "I don't understand." It was as though death had entered the room, shrouded and armed for slaughter.

"This is how I wanted to do it. I wanted to be able to say it to your face. I wanted to walk away with a happy memory of you. Of us. Of…this," and he gestured toward the bed, toward her.

"Are you sick, is something wrong?"

"We're leaving, Janet and Andrew and I. We're moving to California. I was offered a job there with a consortium of architects in San Francisco."

She could barely take it in. It was as though someone in authority had announced that the axis of the earth had shifted. The effects of it were inescapable: the ice age would be here in a matter of weeks.

"We're going to live in the city, or maybe in Berkeley. We're putting the house on the market tomorrow morning. I start work the first week in September. We hope to be out there by June tenth to find a place to live and a school for Andrew. He just has to finish his school year here."

"That's in three weeks. And you're only telling me this now?"

"Rachel's spending the summer with us out there before she heads back to school."

Amelie looked around the room as though she had suddenly found herself in strange surroundings. "I don't understand," she said, and he must have been able to see it, the incomprehension in her eyes, her crooked, confused smile, her hands as they inarticulately played the air before her. She felt something disconnect inside her, as though everything she believed in and trusted had vanished.

"But—when did this happen, Ben? Couldn't you have warned me?"

"I didn't know about it until I was offered the position."

"But you must have applied for it, you must have brought yourself to their attention, people don't just offer people jobs without meeting them."

"The person who arranged this for me was one of my professors at the university. He knows my work, he'd been following my career. I had lunch with him in LA. Things just…happened." He smiled and she wanted to slap that smirk off the face of the earth.

"And you couldn't tell me that all this was in the works?"

"It wasn't easy," he said.

She sighed. There was no point in going on.

"So you're essentially leaving me for Janet."

"It'll be best for everyone that way."

She watched as he began to dress, she saw his average-size penis flop behind the black cotton of his underpants, she watched him button his shirt. It would be the last time she would see him naked, the last time she would be with him.

He was right: if only she had met him earlier. If only she had known him one day before he had first laid eyes on Janet. If only she had grown up next door to him, gone to school with him, attended college with him. If only she had been there at the beginning when they were both nine years old and holding hands on the porch swing. She could have shaped him into the man he should have become. Honorable. Decent. Loyal.

She lay back in bed and pulled the covers up to her chin. She felt as she did when as a child she would become feverish and shaky, when only warmth and shut eyes and the ministrations of her mother could relieve her pain.

Once Ben was dressed he stood over her bed. He said, "Well. I guess it's time, Amelie."

He actually had the nerve to hold out his hand for a shake, and after staring at said appendage for ten seconds she closed her eyes. And he walked down the stairs and let himself out.

Two years, she thought, and it was like a fast montage from a feature film, all the meals, the laughter, the flirting, the sex… And now the movie was over. There would be no sequel. The theater was dark. The audience was gone; the popcorn was going stale.

Amelie in love slept alone.

56

ACCORDING TO THE TV NEWS AT SIX, THE ACCIDENT was now being treated as suspicious. As there was evidence of two different sets of tire tracks, police had concluded that another vehicle had been involved. Sideswiped? Maybe. Deliberately forced off the road? Possibly. Witnesses were being asked to step forward. So far there was no one. "The vehicle," the reporter said as she stood in front of the wreck as it was being hoisted and towed away, its roof peeled back like a tin can, "was registered to a local woman, Jane Baron."

Amelie's hand went to her mouth. A week from now she was supposed to be meeting with a book group at the Baron woman's home. Amelie hardly knew her: a face and wave from behind the wheel of a Mercedes in the school driveway.

The air was heavy, laden with moisture and threat. She felt off-balance, as if in some deeply obscure way this death had caused a rent in the fabric of her own world. Her cell rang, she said, "Hello?" and there was a pause. She was about to end the call when—

"Amelie?"

She had no idea who this was.

"It's…Janet."

"Oh. Yes. Hi. Sorry." She switched off the TV.

"I just wanted to let you know… That thing we talked about—? Well, it's been taken care of. Everything's been solved. My husband and I are moving to San Francisco before the end of the summer." The words came out as a simple fact, with no nuance or stress. The woman sounded distant, even dazed, as though she were communicating from the Siberian outpost of a dormant marriage.

"Oh, that's a surprise," Amelie said brightly, hoping she gave the impression that this was news to her.

"I know it's kind of sudden, but Ben's been offered a very attractive position I've encouraged him to take, and I'll be running my business from our West Coast office in San Francisco."

"Well, congratulations, Janet. It all sounds very promising."

"I feel like our move will change everything. Both for him and for me. I know it sounds like a cliché, but it'll give us both a fresh start. Something I think we really need right now, and it'll put us on a new footing in our relationship. Especially as there won't be any…distractions," she added.

Amelie was surprised to feel her eyes well with tears. Something about the call—about hearing it not from Ben but from his wife—struck her with even greater force. This was not some speculative planning on Ben's part, not a bout of wishful thinking. Now it was real. Now it was final.

"Amelie…? Everything okay?"

"Yes, I'm just…" and she sat. "There's one other thing. I just want to say that I'm sorry, Janet."

"But for what, Amelie?"

"I mean, he's probably told you everything, and I'm…just glad you've worked things out. I am. Really." And a single tear fell from her left eye. "You deserve to be happy."

"You have nothing to apologize for, Amelie. Nothing at all."

Now it was Amelie's turn to fall silent as she wiped the tear away. She had no idea why she'd said it. Maybe it was a matter of clearing the air of any bad feelings. But Janet wasn't even considering Amelie's apology for what it was. She was proving to be a far more decent person than her husband. Without even asking for forgiveness, Janet had just granted her exactly that.

"I...I'm also sorry that you're leaving. I've enjoyed getting to know you."

"And I feel likewise, Amelie. But you'll still have a faithful reader three thousand miles away." And she laughed a little. "I can't tell you how much I'm looking forward to your next book. I have a feeling it's going to be amazing."

Amelie wiped away a tear from her cheek. "Well, I hope that you'll at least find it edifying."

"So I'm just tying up loose ends," Janet went on. "Saying my goodbyes, dealing with unfinished business," and she laughed a little. "And also just to say thank you for being a good listener. It's helped me come to a number of decisions that I think will make things better in my life. And Ben's."

Later, Amelie knew, she would have to parse what Janet said, seeking the subtext, possibly even finding herself in the spaces between the words.

"Did you hear about the accident?" she asked Janet.

There was another pause. The sky swelled with distant thunder. "Oh yes. It was very sad. I mean, what a horrible thing. Funny how things can change in the blink of an eye."

Amelie said, "Did you know the woman—the one who died in the accident?"

"Janey Baron…? Well, yes," and there was the hint of a smile in Janet's voice. "I knew exactly who she was."

57

Now it was morning. In the hours to come Ben would meet with a broker, and a sign would be mounted on a stake and driven into the heart of his front yard, *For Sale Exclusive*. There would be an open house on some future Sunday, and balloons would be tied to the sign and anyone who desired could traipse around Ben the architect's house: a place of absence, of life abandoned, where something of him might linger, a breath taken, one last thought for Amelie Ferrar.

She kicked off the duvet and sat up on the side of the bed and rubbed her face with her hands. Richard had left her. Ben had left her. He had Janet and he had Andrew and he had his new job and he didn't need Amelie. *Hasta la vista, baby.*

She lay in the bath for twenty minutes and stared at the sky through the high window, a tree branch in full leaf waving and shifting in the breeze. She thought of Ben and her in bed one languid afternoon. The memory had lost its sweetness and had become merely wistful, and she knew that one day, like all memories, it would become just another still life, something she could view dispassionately before moving on to another. But there was no consolation in that, because *one day* could be a month from then, a year later, five years from now. Or maybe even never.

She was now just another woman Ben had bedded, one among

a long string of them. Amelie, however, was different. She had never forgotten the men she had loved. She kept memories of what they had done together, the concerts they attended, the movies watched, the dances danced. It even included Richard, because, really, there were the good times, the not-so-good times, and the slightly better times before everything had turned bitter and ugly, but there was always Nina, and because of her Amelie would never forget him.

Love in and of itself was something permanent, like a tattoo that fades with age but never entirely disappears: the people might drift off and depart or even die, but what she and Ben had shared would always remain behind, a ghost in the heart of memory.

In another week Nina would be home from college, and Amelie would put Ben aside and enjoy the time she'd have with her daughter. She would sit at her desk and shape her words into sentences and paragraphs and pages and chapters, and within them would be the work she had always been reaching for but never quite achieving: her story. A woman, her days numbered, who could now finally live to the fullest. All she needed was the right conclusion. Because, in fact, she knew that her story would begin at the end.

She rose from the water and reached for the towel and wrapped it around her. She caught her reflection in the mirror and was startled to see she couldn't recognize this other woman. As though someone had joined her in the room and had all along been standing there, silent and watchful. She looked again and thought, *Yes. Now I know. I know who you are. I know what you've done.*

I know all about you. And him.

And her.

And then it snapped.

She screamed and screamed, tearing at her hair, punching the air, until everything went still and she knew exactly what she had to do.

The universe has a thin skin. All you have to do is blow a hole in it to change everything.

58

IT WAS A PRETTY SHADE OF TIFFANY BLUE, AS THOUGH instead of a lethal weapon it was a rare wildflower, or the name for a perky little assassin with vivid eyes and devastating aim: *Tiffany Blue, Angel of Death.*

There was no point in taking lessons or visiting a firing range; she knew how it worked. You found your target, you aimed your weapon, you pulled the trigger. The heart or the head: either way, it brought things to a proper, unambiguous end.

She dressed carefully: one had to look one's best in such circumstances. She smiled at the woman staring at her. What pretty blue eyes she had. What things they had seen. What stories they could tell. She wondered if the stranger were going to say something, but the woman just smiled approvingly back, almost as if she harbored a secret she would one day share with her. She'd had enough of secrets by now. Enough of lies, of unintended smiles, of soft words and empty promises. She felt the weight of the gun in her hand. She nodded a little, smiled back, mouthed a word of farewell to her victim, closed her eyes, and pulled the trigger.

59

THE OTHER WOMAN WAS IN TINY SHREDS ALL OVER the floor and the dresser, fragments of blue eyes and blond hair, the thousand shards of Amelie Ferrar. And now, she knew, there was only one of her.

Her ears ringing, she went into the bathroom and carefully put on her makeup, lipstick, a little blush, some eyeliner and mascara. Killer eyes, the photographer had told her. Just as fatal as ever.

She wondered what she should wear for the big event. Should she try her black dress? She took the hanger from the closet and slid the dress over her head. She shimmied a little to let it fall properly, slipped on her glasses, and there she was, a unity of look and attitude. The rain had stopped and the sun had started to break through the clouds. She thought of the cop who had stopped her and then recognized her at the accident scene. Was he keeping an eye out for her? Would he follow her once again to the scene of the crime? And would he be gentle with his handcuffs?

She fingered away a stray spot of lipstick, and then brushed her hair again and again until all the little glassy bits of Amelie had fallen to the floor.

It was funny.

It was funny because lately people had come to photograph and interview her, readers had seen her picture, read her words. In her photos she was crisply defined: the blond of her hair, the blue of her eyes, the little lines around her mouth that she'd grown to like. Dressed to be photographed, she was a woman who, when she walked out of a room, left behind a shimmering impression in the air, like a ghost in a house that had seen violence within its walls, murder or passion. Yet beyond the image, behind the eyes, as much as she wanted to pretend she was at peace with herself, there was only the disarray of something breaking down, a many-limbed monster slouching toward chaos.

She went out to her deck and leaned against the railing and smelled the air and understood that something within her was still alive, a creature that existed separately from the person known as Amelie the Lover. This entity had one option that possessed a measure of purity. It was how she measured the final twists in her novels. Unexpected, unanticipated, firmly grounded; in the end utterly inevitable. People would say: *Ah, yes. How fitting.*

She shut her eyes and shook her head a little. She put the gun and both boxes of ammunition in her bag and walked away.

60

SHE DROVE SLOWLY THROUGH THE VILLAGE, PAST THE Coach & Four and Zeke's Bar and Grill, past the gourmet shop where she bought her soup, and the bakery where for years she had bought Nina's birthday cakes, and found herself in the winding lanes beyond, by the paddocks and the drowsy sunlit horses, the old-money farms, the soulless supersize McMansions, the gas stations. Children stood in line at an ice-cream stand while others peered down at her from passing school buses. She slowed when she came to Ben's street and saw his wife taking groceries from her car. Janet turned to look and waved her over.

"Amelie. What a surprise!"

"I just wanted to say goodbye." She held out her hand, and Janet reached into the window and held it for a moment. "I wish you all the luck with the move. You and Andrew and…Ben."

"Thank you. You're so kind to say that."

"Well, I have errands," Amelie said, and Janet said goodbye and smiled and turned to reach for another bag, and now Janet was lying on the ground bleeding from her head, her legs splayed in this moment of tragedy and surprise as apples rolled away and boxes of linguini and Cap'n Crunch tumbled onto the sidewalk, as the woman began to convulse in her final moments on earth. Amelie drove on without once looking back.

But that didn't happen. Janet hoisted her shopping, her son's treats and breakfast cereals, and watched as her husband's lover turned the corner.

Amelie's cell rang. "It's me," the woman said.

"Janet?"

"Laura."

"Laura," Amelie said. "Yes. Hi."

"You heard about the accident, how it was Jane Baron's car?"

Amelie listened. The woman sounded shaken, just like before when she called.

"Of course, yes, it's...it's horrible."

"The police just released this. It wasn't Jane, it was Linda Kinsman. You'd met her, hadn't you?"

"Yes, I think so." She tasted blood in her mouth, and when she probed with a finger she discovered a tiny sliver of Amelie stuck to the inside of her cheek. She pulled it out and launched it out the window into the slipstream. Another little piece of her heart, gone with the wind.

"One of her kids was in your daughter's class until she transferred," Laura said.

"I don't understand, what are you trying to tell me?"

"It was Jane Baron's car. But she'd let Linda borrow it. Linda lived across the street from her. Her car was in the shop, and she was late picking up her youngest from school. So Janey let her use hers."

"Jane's still alive?"

"She's getting ready to move to San Francisco in another month. So we're still looking forward to you visiting our reading group next week."

It suddenly, blindingly, came to her: the day when she and Ben lay together on the bed as a shaft of sunlight fell over them. She reached down and touched him in a playful way. *Come on, Janey,* he'd said.

Janey.

Janey Baron.

She's getting ready to move to San Francisco, Laura had just told her.

Janey. Ben. Janey and Ben. San Francisco.

Janey's car.

She may have been forced off the road, the police had said.

Janet...

61

AMELIE CLICKED OFF AND PULLED TO THE SIDE OF THE road. She flipped down her visor and opened the mirror, and the person she saw was looking at her with a mix of contempt and pity.

Well, she said, and closed her eyes.

And now she opened them.

It was open and shut, she now saw. Absolutely airtight. Amelie had been the cover for Ben's *other* affair. He had sacrificed her for Janey Baron, leaving Amelie to take the fall had Janet ever found out he was cheating on her. Once again he had the ideal arrangement: his family intact, his lover across the bay, no one any the wiser. The perfect life.

When she arrived home there was a police cruiser parked at the top of her driveway. She came to an abrupt stop. It made no sense, a police car at her house. It was the same cop she'd seen before, the one who'd followed her, the one from the accident scene. He walked over to the front of her car, looked down, then looked at his pad. She thought: *Nina.*

"What's happened? Is it my daughter?" She could hear herself shouting as she flung open her door.

"Nothing like that. I just need to confirm your identity. You are Ms. Ferrar? Ms. Amelie Ferrar?"

She nodded.

"Can I have a couple minutes of your time? I just have a few questions for you."

"What is this about, Officer?"

"Can we...?" He nodded to the front door.

He sat across from her in her living room and took out his pad. "It's probably nothing at all, but I just need to clear up some things regarding the fatal accident that occurred yesterday."

It took her a few seconds. "Yes. Of course. It was terrible."

"And I remember you driving past it, maybe half an hour after the police arrived there. Am I correct about that?"

She nodded, still not understanding what this had to do with her.

"And you were heading where at the time...?"

"To town. To get my lunch. What exactly is the problem here, Officer?"

"And that was the first you'd seen of the accident itself?"

"Well, yes, of course," she said.

He took a breath. "Here's the situation. Just after the accident, a local woman happened to be driving on the same road. She identified your car as moving at considerable speed in the opposite direction." He shut his pad. "Away from the accident scene." He looked at her and waited.

"But how could you know for sure when it happened?"

"The victim's wristwatch was crushed, and we could determine the moment she was forced into the tree. This witness was the one who called us to report the accident in the first place. And from her testimony we feel pretty sure that a second car was involved. Unfortunately the tread marks had been affected by the rain, so they can't be used as evidence. We believe it was this car that forced the Mercedes off the road at a high rate of speed."

Amelie swallowed hard. "This is crazy. I wasn't anywhere near it until you saw me."

He looked at her. "Did I say that she said it was your car?"

"No, but it sounds like you're—"

"Let me continue. Apart from any sort of road-rage incident, there may have been a motive involved. That the victim's car was somehow targeted by the driver of the other vehicle." He opened his pad again, and then his phone rang. "I need to take this, Ms. Ferrar." He said, "Yes. Yes, I'm here now... I understand." He glanced at his watch and made a notation on his pad.

Amelie got to her feet, and he took the phone from his ear. "Please remain seated," he said, pointing his finger at the sofa. He finished his call and referred to his pad.

"It gets a little more complicated. The witness was able to remember the first three letters and numbers of the license plate of the car she saw speeding away from the scene." He held up the page for her to see. "An exact match to yours, as you can see." And then he closed it.

"I'm really not understanding this, Officer."

"I'm afraid you've become a person of interest in our investigation. I'm going to ask you not to leave the area for the next thirty-six hours, and—"

"This is crazy. You're accusing me of forcing that other car off the road? Why would I do something like that? I didn't even know the driver."

"I'm only saying the witness identified that Volvo that you just now drove up in. Color and license plate. As you may already know, the Mercedes was registered to a Ms. Jane Baron, but was being driven by her neighbor, a Ms. Linda Kinsman. This witness—I can't, of course, reveal her name—stated in a written, sworn statement that you and Ms. Baron had recently had a heated argument over a personal matter. Something about a man you both knew. This constitutes a potential motive."

When Amelie again stood abruptly, he gestured for her to sit.

"Look," she said. "I hardly know these women. Someone's making all this up."

He stood and slipped his pad inside his pocket. "I'm going to ask you not to leave the area until this matter is cleared up. And we'll need you to come in for further questioning sometime in the next day or two. So I suggest you call your attorney, Ms. Ferrar."

She watched from the doorway as he drove away. *This is how it ends. This is the way Janet had wanted it to turn out.* She had written Amelie into her own story.

But one good story deserved another.

62

FOLLOWING THE LONG DRIVEWAY, AMELIE PARKED
and walked into the building. People happily greeted her, and
she ignored each and every one of them, because she was no
longer the person they knew but someone else. She opened the
door to the classroom and said to the teacher, "I've been asked to
give Andrew a lift again today. His father called and was hoping
I might do it, and as I was passing, I didn't mind. Is it okay if we
leave a few minutes early?"

"His father never left word for us."

"It was a last-minute thing. He's running late in a meeting in
Boston."

The teacher looked as if she was trying to read Amelie's expression. Amelie smiled a little.

"Sure," the teacher said. "He's all yours."

Together they watched the boy gather his things: backpack,
Spider-Man lunch box, lacrosse stick. He looked at her and
she smiled. The teacher touched his head, wished him a good
weekend.

They walked out together just as other cars, other parents,
began to arrive. She switched on the ignition and released the
brake. Locking all the doors, she drove slowly out of the driveway
and onto the road.

He said, "Did my dad call you?"

She said nothing.

"I don't have a piano lesson today."

"I know, darling."

"I'm thirsty."

"I'll get you something in a little while. It won't be long now."

"And I'm really tired."

She wanted to reach out and take his hand, for he was innocent and his voice was high and sweet and she was moved by him, and she did it, she gently took hold of his hand. The fact that he didn't try to slide it away or shake it off cheered her, because now she knew that he was in her world, just as she was in his. She drove through the village. She drove through another and another and another, moving north into the late afternoon.

"I thought you were taking me home," he said.

"I am, darling. I'm taking you to where you belong."

"But this isn't—"

"You'll see, eventually. And then everything will be exactly as it should have been. Right from the start."

The smell of the sea was in the air, and the cars and trucks on the interstate moved swiftly as headlights began to come on. The blue of the day had given way to the gray obscurity of evening. Andrew's eyes were closed and his breathing was steady. He was so at ease that he had succumbed to sleep.

When he roused it was already night. He knuckled open his eyes and looked around. The air outside had grown a chill, even though summer would be upon them in a matter of weeks, and she turned up the heat a little.

"I'm hungry," he said.

"We'll eat soon."

"Promise?"

She turned her smile on him. "Of course."

"Then are we going to see my father?"

"In a way."

He looked at her as if all of a sudden he didn't understand what she was saying.

"I'm going to tell you a story, all right? It begins at the end."

He looked at her and furrowed his brow. "I don't get it."

She smiled. "You will, one day."

In nine or ten years he would be the very image of his father, and then he would mature and grow and become the man his father should have been. And then he would be all hers. Forever and ever.

"Close your eyes, Ben," she said. "Put your head back and close your eyes. We'll be there soon."

Reading Group Guide

1. What do you think was the author's purpose in writing this book? Is there a message you think he's trying to convey?

2. Amelie's affair with Ben, a married man, is morally question-able. At what point do you think she crosses the line? Do you think it is okay to have an affair out of love, like Richard and Sharon?

3. Ben is involved with three women: Amelie, Janet, and Janey. Are there parallels between these women? What are their key differences?

4. Infidelity is a strong current throughout this book. Do you think it's worse to be in Ben's position (married and having an affair) or Amelie's position (having an affair with a married person)? Are they comparable? Is one party less guilty than the other?

5. Amelie encourages emotional honesty with Nina but fails to share any of her own personal life. In what ways could Amelie have communicated with her daughter better? What

kinds of things should you share with a child who is grown up? Discuss how parenthood is portrayed in the story.

6. At forty years old, both Amelie and Janet struggle with the aging process. Describe what parts of getting older bother them the most and why. Do any of these bother you? Do you think they would bother you as much as Amelie and Janet?

7. Describe the way that Amelie and Janet's 'friendship' develops. Do you think Janet knew about the affair the whole time? What are her motivations in befriending Amelie?

8. As Amelie unravels over Ben and her new book, she starts to confuse fiction with reality. Can Amelie's narrative voice be trusted? In what ways do you think she's reliable? Are there parts of the book that make you question the story she gives you?

9. Amelie, Ben, Janet, and Richard are all deeply flawed characters. Do you find yourself sympathizing with any of them? In what ways?

10. Amelie's relationships with men are fraught with tension, starting with a father who abandoned her when she was a little girl. In what ways do you think this shapes her behavior as an adult? Can any of her actions be excused because of this?

11. Amelie worries that people in her community know about her affair with Ben. If you knew, would you feel responsible for telling someone that they're being cheated on? Why or why not?

12. Describe the moments in this book that you found most tense. What would you do if you were in Amelie's position? In Janet's?

13. What do you think happens to the characters after the end of the story? What do you think happens to Ben? What is Amelie planning?

14. Ultimately, do you think that Amelie is a good person? Why or why not?

A Conversation
with the Author

**Was it difficult for you, a man, to write a novel in which the
main character is a woman?**

I'd done it once before, in my fifth novel, *Breathless*. The main
character in that book, a Boston-based historian whose husband
has either been murdered or committed suicide, is distant and
cool. Amelie is a more complex character with a wicked sense
of humor and, of course, a vivid, sometimes fatal, imagination.
I think—I hope—readers might enjoy being with her in these
pages.

I've also been asked this question before in press interviews
when *Breathless* was published in 1996, and as I pointed out then,
male writers have often created memorable female characters:
Flaubert and Tolstoy, just to name two—much greater authors
than I, of course.

As with any protagonist, female or male, it's a matter of getting
under the skin of the character, of living long enough with her
to be able to bring her to life as an individual, working from the
inside out. You may notice that apart from Amelie's blue eyes and
blond hair I never physically describe her—I leave that up to the
reader's imagination.

Why make your main character a writer? Doesn't a writer, well, just sit and write?

The question implies that writing is not an active occupation, that it's merely a matter of fingers on keys and tap-tap-tap several hours a day. In a way, that's one of the points of the book. Can writing break out of the imagination and the words and begin to alter reality? Can reimagining reality somehow lead us to bend it, break it, change it?

Amelie treats writing as a kind of weapon. She has her entire community under her fingers, drawing characteristics from people she sees every day, even from her ex-husband. It's only when she meets her lover's wife that, in her imagining, writing can create a whole new reality—and a possible new future. That's the game of What If, and all writers—indeed all human beings—play it. It's only when we act upon it that we tip into both obsession and then, sometimes, tragedy.

But being a writer comes into play in her affair with Ben. There Amelie has a second life—like a spy she has to create with him a whole new set of codes, alibis to be hauled out should they be seen together, and, in her case, the chance to create a future featuring Ben. In its own way, *If She Were Dead* is a tale of espionage and betrayal.

How did you go about writing *If She Were Dead*? Did you begin with a character, or was it a concept?

I'd begun writing the novel under a different title some twenty years ago. I had the ending first. It came to me in a flash: this combination of a woman's revenge and of trying to right history—and the future—in her favor. I thought of it then as a version of the 1965 movie *Repulsion*, starring Catherine Deneuve, whose life in a London flat begins to fall apart—literally as well as figuratively. It was a kind of horror movie, really.

I'd return to the book at least once a year, refining the prose, tinkering with the plot, searching for the story that now stands. It was always moving towards becoming a psychological thriller. I now think of it as *Repulsion* crossed with *Big Little Lies*—the HBO series, not the book, which I haven't read. So that while Amelie's world is falling apart, she's also strong enough to deal with it in her own wicked way.

If She Were Dead is largely about a woman obsessed. How difficult is it to write about obsession?

Not at all difficult. Obsession is, after all, what we find in literature. Hamlet is obsessed; Raskolnikov in *Crime and Punishment* is obsessed. So is Tom Ripley in Patricia Highsmith's series of books about him. Emma Bovary. Anna Karenina. Both profoundly obsessed characters, especially when it comes to the men they love.

Character must be action; a passive character is inert, it is someone to whom things happen, a kind of punching bag for the gods. Obsession drives a character, compels her or him to act in a certain way, whether logical or impulsive. And then the consequences come tumbling down.

What were your influences for this novel?

I think of this as my Beryl Bainbridge novel (I even named a street in the book after her). In her time she was quite famous, bringing out a book every year, and eventually becoming Dame Beryl Bainbridge. I'd read her 1974 novel *The Bottle Factory*

Outing and was immediately taken by how she balanced the black humor of the book with the growing horror of how the story was developing; something in common to many of her books. I corresponded with Beryl for a year before meeting her when I moved to London. One of the first things she said to me on our way up to her study was, as she pointed to a high corner in the stairway where what looked like a bullet hole could be seen: "That's where my mother-in-law tried to murder me." I've read all of her novels, and consider her a kind of secret influence on my own writing.

Finally, you chose a scene from an old movie, *Double Indemnity*, for the book's epigraph. What made you choose it, and how does it relate to the novel itself?

Film noir, among other things, deals with passions gone awry due to misread cues, as one sees in the best of that genre, whether *Double Indemnity*, *In a Lonely Place*, or *Out of the Past*. I chose the scene I quote, in which Walter and Phyllis try to outguess each other, as a kind of comment on what we're about to read: a novel in which each of the three main characters—Amelie, Ben and Janet—has his or her own scheme brewing. It's just a matter of which one will succeed.

About the Author

J.P. Smith was born in New York City and began his career as a novelist when he moved to England, living with his wife and daughter there for over five years. As a screenwriter he was an Academy Nicholl Fellowship semifinalist. *If She Were Dead* is his eighth novel.

Visit the author at jpsmith.org.

Read on for a look at
J. P. Smith's *The Drowning*,
now available from
Sourcebooks Landmark

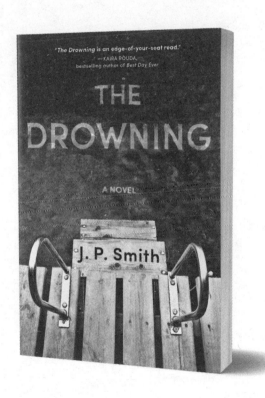

PICTURE THIS: A STILL, STARLIT AUGUST NIGHT, AS warm and clear as it had been all day and the day before and the same as it will be tomorrow. An open field, surrounded by pine woods so dense and dark that the seam between sky and earth has vanished. Soon, the campers will be packing their T-shirts and shorts, their tennis racquets and baseball gloves and bags full of dirty laundry, and heading home to New York, to Connecticut, to New Jersey and beyond.

Campfires light the faces of the boys as they sit in circles: the younger ones toward the center of the field, the older campers by the edge of it, nearer the woods. Dinner—hot dogs on sticks cooked over open flames, potatoes baked in foil among the coals, marshmallows blackening on twigs—is over. The fires move from glow into fade into cinders and, in just a few minutes, into ash as, pacing the perimeter of the circles, the counselors tell the same story they've recited from one year to the next, quietly and reverentially, as though it were a secret meant to be kept forever. A tale that was by now as woven into the camp's culture as the songs they sang in the social hall— odes to the outdoors, to teamwork, to Echo Lake and the hills beyond. The boys stare into the dying embers, watching the words come to life or keeping their eyes shut as though wishing camp were already over and they were home, where nothing bad could ever reach them.

"One night, every seven years since Camp Waukeelo was founded in 1937," one of the counselors begins, "long after lights out, a local man, John Otis, would sneak into the camp through the woods behind the bunks and take one of the younger boys." He falls silent, the better to let his words take root in the boys' minds. "Townsfolk said that John was someone who wouldn't stand out in a crowd, just a guy of average height and weight, but"—he pauses a moment—"with the eyes of a dead man. When you looked into them, you felt the temperature drop."

Another counselor is deeper into the story as he walks behind his circle of campers. "...because the seven- and eight- and nine-year-olds—you know who you are—are easy to grab. Easy to silence. Easy to make disappear..."

A third is saying, "...so the first to vanish was in July 1944, wartime, on a warm night just like this one." A few of the youngest campers try to stifle their crying. The counselor goes on. "The next to disappear was seven years later, in 1951—in fact, on this very date."

A fourth counselor says that John Otis was always watching from the hills behind the bunks, observing the boys line up for the morning flag-raising or jumping into the lake off the dock, deciding which one he would take next. "He might even be out there now, in the woods," the counselor said, and eight pairs of eyes looked up. "Watching. Thinking. Making his choice."

Apart from the counselors' quiet voices and the crackling of the campfires, there is nothing but silence. The campers are already wrapped in narrative, ensnared by words, at the mercy of their imaginations.

"He always goes for the loner," another counselor is saying, and some of the boys look around, wondering which of them that might be. "You know who I mean…the kid who doesn't really participate, who keeps to himself." A few of the campers look shyly down, because they know he's describing them.

The story always ends the next morning when the other campers in the boy's bunk notice his empty bed and wonder where he has gone, leaving no trace or clue behind. Had he been murdered, or was he with all the others who'd been taken by the man who lived high up in the hills in a place none of them had ever seen?

Over time, the legend of John Otis had gathered more details, and these, in turn, were passed along year after year to the campers. It was said that something very bad had happened to John late in the 1930s, when he was growing up in the house built by his father. His mother had disappeared soon after her only son was born, and there was talk of an older sister, though as there was no record of her birth, it was assumed she was delivered at home. And probably even died there.

One day John was at school, a withdrawn and uncooperative and sullen child, talking back to his teachers and picking fights, and the next he was absent, as he was the next day and the day after and then forever. Any attempts by law-enforcement personnel or school administrators to reach his house were met by a pair of watchdogs and, on more than a few occasions, John's father in the doorway, shotgun in hand.

It was felt in the community that what had befallen young John was no longer of interest. He was either dead or being raised outside of society by his father, whose reputation for belligerence and outright violence was well known in the Berkshires. People steered clear of the old man on his rare appearances in the neighboring towns, where he'd buy slabs of meat and bottles of cheap whiskey, along with cases of baby food. After several years had passed, when his father must have been long dead and everyone presumed his son was also gone, John Otis drifted into a kind of malevolent afterlife, a rumor trapped among the hills surrounding the lake. Sometimes campers claimed to have seen him as an adult, in a rowboat in the middle of the lake at sunset, looking their way from the shadow beneath the brim of his hat. Or standing by the edge of the baseball field, among the trees, watching and smoking; vanishing when they turned to alert a counselor.

The sound of rustling in the woods behind the bunks was John Otis; the spark of fireflies was John's eyes. The very thought of him meant he was right behind you.

Within the fictions told and retold, embellished over the years at campfires and in bunks late at night, John Otis was even more vividly alive. If questioned by a camper who had heard the story the year before, counselors would only say that they had miscounted, that *this* was the seventh year.

The same names were repeated. There was Scott Gardner, the kid with the spiky black hair. Seven years before Scott disappeared, Jake Kaufman had been lifted from his bed in the middle of the night, and none of the others in his bunk saw or heard a thing, though in the morning, as the counselors savored in the telling, his bed had been made as neatly as he had left it the day before, except that an antique doll lay in his place, both its eyes gouged out. In early August of 1972, Billy Olsen had chased a ball into the heavily wooded area known as the Pines and never returned. Were they kept prisoner by the man? Tortured? Murdered? Were they there still, their cries unheard as John Otis descended the stairs to the dirt cellar of his ramshackle house?

Sometimes, the counselors would show the boys photos of the allegedly missing campers, in the dusty, leather-bound books kept on a shelf in the social hall, the name of the camp leafed in gold on the covers. There was the pale, blond seven-year-old Henry Cassidy, summer of '44, the faded one sitting in the front row, looking a bit lost. There was chubby, smiling Aaron Blume who vanished two days after the photo was taken in August 1958. And skinny nine-year-old Richard Ivory, all angles and sunken cheeks, who went missing in 1965.

Now it's time to go. The boys are silent as they follow the beams of their counselors' flashlights on the path through the woods back to their bunks. And when they do speak, it's quietly and with wonder, because fear has been given a name and a reality all its own.

"Do you believe any of that?" one of the eight-year-olds asks, and the boy walking beside him, Joey Proctor, says he thinks it might be true. The next night, Joey won't be there, and would never be seen again.

One day, many years later, a counselor would point to Joey Proctor's face in the camp photo and tell the boys about John Otis and how one day Joey was there, and the next he wasn't. Joey had become part of a legend, and that was where he lived from the day he disappeared until the morning, twenty-one years later, when it seemed he had come back to life.